C. C. Goodwin

The Wedge of Gold

C. C. Goodwin

The Wedge of Gold

ISBN/EAN: 9783743329270

Manufactured in Europe, USA, Canada, Australia, Japa

Cover: Foto ©Andreas Hilbeck / pixelio.de

Manufactured and distributed by brebook publishing software (www.brebook.com)

C. C. Goodwin

The Wedge of Gold

WEDGE OF GOLD.

BY

C. C. GOODWIN,

EDITOR DAILY TRIBUNE.

1893.
TRIBUNE JOB PRINTING COMPANY,
SALT LAKE CITY, UTAH.

CONTENTS

THE WEDGE OF GOLD.

CHAPTER I.

THE MINERAL KINGDOM.

The splendor of the world is due to mining and to the perfectness of man's ability to work the minerals which the mines supply. The fields of the world give men food ; with food furnished, a few souls turn to the contemplation of higher things ; but no grand civilization ever came to an agricultural people until their intellects were quickened by something beyond their usual occupation.

How man first emerged from utter barbarism is a story that is lost, but when history first began to pick up the threads of events and to weave them into a record, the loom upon which the record was woven was made of gold. One of the rivers that flowed through Eden also "compassed the whole land of Havilah, where there is gold ; and the gold of that land is good."

" Tubal Cain was an instructor of every artificer in brass and iron." Abraham and Jacob bought fields with money, and when, Pharaoh sought to make Joseph next in power to himself, he took the ring from his finger and put it upon Joseph's finger ; and he put a chain of gold about Joseph's neck. Thus the grandchildren of Adam, in Holy Writ, were artificers in brass and iron, and when civilization in

Egypt began to make an impression upon the world, its sovereigns had already discovered the omnipotence of gold.

Assyria, that came next to be the concernment of mankind, had men who could perfectly fuse gold and glass, and their work is still an object of wonder to the world. Their queens wore raiment which was woven from threads of gold.

The splendor of the Hebrew nation culminated when the roof of their great temple was laid with beaten gold, and when all the magnificent furnishings within the temple were wrought from gold and silver and brass.

The invincible Greeks had chariots and javelins of iron, helmets of gold and brass, and now as their tombs are rifled there is found beside where their bones went back to dust the metal implements with which they wrought, and the imperishable coins with which they carried on their commerce.

The power of Rome came when her artisans learned how to fashion the short sword, and her soldiers learned how to wield it, and her splendor came when, through conquest, she brought under her dominion the gold fields of Spain and Asia, and learned the power which money carries with it. Her civilization began to recede when the money supply began to fall off, and when it became too precious for the masses to possess it, then the race degenerated until the men were no longer fit to be soldiers, the women lost the grace to become the mothers of soldiers, and darkness settled upon Europe.

England remained little more than a rendezvous for wild tribes until her people learned mining and began the study of how to reduce the metals which the mines supplied, and her advancement since can be rated exactly by the progress she has made in bringing the metals into effective forms and combinations. When first the rude Saxon acquired the art to mend the broken links in a knight's armor, and how to temper one of the old-fashioned two-handed swords, it was possible to comprehend, that from that germ would expand the brains that would by and by construct a steel ship or bridge ; when the first rude spindle was fashioned, all the commencement necessary to create and work the world's looms was made.

Out of these accomplishments, commerce was born ; foreign commerce required ships, and so the ships were supplied ; with commerce was developed a financial system, and soon it was discovered that after all the chiefest power of the world was money ; that the swiftest way to win money was to perfect machinery so that out of raw material forms of beauty and of use could be wrought, and thus in regular chain the majesty of England expanded from the first day that an Englishman was able to convert from the dull iron ore something which the world would want, until ships laden with her wares reached all the world's ports, and to barbarous lands she became an iron nation more terrible than the first iron nation.

The world's highest civilization does not come from the fruitful fields, but from the darkness of the deep mines. Power and independence come with the digging and working of the baser metals; full civilization waits upon the production of enough of the royal metals to give to the people wealth in a form that enables them to command the best attainable talent and forces to serve them, and enough of leisure to enable them to put forward their best efforts.

Below the surface of the story which makes this book is a deeper story of what may be performed by brave hearts when they leave the fruitful fields behind them and turn with all their hearts to woo the desert that turns her forbidding face to them at their coming, and holds, closely hidden within her sere breast, her inestimable treasures.

CHAPTER II.

"What think you of it, Jack?"

"It is growing soft in the drift, Jim; the stringers of ore are growing stronger and giving promise of concentrating soon."

"So it strikes me," was the response, "and when Uncle Jimmie Fair was down here an hour ago, I put two things together, and they have kept me thinking ever since."

"And what were the two things, Jim?"

"Why, Jack, did you hear him sigh as he moved the candle along the face of the drift, and hear him say, 'You are doing beautifully, my sons, beautifully; I never had better men,' and then sighed again, and added, 'I fear it's no use; I fear we shall have to drop the work soon?' That was one of the things. The other was the light in his eyes when he examined the face of the drift. If I were a gambler, Jack, I would 'copper' what he said and wager all I had on the twinkle of his eyes."

"It looks good in the drift, surely; and, Jim, if we break into an ore body any time, it will not surprise me."

"Nor me, either, Jack; and if we strike ore here, it ought to be good, because, as I reckon it, since we left the Gould and Curry shaft, we have drifted out of the G. & C. ground, clear through the Best and Belcher, and some distance into the Consolidated Virginia, and by the trend of the lode, if we could find an ore body here, it would be in regular course from the Spanish and Ophir croppings."

" How long have you worked here, and how much have you saved, Jack ? "

" It is three years and a month since I went to work in the Belcher," was the reply ; "I made $400 in Crown Point stocks, and I have saved altogether $2,800 and odd."

" I beat you by a year's work, Jack, and I have, I believe, $3,300 or $3,400 in the bank. Suppose we try a little gamble in stocks. If we could get an ore body here, this stock would double in a week, and it will not fall very much lower if we do not find anything."

" All right, Jim, if you say so. Meet me to-morrow at eleven o'clock at the California Bank, and we will put in and buy a few shares."

" Agreed," was the answer ; " but our twenty minutes are up and we must go. But, Jack, *mum* must be the word."

" Mum goes," said Jack.

It was a queer spot where this talk was held. It was by the air-pipe in the drift which was run from the 1,200-foot level of the Gould and Curry shaft on the Comstock ledge in Nevada, north toward where the great bonanza was found in the Consolidated Virginia Mine. In the face of the drift the temperature was 120 degrees, and miners could work for

only forty minutes and then had to retire to the air
pipe to cool off. It was while resting at the air-pipe
that these men, James Sedgwick and John Browning,
talked.

They were stripped from the waist up ; all their
clothing consisted of canvas pantaloons held up by a
belt, and miners' shoes ; they each had a little band
around the head in which was fastened a miner's
candlestick. Thus exposed, in the candle-light, they
were handsome men. The excessive perspiration
caused by the heat of the mine made their faces as
fair as the faces of women, and as they lounged, half-
naked, carelessly in the drift, their muscles stood out
in knots, and in the dim light of the candles, as they
rose to return to work, their movements were supple
and elastic as those of caged lions. The one who
answered to the name of Browning was shorter than
the other by an inch, but deeper-chested ; the candle-
light showed that his eyes were blue, and his mustache and short curly hair were of chestnut color.
The other was a little taller, but not so compactly
built, and in the uncertain light his eyes, hair and
mustache seemed to be black ; but really his eyes
were gray and his hair brown. Both were young,
perhaps twenty-seven or twenty-eight years of age,
and both were perfect pictures of good health and
good nature.

Their shift was from four in the afternoon to midnight; but when at midnight they went back through
the drift to the shaft to be hoisted to the surface, the
night foreman informed them that there was some

trouble with the cage ; that while they could still hoist rock, it was not deemed safe to trust men on the cage, and, accordingly, some blankets, mattresses, and supper had been sent down, and they would have to spend the night in a cross-cut running from the shaft.

The other miners growled. These two made no complaint, but ate their suppers, then took their beds and spread them in the cross-cut. Sedgwick and Browning went farthest into the cross-cut, made their beds together, and lay down. When they knew by the breathing of the miners nearest them that they were asleep, in low tones they began to talk.

Browning was the first to speak. " By Jove, Jim," he said, " that cage story is too thin. It worked all right up to ten o'clock, for Mackay and Fair both came down and spent a good quarter of an hour in the end of the drift and kept tapping around with their hammers. I was mean enough to watch them on the sly and saw them both taking samples. If you keep awake, you will see John Mackay down here again by six o'clock in the morning, and you may make up your mind not to see any more daylight for three days or a week to come ; that is, if the drift keeps on improving."

" I believe it, Jack," said Sedgwick ; " did you notice that the last blast left nearly the whole face of the drift in ore ? Then, did you notice as we met the car coming out, it had long drills in it, and the shift boss was following it up close ? No blasting will be done to-night, but the drillings will be saved for assay, and I tell you the plan is that we shall tell no tales out of school. Believe me, that cage will not be safe again till as much stock shall be taken in as is needed by those in control."

"And so," said Browning, "when we get to the surface our little money will not buy enough stock to make it any object."

"I have been thinking of that," said Sedgwick, "and it makes me hot, for all day I have been dreaming of doubling my money."

"I have a notion," said Browning, "to try to work my way out on the ladders.

"That will not work," replied Sedgwick; "I looked, and all the lower ladders have been taken down."

Then a long silence followed, until at last Sedgwick spoke again. "I have it, Jack," said he. Lighting his candle, he groped around in the cross-cut, and found a splinter from a lagging. Fishing out a stump of a pencil from the pocket of his pantaloons, he said, "Where is your money, Browning?"

"In the California Bank," he replied.

"All right," was the response. Then on the splinter he wrote for a moment, and then said, "How is this?" and in a whisper read: "California Bank, Please pay to John W. Mackay whatever funds may be to our respective credits."

"What is your idea, Jim?" asked Browning.

"I mean to lay for Mackay, and when he comes

down ask him, quietly, to read the writing when he gets up into daylight."

" But what will he think we want ? " asked Browning.

" He will know mighty quick," said Sedgwick ; " he knows where we work; he will understand that we know what we see, and that while we do not intend to give away the information, at the same time we do not want to 'get left out in the cold' on this deal."

" What think you he will do ? " asked Browning.

" If he believes it safe, and the right kink is on him, he will draw our money and buy us some stock," said Sedgwick. " He made his money that way, and it is not long since he was a timberman on this same lode."

" Why not word it differently, and ask him squarely to buy the stock ? " asked Browning.

" Why, Jack," was the reply, "that would be a dead give-away. He would never present such an order at the bank. It would be a notice to every man in the bank and every friend of every man in the bank, and that would mean everybody in town, that the miners who were kept down in the deeps were trying to buy the stock of the mine. I would rather risk it this way."

" All right, everything goes," said Browning, and both signed the order.

Then they talked for a long time. They had known each other slightly for a couple of years, having met first in the Belcher lower levels, and being thrown together in work on the face of the drift from the G. & C. shaft, they had, during the previous few days, each found that the other was a good and bright man, and had grown more and more intimate, and a warm friendship had sprung up between them. As they lay down again, Browning said to Sedgwick, " How did you come to be here, Jim

" Fate arranged it, I guess," was the reply. " You see, my home was in Ohio, in the valley of the Miami. My father had a big farm—400 acres—but there were two boys older than myself, and they needed the land. I took to books naturally, and the plan was to give me an education, and then add a learned profession, or set me up in some little business. So I went to school, and after awhile was sent to Oberlin College. Queer old place, that! Great place for praying and for teaching the universal brotherhood of man! The result, I used to think, was that a colored man commanded a premium over a white man there. I worried the thing through for three years and a half. There was a young mulatto student in the school named Deering, who was a great deal too big for his clothes. He was inclined to force himself into places where he was not wanted, and at anything like the manifestation of a desire to dispense with his society, he grew saucy in a moment. I did not mind him, but he was vinegar and brimstone to a young student from Tennessee, a slight, weakly lad, but as brave a little chap as you ever saw, named Thorne. Well, one day, for some impertinence, Thorne struck him. Deering was an athlete; he weighed twenty pounds more than I did, fifty more than Thorne, I guess; he was quick as lightning, was most handy with his props, and in an instant he smashed poor Thorne's face with a blow which knocked him half senseless.

"I sprang to Thorne, at the same time telling Deering it was a cowardly act for one like him to strike a little fellow like Thorne. He answered something to the effect that for a trifle he would smash me a good deal worse than he had Thorne, and—well, in minute more there were lively times in that neighborhood.

"It was a tough scrap. It was out on the green; the students gathered around us, and while some cried out to stop us, others shouted, 'Fair play!' and so we were not interfered with. I remember saying to myself, 'If I win, it must be a triumph of race and mind over matter;' but, Jack, that was mighty lively matter. We both had been rowing and practicing in the gymnasium; we were both as hard as iron. Deering was as supple as a boa-constrictor, and had a fist like a twelve-pound hammer. Later, the boys told me the fight lasted twenty minutes. The last I saw was Deering knocked out on the ground, and then my eyes closed, and the boys led me to my room. They swathed my eyes with raw beefsteaks and raw oysters, rubbed me down, and put me to bed. It was ten days before I got out; it was two weeks before Deering did. Then there was an investigation. It was shown that I took up a fight that Thorne commenced; that Thorne had gone for a gun in case I should get the worst of it. So Deering was reinstated, and Thorne and myself expelled. At the time I had a silver watch and four dollars in money. I sold the watch for fourteen dollars. I wrote the facts to my father, and told him I was going West, for he is a straight-laced Presbyterian; I knew he would feel eternally disgraced by my expulsion, and I did not want to hear his reproaches. Thorne wanted to give me money, but I told him I had plenty.

"I worked my way to Texas, and stopped one night at the house of a big cattle man named Thomas Jordan. I had just $1.50 left. He worked out of me my history, and when I explained why I was expelled from school, he laughed until he cried, and said: 'And yo' licked the coon!' and then went off again into a mighty fit of laughter.

"He was a man about thirty years of age, spare built, but wiry as an Indian. He had black hair and eyes; he was not educated, but was naturally a bright man; was brave as a lion; could ride like a Comanche; was a splendid shot, and had been West; took up a gold mine in Arizona, opened it, and sold it three years before I met him for $25,000, and with that bought the ranch and stock. He was originally from Tennessee; when a boy was in the Confederate army; had been knocked about until he was a perfect man of affairs, and the heart within him was simply just royal.

"Next morning, as we went out from breakfast, his vaqueros were trying to ride a vicious horse. He was a big buckskin stallion, six years old, and strong and

fierce as a grizzly.   The horse tossed three of them,
one after the other, out of the saddle; neither one
asted a minute on his curved back.   I was watching
the performance when Jordan came up to me and,
laughing, again said : ' But yo' licked the coon !'

"I said, 'Yes, but that was not much to brag
about.'

" ' Yo' licked the coon, but was afeerd to meet the
governor, eh ?' he said.

" I answered, 'That is about the size of it.'

" ' And yo' did not go home ?' he said.

" ' No,' I replied.

" ' Did not send for any money ?'

" ' No.'

" ' How much did yo' have?'

" ' Four dollars, and a watch which I sold for fourteen dollars.'

" ' How much have yo' left?'

" ' I believe, $1.50.'

" ' What are yo' going to do ?'

" ' Going to work.'

" ' Wat at?'

" ' Anything I can get to do.

" ' Will yo' work for me ?'

" ' Yes.'

" ' Know anything about herding and driving cattle ?'

" ' No, but I can learn it.'

" 'All right, what about wages ?'

" 'Anything you like.'

" 'All right,' said Jordan, ' I will have the boys fix
yo' up a gentle mustang and give yo' a show.'

" I had overheard the cowboys the previous even-
ng telling about a ' gentle broncho ' that they had
given a 'tenderfoot,' and how the tenderfoot was
'jolted.' I reflected that I was in Texas and might
just as well establish myself at once. When a boy,
I could ride anything on the farm or in the township.
So I said :

" ' Mr. Jordan, let me try the buckskin.'

" ' What !' said Jordan, 'would yo' mount that
wild beast ? He's a devil. My best riders cannot
sit him. Indeed, he has tossed half the cowboys in
Texas.'

" ' Let me try him,' said I.

" ' *All right*,' said Jordan, ' come on.'

" We climbed into the big corral. One of the
boys threw a rope upon the horse, drew him up to
the center post, blinded him, and said to me :

" ' Young feller ! If you ride him, you'll be a good
one, shore 'nough.'

" I took off my coat, vest and suspenders, tied a
heavy handkerchief around my stomach, fixed the
saddle, sprang upon the horse, and the blind was
drawn off at the same moment. Then for ten minutes I had a game as lively as I had experienced with
the coon. How he did jolt me ! But I sat him. Then,
when all his other tricks had failed, he started in a
run for the center post of the corral, with the intention of raking me off. But it was his side that struck
the post ; my knee was on top of the saddle, and

when the rebound knocked him away from the post it was not a second until I was back in the saddle; and then I assumed the offensive and drove the rowels into him.   Between the shock of the blow and the surprise of the rowels, he gave up, made a feeble jump or two, stopped and stood trembling.

" I dismounted, and the cowboys threw up their hats and cheered the ' tenderfoot.'   Then I took down the reins of the hackamore (the Mexican Jaquema), bent the brute's head around, and tied him in a half circle to his own tail.   Then, borrowing a cowboy's whip, I tapped him gently with it, and kept him turning and tumbling until he was covered with foam, and I saw he was completely subdued. Then I untied the rope, gave him his head, and then sprang again (without a blind this time) into the saddle.   He moved off in a walk; then I trotted him, then put him in a gallop, and after circling the corral two or three times, reined him up to the cowboys, stopped him, and dismounted.

" ' No wonder he licked the coon ! ' said Jordan.

" And one of the cowboys standing near said, ' Bet y'r boots ! '

" I went to work and was a cowboy for a year, and it was a happy year, for I had no trouble and any number of friends.   I could ride and shoot with any of them, and soon learned to throw a rope.   My riding the big stallion gave me a mighty prestige, for I learned later that many had tried him and no one had kept the saddle for two minutes.   He was my vaquero horse, and many a cowboy stopped and looked as I rode by.

" I had been with Jordan but a short time when one evening he brought a book and said :

" ' Jim ! look at this. A preacher-lookin' chap stopped over night har a year ago and went off in the mornin', and forgot ter take it. See if yo' don't think it's ther durndest stuff yo' ever seen ! '

" I looked at the book. It was the Iliad, Pope's translation.

" 'Why, Jordan,' I said, ' this is a wonderful book.' Then I briefly explained what the great epic was, who the Greeks and who the Trojans were, the cause of the war between them, how nations fought in those days, what gods they worshiped, and added, ' Let me read you a little of it.'

" ' Why, in course,' said Jordan. ' If yo' ken make a blamed thing out er it, we'd all like to har it ; wouldn't we, boys ? '

" They all assented. I was just out of school and read pretty well.

"So I opened the volume at random and it happened to be in Book XVI., where Pelides consents that Patroclus shall put on his own armor and lead his Myrmidons into the fight, where Achilles arouses and sets in array his terrible warriors, has the steeds yoked and prays Dodonian Jove to give to his friend the victory, and then to grant him safe return. After reading ten minutes, I closed the book, and asked Jordan if I should read anymore.

" ' Sarten,' he said. ' That war fine. It are like

that mornin' at Murfreesborough when all thar
bugles war callin' 'nd ther big guns war beginnin' ter
roar.'

"Then I opened at the beginning and read right
along for an hour.   All the company were greatly
excited, declaring 'it war fine.'

"I read to them every evening the winter through,
read the Iliad entire, and in the meantime Jordan
had sent to Galveston for more books, begging me
to select them, and declaring he would fill the house
with them if I would only 'steer his buyin' so as not
by his purchases 'ter make a holy show' of himself.

"When finally the great annual round-up came, I
held my own with the best riders, on trial I could
draw and shoot with the quickest and surest shots,
and could handle a rope fairly well.   I enjoyed the
life.

"Generally every one was my friend, but there was
one rough customer, a man named Turner, who did
not like me, though I had never done a thing in the
world to offend him.   He made his boasts that no
one had ever 'got away' with him or ever would.
He had a tough record and many people feared him,
for he was a powerful man physically, and cruel in
all his instincts.

"One day something was needed from the station,
and I rode Buckskin down to get it. The station was
a couple of miles from Jordan's house.   Thirty or

forty cowboys were there on a lark, and all had been drinking a little.

"They hailed me boisterously and wanted me to drink. I laughingly told them I never drank, and good-naturedly threatened to make it hot for the whole band if they did not behave themselves. I had neither coat nor vest on, and they could all see I had no weapons about me. They all laughed, for they were a jovial, good-hearted crowd.

"But just then this rough Turner showed up and said: 'Who is threatening to make it hot for us?'

"Half a dozen of the boys explained that I was only joking, but Turner was bent on mischief.

"'He won't drink with us, hey? Well, we'll drink with him,' he said, and turning to me ordered me to call up the crowd and treat, or tell the reason why.

"I replied that one reason was that I did not very often drink, and another was that I never drank on compulsion.

"He was frantic in a moment, and suddenly drew his revolver. I caught the barrel and turned it up just as he fired, then took it from him, handed it to one of the boys, and told him to keep it until Turner had time to reflect on what a fool he was making of himself.

"He was only the more furious at that. He sprang backward two or three feet, then drawing a huge knife made with it a savage lunge at me. I seized his wrist, and after a brief struggle wrenched the knife from his hand, but still holding his wrist told him that unless he grew quiet I should have to box his ears.

"The boys laughed and jeered at this, which only further incensed the ungovernable brute, and he declared that he would give $100 for the chance to whip me in a fair fist fight.

"At this I released his wrist and told him he should be accommodated. The boys gathered in a ring around us. Turner came at me like a wild beast, but ' he had no scientific use of his hands and I had had a little practice.

"I knocked aside his blow with my left, and with the open palm of my right hand gave him a sounding box on his left ear.

"The cowboys yelled with delight at this, crying, ' Turner, did you hear that ?'

"Turner rallied and made another rush at me. This time I struck his blow aside with my right hand and boxed his right ear with the palm of my left hand.

So the business continued for several seconds. I never closed my hands, but just boxed him right and left, the boys fairly screaming with joy, until I finally gathered all my strength and gave him one resounding cuff that sent him full length to grass, the most abject-looking, baffled bully that I ever saw.

Seeing how completely whipped he was, I went to him, and taking him by the arm, said, ' Turner, you were right about my treating ; come in and take a drink with me. There's nothing like exercise to make one thirsty.'

" But he would not drink. He arose, skulked away, got his gun and knife, mounted his mustang, and left that part of Texas.

"Next day the boys told Jordan about the scrap, and he danced for joy. He at once rode away to the station to get all the particulars, and when he returned at night he called me aside and said, ' Jim, yo' is thinkin' of leavin' har. We couldn't get along at all without yo'. I seen my lawyer ter-day and told him ter make a deed o' half this ranch 'nd stock ter Jim Sedgwick, and so thar firm now war " Tom and Jim" er " Jim and Tom," I don't give er continental which.'

" Of course I could not accept the gift, but it took me three days to satisfy the great-hearted man why I could not. I told him I was bound to go further West, that his heart had run away with his head, and he yielded at last, but insisted that the offer was a ' squar ' one and would last always if I ever came back.

"When the year was up I had saved $212 at regular cowboy wages and would accept no more, though Jordan begged me to take ' sunthun decent.'

" I came West, learned a little of mining—how to hold and hit a drill—in Colorado, then took a run up into Montana, came down across Idaho and finally reached this place. Liking the ways of things here I went to work. I have not missed a dozen shifts in three years."

Browning chuckled at the story, and when Sedgwick ceased he said :

" Isn't it jolly queer that we have been thrown together? My home was in Devonshire, England. My step-father was a merchant who finally became a half banker and half broker. When I was a little kid my mother died, and my father after a while married a widow who had a little daughter five years younger than myself. My father died, and my step-mother married a man named Hamlin.

"When I became twenty-two years old, my step-father wanted me to marry this little girl. I declined, first, because she seemed to me a sister, and second, I was head and ears in love with the step-daughter of the village barrister. The girl was my sister's running mate, so to speak, and though I had never said one word of love to her, my heart was on the lowest level in the dust at her feet. It was, by Jove!

" In those days I was a bit wild, I guess. I did not get out of school with much honor. I used to ride steeple-chase and hurdle races and dance all night. Sometimes, too, I had a scrap, and was careless about the money I spent. The old barrister—his name was Jenvie—believed I was the worst kid in the United Kingdom. One evening Rose Jenvie—her real name was Leighton, she was my glory, you know—had been visiting my foster-sister, and remaining until after dark, I walked home with her. It was a starlit night in summer, and we talked as we walked as young people do. The gate to the path leading up to her house was open, and I continued to walk by her side until we were almost at the door, when the 'Governor' sprang up from a bench on the little lawn, where he had been sitting, and, rudely seizing his step-daughter by the arm, broke out with a torrent of insulting reproaches that she should dare to be walking alone at night by the side of the most worthless scapegrace in all England.

"The dear girl tried to explain that my part of the affair was merely an act of courtesy, but the old chap was hot, and that only made him rave the worse.

"I stood it a minute, and then said, 'Never mind, Miss Rose! You go within doors, please, and your governor will feel better when he has time to think.'

"At this he turned upon me, ordered me off the grounds, and added that if I did not go at once he would kick me over the hedge. Then I laughed and said : 'Oh, no, Mr. Jenvie, you certainly would not do that.'

Something in my voice, I guess, vexed him, for he sprang at me like a Siberian wolf. He was a big, hearty fellow, about forty years old, and the blow he aimed at me would have felled a shorthorn. But I knocked it aside, as he made the rush, which swerved him a little to one side, and the opportunity was too good. Bless my soul! Before I thought, I planted him a stinger on the neck, and he went down like a felled ox. And he lay there for fully a minute. The beautiful girl never screamed or uttered a word, except, 'O, Jack, I hope you are not hurt!' She had never called me Jack before, and by Jove, it sounded sweeter to me than a wedding march. The old chap in a dazed way rose up on his hands. I saw he was coming out of it, and with a hasty 'Good night, Miss

Rose,' I got out of the way.   I went home and told
my governor the whole story, and wasn't he mad!
Jenvie was his closest friend, you know, and so
he ordered me to go and apologize to the old barrister.   I told him flatly I would not.   Then he
ordered me out of the house, and, first bidding
mother and sister Grace good-bye, I left.   I had four
pounds six, and with it I went down to an old aunt's
of mine in Cornwall.   After three days there I met
some miners, had a night with them, which ended by
their initiating me into their clan.   Next morning,
thinking it over, my better self asserted itself, and the
whim took me to learn the mining business.

"I worked a year, and when off shift I read all
the books on geology and mining that I could find;
I found a pamphlet telling me all about this lode and
its possibilities.   I had worked steadily and had saved
money enough to pay my way here; I came, and
went to work the second day after arriving on the
lode."

'What are your plans, Browning?" asked Sedgwick.

"I have no certain plans," was the answer.   "I
have just lived on an impossible dream, you know,
of making £5,000, then going back, and if Rose
Jenvie is not married to try to steal her away.   If I
could make a good bit of money I would buy a place,
a big tract of downs in Devonshire.   I could, by
draining it and running it my way, make it double in
value in three years."

"And I," said Sedgwick, "have been nursing just such another dream, which is to make $30,000 to go back and cancel the mortgage of $5,000 on the old home place, and then to buy old Jasper's farm on the hill. It is a daisy. It contains 300 acres and is worth $40 an acre. If I could do that, I believe I could reconcile the old gent, and make him think I was not so mightily out of the way after all when I fought at college and ran away. But$ 30,000—good Lord! when will a man get $30,000 working for $4 a day on the Comstock?"

"It is a close, hard game," said Browning. Then there was silence, the candle burned out, and in a moment more both miners were asleep.

CHAPTER III.

The men awoke early, and, as Sedgwick had predicted, by six o'clock, the superintendent of the mine came down and went to the end of the drift. On his return to the lower station of the shaft, Sedgwick approached him, and holding out the bit of lagging, said in a low voice: "Mr. Mackay, there are a few words written on that. Will you not kindly carry them to the surface and read them?" Mr. Mackay took it and put it in the pocket of the gray shirt which he always wore in the mine, saying jokingly: "Tobacco needed on your watch?" "Worse, even," answered Sedgwick, and walked away.

When the men were allowed to go above ground, five days later, they found that Consolidated Virginia had jumped from $4 to $11 per share. Sedgwick and Browning went straight to the bank and asked how their accounts stood. They found that $2,800 from one credit, and $3,200 from the other had been withdrawn. They looked at each other and smiled, but said nothing. Passing outside, they exchanged opinions and both concluded that if Mackay had bought the stock promptly, it must have doubled already. But both agreed that they would say nothing; rather, would let matters drift. So days and weeks rolled by, until finally the stock touched $30 per share, when one morning each received a note to call at the bank.

They went together, and were informed that 2,000 old) shares of Consolidated Virginia had been placed to their credit, and that it was at their discretion to realize upon it, or permit it to remain longer. The news fairly took their breath away.

" How about making $30,000 at $4 per day, Jim ?" said Browning.

" How about £5,000, the old barrister's step-daughter, and the downs in Devonshire, Jack ?" said Sedgwick.

They went to their room in the lodging house to talk over what was best to do.

" When we sell," said Sedgwick, " I am going to Ohio."

" And I to old England," said Browning.

" And how can we give any expression of our gratitude to John Mackay ?" asked Sedgwick.

" Let us go down and tender him half our stock," said Browning.

" A good thought," said Sedgwick. So down to the Consolidated Virginia office they went at once. They gained an instant interview with Mr. Mackay, and, thanking him warmly, told him they had thought it over, and determined that he was entitled to half their shares.

" That's clever of you, boys," said Mackay, " but

that is too big a commission.   How much did you say the order on the splinter had brought you?"

Sedgwick replied that they had 2,000 shares, and that the stock was selling at $30 on a rising market.

"Well," answered Mackay, "that will be $10 for one, will it not?"

They answered, "Yes."

The Bonanza King thought for a moment, and then said: "It is this way, boys.   I have been pick-ing up a few shares of the stock on my own account lately, and do not need any ready money at present, but there are a good many sick and bruised miners down in the hospital.   If, when you sell, you can see your way clear to send them down a few dollars, that will do more good than to divide with me, for I would be liable to lose the money any day in these crazy stocks."

They thanked him with swimming eyes and broken voices, and started to retire, when he called them back, and said: "I bought that stock because I noticed that you were not just like some of the others down in the mine, and I knew if the money should be lost you would neither of you reproach me.   But I called you back to tell you that while I do not think there is any hurry about selling your stocks, dealing in mining shares is a risky business, as a rule, especially when you have nothing but a guess to go on; and I do not believe I would, if in your places, take that up for a business."

Then some one else came in, and the miners retired.

They determined not to sell just then, and both went back to work at 4 in the afternoon of that day.

The young men continued their daily toil. After the stock reached $35 per share, it hung at that figure for a long time, but they felt no uneasiness. They saw the hurry of the work in opening the Consolidated Virginia and the C. & C. shafts; they saw a new great quartz mill being erected, but they saw something else which pleased them much more, which was that the more the great ore body was sunk and drifted upon, the bigger it grew. In the early winter of 1874–5, the stock began to climb up. It jumped to $80, then $85; then, almost in a day, to $115, and so on up to $220. The strain on the minds of the two young miners was very great, but they held on. There was another little lull, and then towards spring it started up again.

When it reached $480, Browning said to Sedgwick: " Bless my soul, Jim, I have not slept for three nights. I have been thinking that hundreds of people have been waiting for the stock to touch $500, and when it does, they will unload and break it down. Had we not better sell? It will give us as much money as we can manage."

" I guess you are right, Jack" said Sedgwick. " I believe it will still go a good deal higher, but if it does, let those who buy our stocks make it. As you said, it will bring us as much money as we can manage. It takes a brave man to sell on a rising market. Let us be brave."

So they gave the order for the sale of the stock,

but that day it jumped to $520, and when the returns were made, they found to their credit, $1,040,000. The stock touched $900 per share a few days later.

The result well-nigh paralyzed them. "At $4 per day, this is not bad, Browning," said Sedgwick.

"This secures the hill farm of old Jasper—three hundred acres at forty dollars per acre—does it not, Sedgwick?" said Browning.

They ordered $10,000 to be placed to the credit of the hospitals and bought exchange on New York and London for $1,000,000. The rest they took with them in money.

In dividing there was a little dispute. Browning insisted that he was entitled to only forty-six and two-thirds per cent. of the amount, as his money was as seven to eight of Jim's.

"Why will you bother me with those vulgar fractions, Browning? Try to be a gentleman," said Sedgwick. "We share alike on this business, remember that; and say what a country this is to get rich in at four dollars a day!"

So it was settled. Their friends were told they had made a little stake, and were going home; the good-byes were spoken, and the young men turned ·their faces eastward.

CHAPTER IV.

SMILES AND TEARS.

While riding through Nevada, Browning, after a long look from the car window, said :

" By Jove, Jim, but is not this a desolate region? It is as though when the rocky foundation had been laid, there was no more material to furnish this part of the world with, and the work stopped."

"Yes, Jack," was Sedgwick's answer. " I knew an old man once. He was very aged and most decrepit. His face was but a mass of wrinkles ; his back was bent ; he always wore a frown on his face, and every relative he had wished that he was dead. But his bank account was a mighty one ; he had given grand homes and plenty of money to each of his six children ; he still possessed a fortune so large that his neighbors could not estimate it. I never look out upon the face of Nevada that I do not think of that old man.

" The fairest structures in San Francisco were built of the treasures taken from Nevada hills; clear across the continent, in every great city are beautiful blocks which are but Nevada gold and silver converted into stone and iron and glass ; in every State are fair homes which were bought or redeemed with the money obtained here in the desert. Beyond that, the money already supplied from Nevada

mines has changed the calculations of commerce, and
made itself a ruling factor in prices ; it has given our
nation a new standing among the nations of the
world ; because of it, the lands are worth more
money even in the Miami Valley where I was born ;
because of it, better wages are paid to laborers
throughout our republic ; it has been a factor of
good, a blessing to civilization ; and yet Eastern people revile Nevada and look upon it as did the relatives of the old man I was telling you of, because it
is wrinkled and sere and always wears a frowning
face."

As Sedgwick and Browning neared Chicago, the
former began to grow restless, and finally said :

"Jack, old friend, you must go home with me.   It
is something I dread more than riding mustangs or
fighting cowboys.   It is more than five years since I
went away, and it will be just worse than a fire in a
mine to face."

Browning agreed that a few days more or less
would not count. "Because," he said, "if Rose Jenvie
is still Rose Jenvie, it will not much matter; if Rose
Jenvie is not Rose Jenvie, then, by Jove, every minute
of delay in knowing that fact is good.   Besides, you
know, I want to see that three-hundred-acre farm of .
old Jasper's on the hill which you are to buy."

They remained a few hours only in Chicago, and
took the evening train for the valley of the Miami.
The next morning, about seven o'clock, they left the
cars at a little village station, and started on foot for
the old home of Sedgwick, a mile away.

"Browning," said Sedgwick, "it was mighty kind of you to come with me. I ran bare-footed over this road every summer day of my boyhood. In that old school-house I could show you notches which I cut in the tables and benches, and it seems now as though I was choking." They came to the old churchyard. "Hold, Jack," said Sedgwick, "let us go in here and look to see if any more graves have been added since I went away."

They climbed the fence, and Sedgwick led the way to a plot of ground where there were three headstones. "Thank God, there are no new graves," he said. "This was my sister; this, my baby brother, and this, my mother," pointing to the names on the head-stones. "Had my mother been alive, I would long ago have come back."

Then, with more calmness, he turned his steps back to the road, but he was shaking in every limb when he opened the old gate and walked up toward the house. The path was lined with lilacs in full bloom, and a robin in a tree near by was calling her mate. "The same old lilacs, the same old redbreast, Browning," he said, with white lips.

He did not stop to knock, but pushed the door suddenly open and strode within. Walking up to an old man, who was reading his Bible, he said, "Father, I am sorry that I fought the mulatto, if it grieved you, but the black rascal deserved it, all the same."

The old man surveyed him wildly for a moment, then broke completely down, and, wringing the young man's hands, could only sob:

"Thank God, my son, whom I thought was lost, is
back again. Thank God!"

Then the brothers and their wives and children
came in, and there was such a scene that Browning
slipped out, seated himself on the piazza, and mop-
ping his brow with his kerchief, said, "Bless my soul;
I believe I will never go home. There is more real
enjoyment at a miner's funeral in Virginia City; there
is, by Jove.

' But they found him after a little, and Sedgwick
presented him to his kinfolk as his close companion,
and he was welcomed in a way which touched him
deeply, and made him conclude that the world was
filled with good people.

Soon the news spread, and the neighbors began to
pour in, and what a day it was! What old memories
were awakened and rehearsed; what every one had
done; who had died; who had married; all the
history of the little place for all the years.

Going home after a long absence is 'a little
like what one might imagine of a ressurec-
tion from the dead. There is exceeding joy, but
mingled with it is much of the damp and chill of the
tomb. Indeed, going home after a long absence
"causes all the burial places of memory to give up
their dead," and through all the joy there is an under-
tone of sorrow, for all the reminders are of the fact
that the calmest lives are speedily sweeping on; that
there is no halting in the swift transit between birth
and death.

Three days passed, and notwithstanding the enjoyment, Sedgwick found that there was a good deal of trouble worrying the family. The old mortgage of $5,000 was not paid ; rather, it had been doubled to make a first payment on a 200-acre farm adjoining, and with fitting up and stocking the old place, and with bad crops, the debts amounted altogether to more than $20,000. He did not tell any one of his good fortune. He was dressed in a plain business suit, without a single ornament. The watch he carried for convenience was merely a cheap silver watch.

On the fourth day, Browning said to his friend : 'Jim, old pard, I must be off to-morrow. You have had a good visit. Come over to England with me for a month, and help me through with—Rose and the old man."

" Agreed, Jack," said Sedgwick. " I want to fix up some little things here, and I do not want to be around when the fixing shall be understood. It will be a good excuse to get away."

Then going to a desk, he wrote a few words, took a bill of exchange for $100,000 from his pocketbook, endorsed it, making it payable to his father, folded the bill inside the letter, sealed it and directed it to his father ; then putting the letter in his pocket, said, " That will make it all right."

At supper that evening he informed the family that he was going on the early train with his friend and might be gone a month or six weeks, after which he believed he would return, settle down and become steady. All tried to dissuade him, but Browning helped him, telling the family he needed his friend's help on serious business ; and so that night the kindling was put in the kitchen stove, the dough for biscuits for breakfast was set, the tea-kettle filled, the chickens fixed for frying, and the coffee ground.

It was but a little after daylight next morning when, the breakfast over, they were ready to start. They shook hands all round, and when it came to saying good-bye to his father, Sedgwick drew out the letter, and giving it to the old man, said : " Father, when you hear the train pull out of the village, open that letter. It contains a little keepsake for you which I picked up by a scratch in Nevada." And they were off.

When that letter was opened, and the astounding figures on the bill were read and comprehended, what a time there was at that house, and how the neighbors came again to see the wonderful paper, and how it was figured how many farms it would buy, what houses it would build and furnish, and how the boy who had been expelled from school for fighting had done it all! What a smashing of old theories it made, and how every wild boy in the neighborhood to whom the evil example of the bad Sedgwick boy had been held up as an illustration of total depravity and as proof that nothing of good ever came to a youth that would fight and get expelled from school, rejoiced ! To these, what a day of exultation that bill of exchange brought !

But it was only a day, before there began to circulate rumors that the whole thing was but a joke; that the bill would be repudiated when presented for payment, or at most that it was only for $1,000.

Sedgwick, *pere*, with his sons, lost no time in testing the matter. Sedgwick had written in the letter that though the bill was drawn on New York, any bank in Cincinnati would cash it. So they repaired to the city, and calling on their lawyer, asked him to go with them and identify them at some bank, as they desired to get a little check cashed. He complied.

The cashier looked at the bill and asked in what kind of money the payment was wanted.

The old man thought he would give his neighbors an object lesson, and replied that he would take it in gold.

The cashier smiled and asked him how he would take it away.

The old man said, "I do not understand you."

"It will, in gold, weigh about 400 pounds," said the cashier.

At this the lawyer became interested in a moment and said : "Four hundred pounds of gold ! What kind of a check have you ?"

"It is a bill of exchange on New York for $100,-000," said the cashier.

" One hundred thousand dollars ! " said the lawyer ; " Great heavens ! have you found an oil well on your farm, robbed a bank, or what ?"

" No," said the elder Sedgwick, " but my wild boy has come from Nevada, and I guess this is a part of the great bonanza."

Finally $25,000 was drawn in paper, enough to clear up all the home indebtedness, and the rest left on deposit until the son and brother should return; for, as they talked it all over, they concluded that he had left with them all his fortune, except traveling expenses.

CHAPTER V.

Browning and Sedgwick reached New York and took passage on the first outgoing Cunarder. When the ship steamed out of the harbor, it entered at once into a lively sea, and the great craft grew strangely unsteady. Browning was a good sailor, but Sedgwick found it was all he could do to maintain his equanimity. " Jack," he said at last, " this is worse exercise then riding a Texas steer." " Did you ever ride a Texas steer ? " asked Browning. " Indeed I have," said Sedwick. " The cowboys have a game of that kind. When a lot of steers are corraled, they climb up on the cross-bar over the gate ; the gate is opened, the steers are turned out with a rush, and the science is to drop from the cross-bar upon a steer and ride him. If you miss, you are liable to be trodden to death. If you strike fairly, then the trick is to see how long you can hold on. It is rough exercise, but I believe it is preferable to this perpetual rising, falling and rolling. The infernal thing seems to work like an Ingersoll drill. It turns a quarter of a circle on one's stomach with every blow it strikes."

They had sailed into an expiring storm that was fast losing its strength ; the waves were breaking down, and by the time night came on the ship was running nearly on an even keel, only gently rolling as it swept magnificently on its voyage.

The two miners walked the deck, or sat by the rail, until far into the night, admiring the glorified structure on which they rode ; watching the stars and the sea, and saw with other things the beautiful spectacle of another ship as grand as their own, that swept close by them on its way to New York.   Its whole 500 feet of length was a blaze of light, and as the Titans whistled hoarsely to each other a greeting without abating their speed, it seemed to the two landsmen as though two stars had met in space, saluted and passed on, each in its own sublime orbit.

Sedgwick and Browning soon made the acquaintance of several passengers.   A day or two later an animated conversation sprang up in the smoking room.   An American was declaring that his country was the greatest on earth because it could feed the world from its mighty food area.

An Englishman disputed the claim, because the profits of the manufacturers of little England were more than all the profits from all the lands of the United States.

A Frenchman claimed the palm for France, because in France the people were artists ; from a little basis, from material well-nigh worthless in itself, the Frenchman could, by infusing French brain into it, create a thing of beauty for which the world was glad to exchange gold and gems.

Then Browning said ; "You are all right, looking from a present horizon ; all wrong, when the years are taken into account. The great country of the world is to be the country that produces the metals in the greatest quantity and variety, and whose people acquire the art of turning them to the best account. This ship that we are on, a few months ago, was but unsightly ore in the ground. Look at it now! Tried by fire and fused with labor, it has grown into this marvelous structure. England's greatness and wealth are due, primarily, all to her mining. Her civilization can be measured by her progress in reducing metals. She will begin to fall behind soon, for America has, in addition to such mines as England possesses, endless mines of gold and silver, and, after all, the precious metals rule the nations and measure their civilization. It has always been so and always will be. Those mines in America will build up greater manufactures than England possesses; they will create artists more skilled than even beautiful France can boast of. A hundred years hence, all other nations will be second-class by comparison."

The next day the conversation was resumed and carried on with much spirit, until Sedgwick, who had been reading through it all, laid down his book, and in a brief pause of the talk said :

"Neither fruitful fields, rich mines, nor skilled artisans, nor all combined, are enough to make great nations. A hundred nations existed when Rome was founded. They had as fair prospects as did Rome, but ninety of the hundred are forgotten ; the other ten are remembered but as inferior nations. It was the stock of men and women that made

Rome's grandeur and terror.   For five hundred years
an unfaithful wife was never known in Rome.   The
result was Rome had to be great and grand.

    " I stood once on the crest of the Rocky Mountains
in Montana.   Near together were two springs, out of
each of which the water flowed away in a creek.   One
follows the mountains down to the eastward, the other
to the west.   One finds its final home in the Gulf of
Mexico, the other in the Pacific.   The one takes on
other streams, its volume steadily swells ; before it
flows far its channel is hewed through fertile fields ;
gaining in power, the argosies of commerce find a
home upon its broad bosom, and it is a recognized
power in the world, a mighty factor in the calculations of merchants and shippers.

    "But in the meantime it becomes tainted, until at last
when it finds its grave in the Gulf, so foul are its
waters that they discolor for miles the deep blue of
the sea.

    " The other starts with a babble as joyous as the
carols of childhood ; when it reaches the valley it
begins its struggle through a lava-blasted desert ;
when the desert is passed, it has to grind its channel
through rugged mountains that tear its waters into
foam, and at last in mighty throes, on the stormy bar
it finds its grave in the roaring ocean.   Its existence
is one long, mighty struggle ; there are awful chasms
in its path into which it is hurled ; the thirsty desert
encroaches upon its current ; mountains block its way ;
at the very last furious seas seek to beat it back, but

to the end it holds itself pure as when it starts on its
way from the mountain spring.

"These rivers are typical of men and of nations. Some
meet no obstruction ; they glide on, gaining in wealth
and power ; at last, they become in one way a
blessing, in another a terror; but in the meantime,
they grow corrupt because of the world's contact;
and so pass, gross and discolored, into eternity.

"Others have lives that are one long struggle
unheard-of obstacles are ever rising in their paths,
but they fight on and on, and when at last their
course is run, those who trace them through their
careers, with uncovered heads are bound to say that
they kept their integrity to the last, and that all the
world's discouragements could not disarm their power,
break their courage, or dim the clear mirror of their
purity."

Sedgwick ceased speaking, but after a moment,
looking up, he added :   "Not very far from the
sources of these two streams, there is another foun-
tain in the hills, out of which flows another stream as
large and fair as either of the others.   It, too, goes
tumbling down the mountain gorge, increasing in
volume, until it strikes the valley, then grows less
and less in size, until a few miles below it disappears
in the sands.

"This, too, is typical of men and nations.   They
begin life buoyant and brave ; they rush on exultingly
at first, but the quicksands of vice or crime or disease
are before them, and they sink and leave no name.

"The man or nation that is to be great must be

born great. Those who succeed are those who are guided into channels which make success possible.

"The strength of the modern world rests on the modern home. That did not come of rich mines or fields, but of the sovereign genius of the men of northern Europe; and the glory was worked out amid poverty, hardships and sorrows."

But the voyage was over at last, and the two miners hastened to take the train for the home of Browning in Devonshire. They arrived at the village at midnight and went to a hotel, or, as Sedgwick said: "This, Jack, is han Hinglish Hinn, is it?"

Next day was Sunday and Browning was up early. He said to Sedgwick: "Wait until I go and prospect the croppings about here a little. It is a good while since I was on this lead, and I want to see how it has been worked since I went away."

He came back in half an hour a good deal worked up. "Do you know, Jim," he said, "by Jove, they are all gone! That old step-father has 'gone pards with old Jenvie, and they have all moved to London, and are running a banking and brokerage establishment. I have their address and we will chase them up to-morrow, but I do not like the look of things at all. Why, Rose Jenvie in one season in London would blossom out and shine like a gold bar."

"Stuff," answered Sedgwick. "In Texas we always noticed that if we ever turned out a blood mare she was sure to pick up the sorriest old mustang on the range for a running mate. Your Rose would be more apt to pick up a husband here than in London for the first two or three years she might be there."

Said Browning : "I say, Jim, did you mean that mustang story to go for an excuse for Miss Rose calling me 'Jack?'"

"O, no!" said Sedgwick, "when she called you Jack, she was just a silly colt that could not discriminate."

"I see," said Browning, "but I say, Jim, you ought to have been here then. By Jove, she might have even fancied you."

"Don't you dare to talk that way," said Sedgwick, "or I will try to cut you out when we see her, unless, as is quite possible, she has already been some happy man's wife for two or three years."

"Jim, I say, stop that!" said Browning. "It will be time to face that infernal possibility when I cannot help it. Bless my soul, but the thought of it makes me sea-sick."

They breakfasted together, and were smoking their after-breakfast cigars—Nevada-like—when the church bells began to ring.

"When did you attend church last, Browning?" asked Sedgwick.

"I have been a good deal remiss in that," was the reply..

"Suppose we go. It will be a novelty, and you will see more friends there than in any other place."

"A good thought, old boy," said Browning, "and we shall have time only to dress."

A few minutes later they emerged from the hotel,
and proceeded to the old church that Browning had
attended during all his childhood.

Queerly enough, the sermon was on the return of
the Prodigal Son.   The good clergyman dilated on
his theme.   He told what a tough citizen the Prodigal Son was in his youth, how he was given to
boating and steeple-chasing, and staying out nights
and worrying the old father, until finally he ran away.
" Photographing you, Jack," whispered Sedgwick.
When he came to the part where the Prodigal ate the
husks, Sedgwick whispered again : " He means the
hash in that restaurant on the Divide, Jack."

Then the picture of the joy of the father on the
return of this son, and the moral which the parable
teaches, were graphically given.   At last the service
was over, and as the congregation filed out there was
a general rush for Browning, for the whole congregation recognized him, though the almost beardless boy
that went away had returned in the full flush of manhood.   He was overwhelmed with greetings and
congratulations over his safe return, and as Sedgwick
was introduced as Browning's friend the welcomes to
him were most cordial, though there was many a
glance at the fashionably-cut clothing of the young
men.

The people were all in Sunday attire, many of the
ladies wearing gay colors.   The day was warm and
sunny and they lingered on the green, talking joyously, when suddenly a cry of terror arose, and looking, the young men saw a two-year old Hereford bull

coming at full speed at the crowd, and with the evident intention of charging direct into it. Every one was paralyzed; that is, all but one. That one was Sedgwick. Near him was a woman who had a long red scarf doubled and flung carelessly over her shoulder. In an instant Sedgwick had thrown off his coat, snatched the scarf from the woman and dashed out of the crowd directly toward the coming terror. He shouted and shook the scarf, and the bull, seeing it, rushed directly for it. As he struck the scarf, like a flash Sedgwick caught the ring in the bull's nose with his left hand, the left horn in his right hand, and twisting the ring and giving a mighty wrench on the horn, both man and bull went prone upon the turf. But the man was above and the bull below, and clinging to ring and horn and with knee on the bull's throat, Sedgwick bent all his might upon the brute's head and held him down.

Browing was at his side in a moment, and at Sedgwick's muffled cry to tie his forelegs, Browning seized the scarf, lashed the bull's legs together, and then both men arose.

Securing his coat quickly, Sedgwick seized Browning's arm, and said, " Let us get out of this, old man. You told me this was a bully place, but I did not look for it quite in that form."

" Where did you learn that trick ?" asked Browning.

" In Texas," said Sedgwick. " It is a game we play with yearlings there, but we never try it on an old stager, because, you see, if one should fall he

would be in the sump, or in a drift where the air
would be bad in a minute.   That was a big fellow,
but he had a wring in his nose, which made me the
more sure of him, and then you see there was nothing else to do.   I will go to no more churches in
England with you without carrying a lariat and
revolver."

"It was a good job, Jack," said Browning; "by
Jove, it was.   I am sorry it happened, but I am glad
you did it.   I don't believe I could have managed it
any better myself."

The feat was the talk of the town, and it grew in
size with every repetition, and in the next day's
paper it was magnified beyond all proportions.   For-
tunately, the printers got both the names of Browning and Sedgwick spelled wrong, which was all the
comfort the young men had out of it.

On Monday morning the friends went out in the
country and looked over the estate that Browning
had been hoping to make money enough to purchase.
Browning explained his plans for improving it, and
the address of the owner in London was obtained.

In the evening they took the train for London.
The landlord had had a great night and day because
of callers on Browning and his friend, and would take
nothing of his guests except a five-pound note to
hand to the woman from whose shoulder Sedgwick
had caught the scarf.

CHAPTER VI.

BONANZAS.

It was in the gray of the morning when they entered the mighty city by the Thames. They sought a hotel, where they breakfasted; then waiting until business men had gone to their work, they called a carriage and drove to the home of Browning's step-father.

It was Browning's turn now to tremble and perspire. "Bless my soul, Jim!" said he, "no drift on the Comstock was ever half so hot as this, never, by Jove!"

They were admitted and shown to the parlor. Browning asked for Mrs. and Miss Hamlin, and bade the servant say some friends desired to see them.

Who can picture the joy that followed the coming of those ladies into the room! It is better to imagine it.

After an hour had passed, and the tears had dried, and the tremblings ceased a little, Browning's sister drew him a little aside and asked him why he did not inquire about some one else.

"Because," said he, "I dare not."

"Well," said the dear girl, "she is due here even now. If you will go into the library I will meet her, tell her mother has a caller, and propose that we go to the library. When we get there I will lose myself for your sake, and, like the famous witches, ' dissolve into thin air.'"

" She is not married ? " asked Browning.

" No," replied his sister.

" Heart whole ? " Browning queried.

" How should I know ? " answered his sister ; " but there is the door-bell.   Hurry Jack ! This way to the library ! "

Rose Jenvie came in.   Grace met and greeted her in the hall.

" Why, Grace," said Rose, " you have been crying. What is wrong, dear ? "

" Nothing is wrong," said Grace, " nothing at all, and I have not been crying."   And all the time the tears were running down her cheeks.

" Why," exclaimed Rose, " what in the world is the matter ?   What has so upset you this morning ? "

" I tell you, nothing," answered Grace.   " Mamma has a caller in the parlor ; let us go to the library."

Reaching the door, Grace opened it for Rose, and then said, pettishly, " There ! I have forgotten a letter I wish to show you ; go in, and I will be back directly."

Rose naturally walked in, when Grace closed the door behind her, turned the key noiselessly and fled.

The curtains were half drawn, the day was cloudy, and Rose advanced two or three steps into the room before she discovered another occupant.   That occupant rose as she stopped.   She saw a manly fellow with hair cut short and full mustache.   He saw a woman a little above the medium height, with hazel·

eyes, full and proud, a fair, clear-cut face, a slight but
perfectly developed form, and the face wore a look
which it seemed to him was sad, despite its beauty, as
though some thought within made a shadow on the
fair young life.

The young man gazed a moment, then raising and
opening his arms, in a voice that shook perceptibly,
said, " Rose ! "

She gazed a moment, then with a joyous cry of " O,
Jack ! " sprang into the outstretched arms, and for
the first time in their lives their lips met.

There were tears in Jack's eyes ; the tears were
raining down Rose's face, and both were shaking as
with a burning ague.   Browning sank upon a sofa,
still clasping the fair girl in his strong arms, and seat-
ing her beside him.

" O, Rose," he said, " I have dreamed of this meeting ever since I left you, by sea and land, under the
sunshine, in the deep mine's depths, by day and night.
I love you, I do not know when I did not love you ;
I have come for you, will you be my wife ? "

Then Rose said : " You went away without a good-
bye or any message.   You never wrote.   You have
been gone more than four years."   But with a smile
which was enchantment to Jack, she added : " If I
could have found any one to marry me, I would have
shown you, but no one would, because when I was
young I kept such bad company."

Then how they did talk!   Jack repeated all the old
inaccuracies which lovers have called up since the
Stone Age, the burden of which was that the memory

of her face had been his light in the darkest mine ; the memory of her voice had been the music for which his soul had been listening for years.

And Rose told the enraptured young man how hard her lot had been to conceal a love which she had no right to own, because it had never been asked ; how hard it had been for her to simulate contentment and cheerfulness, but after all how it had been her comfort and support, because she had never doubted that he would come back.

Then Jack, between kisses, told his charmer that he had worked every day for years ; that he had gathered up quite a many good pounds ; that if she would be his wife, if nothing could be done in England, they would bid England good-bye and make their home beyond the sea. And she consented, adding : " If you have to run away again, see that you do not go alone. You were always so wild that from the first you have needed some careful person to look after you."

An hour later, Grace came, unlocked the door, and found the happy pair arm-in-arm walking up and down the room. Going up to them, and looking into their faces, she said :

" Why, Rose, you have been crying ; what is wrong, dear ? "

" Nothing is wrong," she answered, " nothing is wrong, and I have not been crying ; have I, Jack ? But, Grace, was it fair to give me no hint, and thus permit Jack to surprise me into giving away something that I ought to have kept him on the rack for a month at least about before conferring ? "

Grace smiled and said : " Are you quite satisfied, Jack ? "

" Quite," he replied.

" And are you as happy as you deserve to be, Rose ? "

" Oh, Grace," said Rose, and then the two young women both cried and embraced each other until Jack gently separated them, and said : " Come, we must find Jim. Jim is my friend. His judgment is perfect, and I must submit this business to him."

" Mr. Sedgwick has gone back to the hotel," said Grace, and a serious look was in her eyes as she spoke.   But in a moment she smiled and said : " When I told him where you were and who was with you, he laughed and said : ' It is liable to be a case of working after hours.   When the young lady succeeds in extricating herself, tell Jack, please, that I have gone out to take in London, and will see him at the hotel when he finds time to call.' "

" And who is Mr. Sedgwick ? " asked Rose.

" The best and noblest man in all this world," replied Jack.

" Oh, Jack ! " said Rose.

" It is true, all the same, my sorceress," said Browning.   " I have seen him tested.   He has been my close companion for lo ! these many months."

" I am jealous of him," said Rose.   " But why did he run away ?   I want to know all your friends."

" I suspect the truth is he left out of consideration

for you and myself," said Browning. "He knew how I felt, and he hoped I would not be disappointed, and I suspect he thought the sacredness of our joy ought not to be disturbed."

"Very fine, of course," said Grace ; "very thoughtful and considerate, but why did he not stop to ask himself if it was quite fair to leave me all alone."

"You are right, Gracie," said Browning, "and this act of his shows an absence of mind on his part that I did not expect."

Then all laughed, but Grace blushed a little while she laughed.

Then Mrs. Hamlin came in. She warmly congratulated the happy pair.

They strolled into the sitting-room, and soon after the mail was brought in. The first things the girls siezed upon were the papers from Devonshire, for they were like other people. Men and women live in a place for years, and daily express the belief that the home paper is the worst specimen they ever saw, but let one of them absent himself or herself for a week, and the same newspaper from the old home is the one thing they want above all others. Glancing over the paper, Grace suddenly looked up and said: "Why, they had a wonderfully exciting episode down in ——— on Sunday last." She had come upon the account of the exploit with the bull, and read it aloud.

The names being misspelled, she never suspected the real facts.

"That was a brave man," she said, when she had

finished. "It must have been splendid. I wish I could have seen it. How it must have astonished those villagers. I would like to kiss the man who performed that feat."

"Would you?" said Jack laughingly. "I will tell him so when I meet him."

"Please do," said Grace. "He must have been a grand matador from Spain," and springing up, she caught a tidy from the furniture, danced around the room with it, holding it in both hands as though bating an angry bull, and suddenly dropping it, made a grab for an imaginary ring and horn, and twisting both wrists quickly, cried out: "Did I not down his highness beautifully?"

"Beautifully," said Browning, "and when I meet the man I will tell him of your vivid imitation."

"And don't forget to tell him I would like to kiss him," said Grace, laughing.

"Maybe I can fix it so you can tell him yourself, Grace."

"Do you know him, Jack?" asked Rose.

Jack smiled and said, "Perhaps."

"What do mean, Jack," asked Grace.

"I know the man, Grace; and so do you," said Jack.

"True?" asked Grace.

"True," said Jack.

"I know him?." asked Grace. "Why, who is there in ——— that would do anything like that?"

"No one that I know of," said Jack. "But you have forgotten a somewhat diffident and reserved young man with whom you were conversing in the parlor an hour ago ? "

Grace grew pale, and sank into a seat. "O, Jack, you don't mean —— ? "

" Yes," he said, interrupting her, "it was Sedgwick, and it was splendidly done, too. It was, by Jove ! "

" Honest? " asked Grace.

" Honest, and I will deliver your message."

Blushing scarlet, Grace sprang up and began to plead.

Browning would promise nothing except that he might possibly put the matter off a little while. " But," he added, " I believe Jim would give more to see your imitation than you would to see the original performance repeated without change of scene."

" Were you not sharp, Jack, to get me to commit myself before ever gaining a glimpse of this wonderful man ? " asked Rose.

"Indeed, was," the replied. " Why, I recall now that once when we were having a friendly dispute, he threatened that unless I came to his terms he would come over here, search you out, and try to steal you away from me."

" But then he had not seen *me*," said Grace, mockingly.

All laughed at that. Rose spoke first and said: " But, if he is your close friend, and has come to England with you, why does he go back to the hotel ?"

Browning smiled and said, "Why, child, save for three days in his own father's house, he has been under no gentleman's private roof for years. He does not know our English methods. And that makes me think; I, too, must go. My own tenure here was a little uncertain, when I went away, and now I, too, am going to the hotel. When my father comes, Grace, you may tell him I have been here, that I called, but that I am staying at the —— Hotel. If he comes and calls upon me, I shall be glad to see him; if he does not, why, tomorrow at ten, if you girls will have your hats and wraps on, I think Jim and myself will be glad to engage you for a drive. Jim has not been forbidden the premises, and he can call for you while I wait outside."

No persuasion would make him remain. Putting his arm around Rose, he drew her to him, and said: "We will give the old folks a chance to do the fair thing; if they will not, what then, little one?"

"Henceforth," she answered, gravely, but low and sweet, "your home is to be my home, your God my God." Then she bent and touched his hand with her lips, and he wended his way back to find Sedgwick.

CHAPTER VII.

A DINNER PARTY.

And Sedgwick, what of him ? He had gone, as he said, "to see Jack through, as Jack had stood by him in Ohio," but when Grace Hamlin—or Grace Meredith, which was her real name—at their summons entered the parlor he was transfixed. Just medium height was she, slight but perfect in form, with darkish-brown eyes and clear-cut features, a golden chestnut curly mass of hair, the hand of a queen, and the hand-clasp of a sincere, true and happy woman. And poor Jim was lost in a moment.

He called up all his self-possession, and did the best he could, but he seized the first opportunity to get away where he could think. Once outside the house, he hailed a cab, told the driver to jog around for an hour or two, and then land him at the —— Hotel. Once started, he settled back and began to cross-question himself, and to moralize over the situation.

"I have seen prettier girls than this one, seen them in Ohio, in Texas, in Virginia City, and they never gave me an extra heart-beat. What is the matter with me now ? When that girl smiled up in my face, welcomed me as her brother's friend, and told me she was glad I had come with him, all the clutches broke off my cage, and I thought I would

64

in a moment bring up in the sump below the 1,700 foot level, smashed so they would have to sew the pieces up in canvas to bring me to the surface. It is a clear case that I am gone, and what the mischief am I going to do? Suppose I brace up and try to win her, and fail, then I shall be done for sure enough. The old world so far has had no particular attractions for me, and were I to ask her to look at me, and she, like a sensible woman that she is, should first look surprised at my assurance, and then respectfully decline, what would there be left for me? Suppose again, I could fool her into accepting, then what? I, a rough Nevada miner, linked for life with a London fairy—beauty and the beast—what would I do with her? In this babel, what could I do? What could she do on the old Jasper farm on the hill? I have it. I won't see her again. I will go and pack my grip, tell Jack I have received a cable which takes me home, and I will leave to-morrow.

"But then I could not go as I came. Those steady brown eyes would follow me; when the sunlight would turn its glint on gold and purple clouds, her chestnut curls would be sure to flash before my eyes, and then there would be a voice crying to me ceaselessly: 'You who prided yourself on being brave enough to do any needed thing, you on the first real trial lowered your flag and fled in a panic.' A nice fix I have got myself into. All my life, through all my dare-devil days, on the ranges in Texas, down amid the swelling clay of the Comstock, everywhere, my soul has been equal to the occasion, and I have been able to acquit myself in a way not to attract attention to my deficiencies. But now my heart has gone back on me; a pair of eyes have confused my vision, and a little hand has knocked me out on the first round. I am in a deuce of a fix, surely." So he rattled on to himself.

The driver was a garrulous whip. From time to time he had been calling down to Sedgwick the names of famous points of interest along the route, which had been unheeded by the absorbed occupant of the cab. Finally the driver explained that a certain structure was Westminster Abbey.

"And what is Westminster Abbey?"

"It is where kings and queens and great soldiers and scholars are buried," said cabbie.

"Burial lots come high there, do they not?" said Sedgwick.

"Why, man, there are no lots sold there," said cabbie. "It is a place which was hundreds of years ago set aside for England's great dead to be buried in. The brightest dream of an Englishman is to rest there at last."

"Do they dream when they get there?" asked Sedgwick.

"Why, man," said cabbie, "when they get there they are dead."

"Great place!" said Sedgwick.

"The greatest in all England," replied cabbie.

"Do you know of any Englishmen who are in a hurry to be carried there?" said Sedgwick.

" O, no," said cabbie, " the best of them are not in any hurry about it."

" You Englishmen must be a queer race, to be always dreaming of going to a place and still are never anxious to start," said Sedgwick.

Cabbie gave up trying to explain the majesty of the great Abbey to one so utterly obtuse as Sedgwick seemed to be. He drove on in silence for h al an hour or forty minutes before he rallied enough to speak again. Then he pointed to a structure and called down to Sedgwick that the place was Newgate.

"What is there peculiar about Newgate ?" asked Sedgwick.

" Why, it is the famous Newgate prison," said, cabbie.

Sedgwick roused himself and asked, " What do they do in Newgate ? "

" What do they do ? " said cabbie, " what do they do ? Why, they hang people there sometimes."

" Get down, please, and ask them what they will charge to hang me," said Sedgwick. He did not smile ; he seemed in sober earnest.

Cabbie looked at him for an instant, then whipped up his horses and hurried him to the hotel. Arriving there, he sprang down and said, " This is your hotel." Sedgwick got out and was walking off mechanically, when cabbie said, " Five shillings, please, sir." Sedgwick, with " O, I had forgotten," handed the man a guinea, and passed into the hotel. Cabbie looked after him, then tapped his forehead as much as to say, " He is off in the upper story," and mounting his box, drove away.

Sedgwick went to his rooms, threw off his coat, opened a window, sat down, put his heels on the table, lighted a cigar which went out in a moment, and an hour later when Browning, radiant, joyous, and exulting, returned, he found him there, still holding the unlighted cigar in his mouth, his feet still on the table, and a puzzled, undecided, and absorbed look on his face.

Browning rushed up to him, crying, " Jim, congratulate me, I have seen her, and it is all settled. She is an angel, Jim, and she has promised to be my wife. O, but God is good to me."

" I am glad, old man, I rejoice with you," said Sedgwick. " I hope with all my heart no cloud will ever cross the sunshine of your lives." Then he relapsed again into his moody way.

" What ails you, Jim ?" asked Browning. " Does this great babel oppress your spirits ? "

" I believe it does, Jack," he answered. " I was just thinking as you came in that I had better pull out for home. The atmosphere here is like a drift without any air-pipe."

" Nonsense," said Browning; "you cannot go You must wait for my wedding. It would be all spoiled without you. I was planning it on the way. It will be in the church, of course, just before midday. You will be the best man—as usual. You and my sister shall do the honors that day. All my friends will be there. I will have the church smothered in flowers. I will corrupt the organist, bribe the choir, double-bank the preacher in advance, and we will all have a rousing time. We will, by Jove!"

Sedgwick smiled at his friend's happiness, and said: " Did you ever think that maybe I would be a little out of training for a performance of that kind? I think I would sooner risk keeping my seat on a wild mustang."

"You can do it, Sedgwick," said Jack. "You must do it. I would not feel half married unless you were present, and then, did you not promise to come and see me through?"

"Who will give away the bride?" asked Sedgwick.

The question seemed to startle Browning. "That reminds me," he said, doubtingly, "that I have neither seen my governor nor old man Jenvie. I left home telling mother and Grace that before I went home to live I would have to be invited by the governor. And that reminds me, too, Jim, there must not be a word about my money. I have only carried the idea that I worked for three years in the mines in America. They will reckon it up and conclude that if I was prudent I may have saved £400 or £500."

" That reminds me," said Sedgwick, "that no one must know that I have anything more than the savings of three or four years' work. It would give you away if the facts were known about my little fortune. But, Jack, could you not get along just as well without me? You ought to be in your own home and ought to enjoy every moment of time, while I am, in this vast waste of houses, what one solitary monkey would be in a South American wilderness."

"I will not hear of it, old pard," said Browning. "You see, if the governor asks me home you will go with me, and we will cabin together as of old. We will, by Jove! If he does not, then you must help me hold the fort in this hotel until I can bring my wife here," and he blushed like a girl when he spoke the word "wife."

The day wore heavily away. It was almost dark when a carriage stopped at the hotel and the cards of Archibald Hamlin and Percival Jenvie were brought in. Browning received them, and glancing at them handed them to Sedgwick, whispering, "They are the old duffers, Jim," caught up his hat, said to the servant, "Show me the gentlemen," and followed him out of the room.

He was absent a full half-hour. When he returned the two old men accompanied him and were presented to Jack. They were very gracious, invited Sedgwick to come with his son and make his son's home his home while in London.

Sedgwick was shy when there were ladies present, but men did not disconcert him.

He thanked Mr. Hamlin for his kind invitation, but begged to be excused, adding, "I am but a miner, not yet a month from underground. I have lived a miner's life for years. You do not understand, but that is not a good school in which to prepare a student for polite society."

" Tut, tut," said the old gentleman, with English
heartiness. " We have a big, rambling old house.
You can have your quarters there. When you
become bored you can retreat to them. You shall
have a key and go and come when you please. We
should all be hurt were not Jack's friend made welcome
under our roof so long as he pleased to remain in
London."

" Well, let me think it over to-night. If I can
gather the courage, maybe I will accept to-morrow,"
said Sedgwick.

Then Jenvie interposed, saying, " Mr. Sedgwick,
let us make a compromise. My house is but a step
from Hamlin's; make it your home half the time.
Really it should be. In England friends only stop at
hotels when traveling."

" Come, Jim," said Jack; " you see it must be, and
that is the right thing. Ours are old-fashioned
people, just up from Devonshire. What would you
have thought had I insisted upon stopping at that
hotel at the station near your father's house ? "

Sedgwick yielded at last. Their trunks were
packed in a few minutes, the bill settled, and they
drove away.

Reaching the Hamlin home they were shown at
once to their apartments, and were informed that so
soon as they were ready dinner would be served.

They were not long in dressing, and together they
descended to the parlor. Besides the family, the
Jenvie family were also present. Grace met them at
the door, shook hands with Sedgwick, and welcomed

him with a word and a smile which set all his pulses
bounding, and, taking his arm, presented him to the
strangers; then shouted gaily: "Follow us! dinner
is waiting."

Sedgwick was given the seat at the right of his
host; Grace took the seat at his right, with Jack and
Rose opposite.

The ladies were radiant in evening costume, and
Sedgwick with a mighty effort threw off the depres-
sion which had burdened the day and appeared at his
very best.   •

Mrs. Hamlin, judging shrewdly that perhaps it
would relieve the stranger from embarrassment to
engage him in conversation, with beautiful tact
brought him to tell the company of his own country,
remarking that "We insular people have but a vague
idea at best of America."

With a smile, Sedgwick replied: "I do not know
very much myself of my native country, for since I
left school (here he glanced at Jack and his eyes
twinkled) I merely wandered slowly through the
southwestern States, almost to the Gulf in Texas,
then bending north and west again, continued until I
reached the eastern slope of the Sierras, and then
made a dive underground and remained there until
Jack determined to go home, and I came along to
take care of him."

Here Miss Jenvie interposed and said: "What was
the most precious thing you ever found in the mines,
Mr. Sedgwick?"

"Considering who asked the question, it would be cruel not to tell you it was Jack," he replied.

All laughed, and Miss Jenvie said : " Is it true, did you and Jack first meet underground ? "

"Indeed we did," said Sedgwick, "and we were neither of us handsomely attired. I thought he was a gnome ; he thought me a Chinese dragon."

Then Miss Grace interposed ; " Mr. Sedgwick," said she, " is not Texas a land where there are a great many cattle ? "

" Millions of them," was the reply.

" And is not that the region where the cowboy is also found ? " she continued.

" There are a few there, surely," said Sedgwick, and looking across the table he saw a smile on Jack's face.

" They are good riders and good shots, are they not ?" Grace asked.

" Some of them ride well, and nearly all of them shoot well," said Sedgwick.

" I would like to go there," said Grace, impetuously ; "it must be a jolly life." Then looking at her mother, she laughed gaily and said : " If ever one of those cowboys, with broad hat and jingling spurs, comes this way, you had better lock the doors, mamma, if you want to keep me."

Sedgwick kept a steady face, but his heart was throbbing so that he feared the company would hear it.

Then Jenvie asked Sedgwick if mining in Nevada was not mostly carried on by rough and rude men.

Sedgwick's face became grave in a moment, as he said : " We must judge men by the motives behind their lives, if we would get at what they really are. There are married men and single men at work in the mines. The married men have wives and little children to support. They wish to have their dear ones fed and clothed as well as other generous people feed and clothe their families. They want their children educated. They have, moreover, all around them examples of rich men who a year or five years previous were as humble and poor as they now are. The young men have hopes quite as sweet, purposes quite as high. This one is to build up a little fortune for some one he loves ; this one has a home in his mind's eye which he means to purchase ; this one has relatives whom he dreams of making happy, while others have visions of honors and fame, so soon as something which is in their thoughts shall materialize.

" Then the occupation itself and the results have a tendency, I think, to exalt men. To begin with, the work is a steady struggle anainst nature's tremendous forces. The rock has to be blasted, the waters controlled, the consuming heat tempered, the swelling clay confined, and to do this men have to employ great agents. A silver mine generally has Desolation placed as a watch above it. To work it everything has to be carried to it. The forest away off on some mountain side has to be felled and hauled to the spot. For many months the great Bonanza has received within it monthly 3,000,000 feet of timbers, machinery equal to that in the holds of mighty steamships has to

be set in place and motion; drills are kept at work
2,000 feet underground, from power supplied on the
surface ; hundreds of men have to be daily hoisted from
and lowered into the depths ; there has to be a precision and continuity that never fail, and the men
who plan and carry on that work emerge from it after
a few years stronger, brighter, clearer-brained and
braver men than they ever would have been except for
that discipline.

" Then what they produce is something which makes
the labor of every other man more profitable, for it is
something which is the measure of values, something
which all races of men recognize at once, something
indestructible and peculiarly precious, which can be
drawn into a thread-like silk, or hammered into a
leaf so thin that a breath will carry it away ; it is the
very spirit of the rock, the part that is imperishable.
Moreover, it is labor made immortal, for, tried by
fire, it grows bright and loses no grain of its weight.
Could we find a piece of the beaten gold that overlaid
the temple of Israel's greatest king, it would, to-day,
represent the labor of one of those miners that toiled
in Ophir and fell back to dust thirty generations
before the Christ was born.

" Moreover, it is and has been from the first one of
the measures of the civilization of nations. Where
gold and silver are in general circulation among the
people they are always prosperous, their children are
always educated, and the advance is so marked that
it can be measured by decades of years. A nation's
decay or enlightenment can be traced by the decreas-

ing or increasing volume of gold and silver in circulation.

" Miners thus engrossed, producing such a substance, and carrying such hopes and aspirations in their souls, as a rule, grow stronger, more manly and more true.

" I do not say that there are not many rough characters among them. I do not say that when the influence of true women is in great part withdrawn from any class of men, they do not more and more gravitate toward savagery, for they but follow a natural law; but the tenderest, truest, bravest, best, most generous and most just men I have ever known have been miners in the far West of the United States."

While talking, Sedgwick had seemed to forget where he was, but as he ceased he glanced across the table and noticed a look of full appreciation on Rose's face, and smiling, he added : " I was talking for Jack's sake, Miss Rose."

It was a pleasant dinner, and a pleasant evening followed. There was a running fire of conversation, broken only when the young ladies sang or played. When Sedgwick first heard Grace sing, he sat, as he said afterward, " in mortal terror lest wings should spread out from her white shoulders and she should disappear through the ceiling."

In point of fact, she sang well, but she was not nearly ethereal enough to want to give up the substantial earth to take to the ether.

But amid all the contending emotions, Sedgwick kept a furtive watch upon the two old men. They were exceedingly gracious, but they gave Sedgwick the impression that they were striving too hard to be agreeable.

Jack was in the seventh heaven. He tried to conceal his joy, but every moment he would glance at Rose Jenvie with a look in his eyes which was enough to show any miner where his bonanza was. Sedgwick was wildly smitten, himself, but he kept his wits about him enough to watch and try to fathom what in the bearing of the old men for some inexplainable reason disturbed him.

When the company separated and sought their respective apartments, Jack went to his own room, threw off his coat, put on slippers and lighted a cigar, crossed the hall, first tapped upon the door of Sedgwick's room, then pushed it open, walked in, closed the door, and then burst out with " Jim, is she not a glory of the earth ? "

" I think she is, indeed," was the reply. Sedgwick was thinking of Grace.

"Is there another such girl in all the world, Jim ? " said Jack.

" I don't believe there is, old boy; not another one," said Sedgwick.

" What a queenly head she has ! What a throat of snow ! What an infinite grace ! 'Whether she sits or stands or walks or whatever thing she does,' she is divine," said Jack.

" She impressed me just that way," said Sedgwick.

" Not too short, not too tall, with just enough flesh

and blood to keep one in mind that while she is divine, she is still a woman," said Jack.

"Only base metal enough to hold the precious
metal in place," said Sedgwick.

So Jack rattled on in the very ecstasy of his love,
and so Sedgwick, quite as deeply involved, replied;
the one talking of Rose, the other of Grace.

At length, however, Sedgwick roused himself and
said: "Jack, old boy, tell me how the old men
received you."

"With open arms," said Jack. "My stepfather
grasped both my hands, said he was hasty in banish-
ing me as he did, that his heart had been filled with
remorse ever since, that he had sought in vain to find
me. And old man Jenvie, with a hearty welcome and
jolly laugh, declared that I served him exactly right
when I floored him ; that it had made a better man of
him ever since, and that he was glad to welcome me
back to England."

Sedgwick listened, and when Jack ceased speaking
there was silence for a full minute, until Jack said:

"What are you thinking of, Jim ?"

"Nothing much," said Sedgwick; "only, Jack, I
have changed my mind. I will stay and help you
through the wedding; only hurry it along as swiftly
as you conveniently can."

"There is something on your mind, Jim," said
Jack. "What is it, old friend ?"

"Nothing, Jack; nothing but a mean suspicion, for
which I can give myself no tangible excuse for enter-
taining," asked Sedgwick.

"Suspicion, Jim! Which way do the indications lead?" asked Jack.

"I will tell you, old friend. In Nevada we would say that these old men are too infernally gushing in their welcome to you. I fear there is something wrong behind it all; though, as I said, it is a mere suspicion which I cannot explain to myself; only, Jack, I will stay to the wedding, and be sure to give no hint to any soul in England that I have more than money enough to make a brief visit, and then to return to America. And do not permit what I have said to worry you, for I have no backing for my impressions."

Then Jack went to his room to sleep and to dream of Rose Jenvie, and Jim went to bed, not to sleep, but to think of Grace Meredith.

CHAPTER VIII.

As we know, Sedgwick went first with Browning to the hamlet in Devonshire where Jack's early home had been. Browning was recognized, of course. An old friend of Hamlin's was at the church, spoke to Jack, and witnessed Sedgwick's encounter with the bull. He knew under what circumstances young Browning left home, and so on that Sunday evening he wrote to Hamlin that his stepson was in Devonshire, told him of the episode at the church, and informed the old man that the companion of his son, though a quiet and refined-appearing man enough, must be a prize-fighter in disguise. He further stated that Jack had told him that he and his friend had been working in the mines at Virginia City, Nevada, for three or four years. He added the strong suspicion that the complexion of the men indicated that they had not been in the mines at all. (His idea of a miner was a coal-miner, and not one from the Comstock mine, where there is no coal dust, and where the thermometer indicates a tropical climate always.)

This letter reached Hamlin early on Monday. Being a half banker and half broker himself, he turned at once to the page in the bank directory, giving American banks and their London connections. He found the Nevada branch bank and California branch bank of Virginia City, and what banks in London

they drew upon, and hastened first to the Nevada
bank's London agency.   He could obtain no news
there.   Then he sought the other, and knowing the
management, he explained to one of the directors
that his son was on the way home, was already in
England, and asked him confidentially, both as a
father and a brother banker, whether any credit had
come for the boy.   The director ran over his corres-
pondence, and, looking up with a smile, said:

"Is your son's name John Browning?   If it is, he
has bills of exchange upon us for £100,000."

The old man was paralyzed.   "It cannot be possible," he said.   "Great heavens!   £100,000!"

"Those are the figures sent us," said the cashier,
"and we received a mighty invoice of Nevada bullion
by the last ship from New York.   There is no
mistake."

Then an effort was made to see if another man
named Sedgwick had any credit, but nothing was
found.   Enjoining upon the banker the utmost
secrecy in regard to his being at the bank, the old
man went away.

The question with him was what to do.   His
business was not very prosperous, because he had not
capital enough.   Then, too, he was in debt to Jenvie.
He wanted the lion's share of that money, and, more
than ever, he wanted Jack to marry Grace.

Then what did Jack mean by bringing a prize-
fighter home with him?   He was worried.   Finally
he determined to consult with Jenvie, his partner.
He knew he did not like Jack, and he had, moreover,

received hints from him that he was getting along well in making 'a match between Rose and a rich broker named Arthur Stetson, who had met her and been carried away by her beauty.

So, calling Jenvie into their most private office, Hamlim bolted the door to prevent interruption, read him the letter received from Devonshire, and told him of the astounding discovery he had made at the ——— bank. The question was, what course to take.

"I believe Rose likes Jack," said Jenvie. "She grieved exceedingly when he went away, though she hid it so superbly that only her mother knew about it, and she has rejected every suitor since except Stetson, and I fear when the climax comes she will reject him. The chances are, when Jack comes they will rush into each other's arms. At the same time, I do not want him for a son-in-law. But I would like to get some of the money into the firm, for we need more capital badly."

They plotted all that day, and next morning decided that on the arrival of Jack they would welcome him; let the matter between him and Rose take its course, but in case of an engagement would prevent an immediate marriage, if possible, and see, in the meantime, what could be done toward working Jack for a part, at least, of his money. With that arrangement decided upon, when a message came from Hamlin's home that Jack had returned and had gone to the hotel, they were ready, and in company went to greet him and escort him home.

Sedgwick had to be invited also, and that suited them, for they both desired to know what kind of a man he was. Both were satisfied, too, that he had no money, or he would have obtained a credit where Jack had obtained his exchange. When, at the first dinner, Grace had drawn from him that he had been in Texas and had seen cowboys, they both guessed where he had caught the trick which he had put in practice in Devonshire, and, thenceforth, save as a careless friend that careless Jack had picked up, they dropped Sedgwick from their calculations.

How Jack got his money was the greatest mystery; and so a few days after his coming, his father said to him: "Jack, I hope you have come home to stay. Look around and find some business that you think will suit you, and I will buy it for you if it does not take too much money."

" Thanks, father," said Jack; " much obliged, but I have a few pounds of my own."

" How much are miner's wages in Virginia City ? " asked the old man.

" Four dollars a day ; about twenty-four pounds a month," said Jack.

" And what are the expenses ? " was the next question.

" Four shillings a day for board ; three pounds per month for a room, and clothes and cigars to any amount you please," said Jack.

" Why, you could not have saved more than £150 or £160 per annum at those rates," said the old man.

"No," said Jack; "a good many may not do as well as that; but I had a few pounds which were invested by a friend in Con-Virginia when it was three dollars a share, and it was sold when it was worth a good bit more."

The old man had learned the secret. He asked one more question. "Did your friend Sedgwick do as well as you did?"

Jack thought of Sedgwick's injunction, so answered:

"He made a good bit of money, something like £20,000, but he turned it over to his father in Ohio. I think the plan is to buy a place near the old home. He only brought a few hundred pounds with him. Indeed, he only ran over to oblige me. We were old friends; at one time we worked on the same shift in the mine."

The old man was satisfied. Moreover, he saw his opportunity.

"What a wonderful business that mining is," he said. "Stetson, the broker over the way, is promoting a mining enterprise in South Africa. According to the showing, it is an immense property. Here is the prospectus of the company. Put it in your pocket, and at your leisure run over it."

Jack carelessly put the pamphlet in his pocket. That evening he was with Rose and remained pretty late. When he sought his room he could not sleep, so he ran over the statement. It was a captivating showing. The mine was called the "Wedge of Gold." It was located in the Transvaal. The main ledge was fully sixteen feet wide, with an easy average value of six pounds per ton in free gold, besides deposits and spurs that went much higher. The vein was exposed for several hundred feet, and opened by a shaft 300 feet deep, wlth long drifts on each of the levels. The country was healthy, supplies cheap, plenty of good wood and water, and the only thing needed was a mill for reducing the ore. The incorporation called for 150,000 shares of stock of the par value of one pound per share, and the pamphlet explained that 50,000 shares were set aside to be sold to raise means for a working capital, to build the mill, etc.

Browning read the paper over twice, then tumbled into bed, and his dreams were all mixed up ; part of the time he was counting gold bars, part of the time it seemed to him that Rose was near him, but when he spoke to her, every time she vanished away. Between the visions he made the worst kind of a night of it, and next morning told Jim that he was more beat out than ever he was when he came off shift on the Comstock.

CHAPTER IX.

HOW MINERS ARE CAUGHT.

Browning and Sedgwick had been in England two weeks. The question of the marriage of Browning and Rose Jenvie had been discussed and decided upon. Neither Hamlin nor Jenvie had interposed any objection to the marriage except on the point of time. They asked, at first, that it be postponed for six months, as Jenvie insisted that he wanted to be certain that Rose had not been carried away by a mere impulse on seeing once more an old friend who had long been absent. Hamlin agreed with him that the young people must be sure not to make any mistake. Jack was impetuous, and Rose, while making no pronounced opposition, quietly said that no tests were necessary; that she and Jack had been separated for a long time and knew their own minds. Sedgwick, when called in, refused to express an opinion, it being a matter too sacred to permit of any outside interference.

. Finally a compromise was made, the time reduced one-half, and the date fixed for the first of September, it being then nearly the first of June. Jack had only agreed to the postponement on the condition that Sedgwick should not desert him, but wait for the wedding. He consented, saying carelessly that two or three months would not much matter to him, but the truth was that the delay urged by the old men strengthened his suspicion that all was not just right. "Those old chaps are too sweet by half," he said to himself. "There is some game on hand to get the best of generous, simple-hearted, unsuspecting Jack, sure, and while I cannot fathom it I will keep watch."

Then, there was the enchantment that Grace Meredith had woven around his life. Every morning she greeted him with a smile, a welcome word and a hand-clasp that set his blood tingling. Her breath was in the air that he breathed, and when at night the hand-clasp and the smile were repeated, and the good-nights spoken, it all fell upon him like a benediction; and, going to his apartment, he would ask himself what his life would be were the smile, the word, and the hand-clasp to be his no more.

After a few days there came a change in Grace. She was as cordial as ever, as gently considerate as ever, but she seemed to lose vivacity. She was often lost in revery ; a sadder smile seemed to give expression to her face ; she did not laugh with the old ringing laugh ; there seemed to come in her look when she suddenly encountered Sedgwick, something which was the opposite of a blush—as opposite as the white rose is to the blush rose.

In those days the steady conscience of Sedgwick was undergoing many self-questionings. Should he offer his love and be rejected, what then ? Should the impossible happen and he should be accepted, what then ? Should he carry the petted London girl to his home and friends in the Miami Valley, would there not be reproaches felt even if not spoken ?

Thus he vexed himself day after day ; night after night he tossed restlessly, and saw no way to break the entanglement that had entwined his life. But he kept watch of Jack and the old men.

Meanwhile, Jack had read over and over the prospectus of the " Wedge of Gold " Mining Company. It was the lamp and he was the moth that was circling around it with constantly lessening circles. His father, to whom he had applied for information, told him that he believed the shares were going at one pound, but that they threatened to be higher within a week, and Jenvie, taking up the conversation, explained that, with a mill built, the mine would easily pay sixty per cent on the investment annually, which would throw the shares up to at least twenty pounds. At the same time both the old men referred Jack to Stetson for full particulars, as they had no direct interest in the property.

After a few days more, the mail from South Africa brought a glowing account of further developments in " The Wedge of Gold," which account found its way into the papers, and one was put where Jack would read it. He had not consulted with Sedgwick. His idea was to make an investment, and when the profits began to come in, to divide with him.

So one morning he went to the office of Stetson and said to the young man : " I have concluded to take the working capital stock of the ' Wedge of Gold ;' and sitting down he gave his check for £50,000. The stock for him would be ready, he was informed, the next day, so soon as it could be properly transferred.

He went out.   The real owner of the property was sent for; the property was bought for £2,000; the deed, which had been put in escrow, and which on its face called for £150,000, was taken up, releasing the stock, and then the old men and the young man rubbed their hands and said to each other that it had been a good day's work.

CHAPTER X.

Sedgwick and Browning had now been several days in London. Every day they had been riding and driving—seeing the sights. One morning at breakfast Jack mentioned that it was Tuesday; that next day would be the annual celebrated Derby Wednesday; that he had made arrangements for as many to go as could get away. The number was finally limited to four—Grace and Rose, Jack and Jim.

This was talked over, and so soon as the arrangements were determined upon, Jack proposed that when the race should be over, instead of coming back to London, they should go on beyond Surrey, down to the seashore in Sussex, where an old uncle of Rose's resided, for a few days' visit. This was, after some discussion, agreed upon; whereupon Jack rose and went out to make a few needed little preparations; the young ladies followed to do some shopping, while Sedgwick went to his room to write some letters.

He finished his letters and was going out, when he met Mrs. Hamlin in the hall. She greeted him and asked him to sit down a moment, saying she wanted to talk with him. He swung a chair around for Mrs. Hamlin, and when she was seated he took another chair opposite, saying: " Is there anything particular this morning, madam, which you desire to talk about?" The old lady looked at him a moment, then said:

"Mr. Sedgwick, I have noticed that since you came to my house you seem to be worried, as though this London roar and confusion oppressed you; and I have seen a look on your face sometimes, which, it seemed to me, if set to words would say: ' I would give anything in the world to be out of this and back once more free in my native land.' It worries me, and I want to ask you if something cannot be done to make your life here more pleasant."

"Why, my dear madam," said Sedgwick, " I never was half so kindly entertained before as I have been in your house. There is nothing lacking, nothing ; and when I think of ever returning all this kindness my gratitude is made bankrupt."

"Still, you have something on your mind. Is it a business trouble? Will you not test our friendship in real truth?" asked the lady.

Sedgwick looked at her seriously a moment, and said : "I have something, but it is not business, that distresses me. But, were I to tell you, it would test your friendship indeed."

"Well," responded the lady, " I want to know it. I hope we can help you."

"Mrs. Hamlin," said Sedgwick, "I was reared a farmer's son. I was a wild boy, I guess. I left school with education not yet completed—left under a cloud, but no disgrace attached to my leaving. I went to Texas and was a cowboy for a year. From there I wandered west, learned the occupation of

mining ; for four years almost every day I have been
underground. I met Jack: we were friends; how
close at last you do not know. We started east ; he
accompanied me to my childhood's home. After a
brief visit I came with him to his. I have been three
weeks under your roof; I am bound by a promise to
remain until Jack's marriage, and, in the meantime,
in spite of myself, I, the farmer, the cowboy, and the
miner, have dared to look upon your daughter, and
my soul is groveling at her feet. I love her with
such intensity that I have feared sometimes I should
break down and beseech her to have pity on me.
Now you have it all. Tell me, I pray, how I can be
true to myself and to the hospitality which you have
extended me until Jack shall be married and I can
return to my native land !"

When he once had begun, his words were poured
out in a torrent; his face was pale ; he trembled, and
his breath came in half gasps.

Mrs. Hamlin was silent a moment. Then, looking
up, she said: " Have you spoken of this to Jack ? "

" Not one word," he replied.

" Or to Grace ? "

" O, Mrs. Hamlin, believe me, not one word."

The lady leaned her head upon her hand for a few
moments. Then, looking up, she said: " You ask me
what to do. I cannot help you. But my judgment
would be that you go directly to Grace and ask her
help. I have not the slightest idea of her sentiments
toward you, but if she does not care for you and
thinks she never can, she will frankly tell you. If

she does love you, she is probably suffering more than you are."

" O, Mrs. Hamlin," said Sedgwick, "are you willing that I shall speak to her, that I shall tell her how much she is to me ?"

" Quite willing," was the answer, spoken after a moment's thought. " Believe me, I never suspected anything of this kind, never in the least, or I should not have stopped you here ; but if Grace loves you I shall be most glad. And one thing more. Should Grace be willing to accept your attentions, for the present, please, do not speak to Mr. Hamlin or to Jack. I have my special reasons for making this request. I ask it because Mr. Hamlin is peculiar, and Grace is my child, in fact, while he is but her stepfather."

Then she arose, held out her hand and smiled. Then her face became grave, and she leaned over the young man, kissed his forehead, and left the hall.

When the door closed Sedgwick put his hands before his eyes as though to ward off a great light ; and when he removed them his lips were moving and his face wore a softened and exalted look, such as Saul's might have worn after he saw the " great light."

Dinner was hardly over that evening when Jack disappeared. He spent nearly all his evenings with Rose, and so his absence was not remarked. Mr. Hamlin had been called away to Scotland for two or three days on business. Mrs. Hamlin, Grace and Sedgwick passed into the parlor. After a little conversation, Sedgwick asked Grace to sing, and as she

went to the piano Mrs. Hamlin arose and left the
room.

Grace struck the instrument softly, and in a
moment began to sing. The piece she selected was
the old one beginning :

> " Could you come back to me, Douglas, Douglas,
>   In the old likeness that I knew,
> I would be so faithful, so loving, Douglas,
>   Douglas, Douglas, tender and true."

There was a strange thrill in the voice of Grace as
the song progressed, and when she reached the
fourth stanza and sang :

> "I never was worthy of you, Douglas,
>   Not half worthy the like of you;
> Now, all men beside seem to me like shadows,—
>   I love you, Douglas, tender and true,"

the last words ended in a tone very much like a sob,
and the singing ceased.

Sedgwick had risen, and walked to the side of
Grace while she sang. When she ceased he said:

" That is a very touching song, Miss Grace. Your
voice vibrates in it as though your heart were
heavy."

" It is," she frankly answered.

He bent and took an unresisting hand and said:
" If you are in trouble, may I not try to be your
comforter ? "

She rose from the piano, and looking up clear and
brave into the eyes of the young man, said: " You
are most kind, but I cannot tell you why my heart is
heavy."

He looked down into her eyes for a moment and

then said: " My heart is likewise heavy, Miss Grace; may I tell you why ?"

" Surely," she answered, "if you have a sorrow, and if there is any balm in this household, it shall be yours."

He took her other hand, and drawing her gently toward him, said: " Come near to me Miss Grace. I am involved in a trouble which I never dreamed of when I came here. Mine has been a harsh life, but I have always tried to meet my fate resignedly. Now I am overborne. Since the first hour I met you, first looked into your divine face, first felt your hand-clasp and heard your voice, my heart has been on fire. You have become my divinity. I worship you. Oh, Grace, can you give me a thread, be it ever so slight, out of which I may weave a hope that some time you will bend, and sanctify my life by becoming my wife ? "

As he spoke, over the pale face of Grace Meredith an almost imperceptible glow spread, as when an incandescent lamp is lighted under a translucent shade ; her eyes grew moist, her lips quivered, she trembled in every limb, and, suddenly dropping on her knees, drew his hands to her lips, kissed them, and murmured : " O ! my king ! "

He caught her to him and cried : " Is it true ? Is it true ? Do you really care for me ? "

She looked up and said : " O, my blind darling, you are so very, very blind ! My soul has been calling to your soul since the first hour you came."

Half an hour later Grace looked up and with a ravishing smile, said: "Do you know, dearest, I believe all my heavy-heartedness is gone."

At last Sedgwick said: "My beautiful, what will your friends say to your marrying a rough miner?"

"What," replied she, "will your friends say if you prove foolish enough to marry a simple English girl, whose horizon is bounded by Devonshire and London?"

His response was : "My adored one!"

Then she crept nearer him, and with serious accent said : "My love, if happily our lives shall be united, whom will it be for, our friends or ourselves? I will tell you. If ever I shall be permitted to become so blessed as to be your wife, it will be with the thought in my heart that we are all in all to each other in this world, and in the world to come."

"In this world and in the world to come," he repeated ; and then, with bowed head, in a whisper, he added : "May I be worthy of such a blessing, and God spare to me my idol, that I may praise Him evermore."

And then they began to talk in earnest. One hour like that is due to every mortal ; no mortal can have more than one such an hour, no matter how long may be his life.

Later they came directly to the subject of their marriage. They agreed that, if possible, it should be on the same day that Jack and Rose should be married. But Sedgwick mentioned Mrs. Hamlin's desire that for the present no one should know of his love or of hers (if it should be returned), and said he believed it best not to mention their relations until the wedding day of Rose and Jack drew near.

Grace agreed with him, except that Rose must be told, saying she would find it out even if the attempt were made to conceal it from her, and added : " Jack and Rose are completely absorbed in each other. They will be with each other most of the time. My father is absent all day, and until late at night. My mother is good, and will not much disturb us. I can look in your eyes every day, kiss you sometimes, and feel your presence like a robust spirit near me all the time." Then, suddenly pausing for an instant, she again broke out with, " Oh, how happy I am ; it seems as though my heart would break with its ecstasy ! " and, springing up, she ran to the piano, and sang a song which filled the room with melody, and caused a linnet that was asleep on her perch to awaken and join her trills to the song.

CHAPTER XI.

The next morning early the young couples started for Epsom Downs. Browning had engaged a carriage to take them, and they started a little after daylight. Early as it was, the procession which annually empties London to witness the great race was in motion. There had been a slight shower the previous evening; every bit of herbage was fresh and beautiful ; the day was .perfect and the ride delicious. When part of the distance had been traveled, Browning, looking back, said: " Grace, I believe I see your destiny coming."

" In what form ? " asked Grace, laughing.

" In a typical cowboy," said her foster brother.

Then all looked, and sure enough there, two hundred yards away, was the broad hat, the nameless grace, the erect form, the man straight as a line from his head to his stirrups, the Mexican saddle, the woven-hair bridle with Spanish bit; all complete except the horse. That was not a steed of the plains, but a magnificent hunter. The girls clapped their hands in delight, and Grace wished he would " hurry up," so that they might get a nearer view.

" Just then a cry arose in the rear, and a horse attached to a broken vehicle was seen coming, running away in the very desperation of fear.

The carriage was driven to the side of the road, and both men sprang out. A dense crowd of vehicles, many of them containing women and children, were just in front, and the thought of that mad horse dashing among them was sickening. But Sedgwick cried out : " Look, ladies, quick ! "

What they saw was the hunter under a dead run, his rider urging him on apparently, and working something in his right hand. The harnessed horse was a good one, but the hunter was gaining upon him, and just as the mad runaway was almost opposite the ladies, the right arm of the rider of the hunter made a quick curve, the looped end of a rope darted out like a bird of prey from the hand; the loop went over the runaway's head; the hunter was brought almost to a dead stop ; the other animal went up into the air, then fell to his knees, then over on his side. Sedgwick and Browning sprang to him, unfastened him from the wreck, got the reins and secured his head, then took off the lariat, let him up, and tied him to the hedge by the roadside.

Browning first turned to the stranger who was coiling up his lariat on the saddle's horn, and said : " That was a good morning's work, my friend ; had that mad horse crashed into the vehicles ahead, he would have killed some one."

" I wur afeerd of that, stranger, and that's what made me think he orter be stopped," said the horseman.

Sedgwick wheeled quickly round when he heard the man's voice, and, looking up, cried : " Hello, Jordan, how did you leave the boys on the Brazos ? "

The man gave one look ; then, springing from his

horse, he rushed to Sedgwick, and throwing both
arms around him broke out with : "Why, Jim; bless
my broad-horned heart, but I'm glad ter see yo'! How
in kingdom cum did yo' get heah ?"   Then he caught
both his hands and wrung them, all the time exclaiming : " Blame me, but I'm glad.   This is the fust
luck I've had in the Kingdom.   Jim, is it sho nuff
you ?"   And he danced like a lunatic.   And Sedgwick, if not quite so demonstrative, was quite as much
rejoiced.

When they quieted down a little, Sedgwick said :
" Jordan, I have some friends here whom I want to
present to you."

His face sobered in a moment.   "I forgot, Jim,"
he said, "thet any one war heah savin' ourselves.
They must think us two 'scaped lunertics."

" That's all right, Jordan," said Sedgwick, and he
formally presented his friend to the ladies and to
Browning.

The ladies told him how grateful they were that he
was near to prevent any damage by the fleeing horse,
and how glad they were to see the actual picture of
how a wild horse is caught.

Jordan blushed like a girl.   " It war nothin', ladies,"
he said ; " only it seemed like it war necessawy sunthin' should be done, and right soon.   So I interfeerd
as well's I could."

" Where the mischief did you get that rig, Jordan ?" asked Sedgwick.

"I brung it with me from ther old ranch ; that is,
all but the hoss.   I didn't know but I mighter want

ter ride, and I knowd I couldn't sit an English saddle a minit."

"And why did you come away, Jordan?" asked Sedgwick.

His face saddened for a moment, and then he smiled and said: "I got tired of ranchin', sold out; but why I come here I've no idee, 'cept it might o' been to stop that thar hoss."

" It was a good idea, anyway, and we are all glad you came," said Rose. " We started to see the great race, and we have seen a greater one," and she smiled as she spoke, until the dark man again colored and said: " Indeed, Miss, it war nothin'."

But the procession grew denser every moment; so Jordan mounted his horse again and rode beside the carriage, and a running conversation was kept up all the way to the great race track.

Jordan was exceedingly interested in the colts as they were brought upon the track.

" They is thoroughbreds, shore. They is beauties," he kept exclaiming ; and as they were stripped for the race, he picked out the one he thought ought to win, and offered to wager hats with Sedgwick and Browning and gloves with the ladies that his favorite would win.

And the colt he set his heart upon came near winning ; he was third among the eighteen starters, and to the last Jordan insisted that he would have won if he had been well ridden.

" He orter won," Jordan said. " The trouble war, his jockey lacks two things ; he don't understand hoss character, 'nd he lacks pluck. He never interested ther colt in him, never rubbed his nose and whispered inter his ear thet his heart would be broke if ther colt didn't win ; so ther colt only ran ter please hisself 'nd never thought o' pleasin' his rider. Then, from the fust, ther rider believed he wouldn't be nearer nor third, 'nd ter do anything a man's got ter believe he ken make it. Menny a grand hoss's repertation has ben ruined by ther fool man as has hed him in charge, and this war ther case terday."

Then he was absorbed in thought for a moment, then went on again as though he had not ceased : " It wer ther same with men. Ez often ez ever ther best men don't win ther prize ; meny er blood man hez been distanced by er mustang."

The race over, they all had dinner together, and with beautiful tact the ladies kept Jordan talking most of the time, and enjoyed his quaint sayings exceedingly.

He had been three months from the United States ; had made one trip to Scotland, one to Wales, one to Paris, and his impressions of the different points and the people he had seen were most vivid and unique.

His talk ran a little in this vein : " Yo' see, up in ther Highlands, I looked fur the lakes and mountains that yo' read to us about, Jim. There is some fine lakes, but mountains ! sho, we can beat 'em in America, all holler. And ez to broad rivers, why, ther Mississippi cud take um all in, and wouldn't know she had a reinforcement ; while pour 'um into ther Colorado gorge and they'd be spray afore they reached ther bottom. I looked for ther pituresk Highland

heroes in ther tartans and with thei bag-pipes ; but
they tho't, I reckon, that I war James Fitz, and wur
all ambushed.   But I did see some pretty girls thar,
'an some powerful fine black cattle.   They war fine—
good for twelve hundred pounds neat.

"The blamd'st thing I seen war in Wales.   I didn't
see that, but hearn.   That war the language.   It's a
jor-breaker, if you har me.   I don't see how the
children up thar learn it so blam'd young.

"Paris is a grand place, a genuine daisy; but I
believe it is wickeder'n Santa Fe wuz when the rush war
to New Mexico."

Grace explained to Jordan that they were going
down to Sussex to visit some relatives of Rose, and
begged him to go along, and bespoke for him a
hearty welcome.

"I'm greatly obleeged, Miss," said Jordan, "but I
must beg yo' ter 'scuse me.   I must see my hoss
home.   I've been ridin' him and teachin' him a few
things, like startin' and stoppin,' for a month.   He
war wild when I tuk him fust, but since he and I got
'quainted, we agree zactly, and I told ther men as
own him he should be home ter night, and I must take
him.   I wouldn't send him by the are-apparent hisself.   Besides, my society accomplishments war neglected some'at when I war young, and I would rather
break y'r heart, Miss, by declinin' ter go, than hev it
broke by my arkerdness 'mong y'r friends."

But he told Sedgwick where he was stopping in
London, and it was agreed that on the return of the
party to the great city they should see more of each

other. So Jordan returnea to London, and the young people took the train for a little town on the coast, not far from Brighton, in Sussex.

They found the uncle and aunt of Rose. A great welcome was given them, and four or five days were delightfully whiled away.

A regiment of English regulars was stationed there. Our party made the acquaintance of the officers and their families, and one day a horseback ride into the country was proposed for the next morning.

It taxed the capacity of the place to supply the necessary animals, and one of the horses brought up, though a magnificent and powerful fellow, was but half broken at best, and he snorted and blowed, and reared and pawed, and took on a great deal.

The company were looking at him, and each selecting the horse that suited him best, when Miss Rose said : "What a pity that Mr. Jordan did not come along ! He would have selected that wild horse."

The colonel of the regiment, a portly man, and a little inclined to be pompous, in a peculiarly English tone said : " Possibly, you know, our young American friend would like to mount him."

Sedgwick affected not to notice the tone or the accent, and answered simply : "I have ridden worse-looking horses. If I had a Mexican saddle, or one of your military saddles, I believe I should like to ride him ; but I am a little afraid of these things you call saddles."

Strangely enough, the officer thought the objection to the saddle was meant merely as an excuse to avoid

riding the horse, and so he spoke up quickly, saying :
" The gentleman shall be accommodated.   I always
have an extra saddle with me; he shall have that,"
and gave his servant directions to go and bring the
saddle and bridle.   When they were brought, Sedgwick looked at them, said they would answer admira-
bly, and throwing the trappings over his left arm,
went up to the snorting horse, petted and soothed
him, rubbed his nose, and talked low to him a moment ; then slipped the bridle on, then gently pushed
the saddle and trappings over his back ; made all
secure, and then, without assistance, mounted him,
talking softly to him all the time.

The horse made a few bounds, but quickly sub-
sided.   They were enough, however, to show the
onlookers that the man on the horse was sufficient
for the task he had undertaken.   Riding back, Sedgwick dismounted, still talking low to the horse and
patting his neck, for, as he explained, " The colt has
a lovely, honest face and head ; he is only timid, and
does not yet quite understand what is wanted of him,
or whether it will do for him to give us his entire
confidence."

The officer who had sent for the saddle had watched
everything ; so when Sedgwick dismounted he held
out his hand and said, heartily: " I beg your pardon,
Mr. Sedgwick, I was mistaken in you.   You do more
than ride.   When mounted, you and the horse
together make a centaur."

With a celestial smile, Miss Jenvie said : " I beg
your pardon, Mr. Sedgwick.   Mr. Jordan is not

needed, except as a pleasant addition to our company."

They all mounted and rode away.   It was a jolly
party.   Grace and Rose rode with two of the
officers ; two of the officers' wives were escorted by
Sedgwick and Browning.

As they rode, Sedgwick kept patting his horse, and
in a little while so won his confidence that he was
able to rub his whip all about his head.

They stopped at a roadside inn for luncheon, and
returned in the cool of the afternoon.

By this, time Sedgwick's horse had apparently
given his rider his full faith, and Sedgwick, in sharp
contrast with the other gentlemen, sat him in true
cowboy style.   They were riding at a brisk pace, when
the hat of one of the ladies was caught in a flurry of
wind and carried twenty or thirty yards to the rear.
The others began to pull in their horses, when
Sedgwick, like a flash, whirled his horse about, and,
calling to him, the horse sprang forward at full speed.
All turned, and the ladies screamed, as they thought
Sedgwick was falling.   He had ridden, not directly
for the hat, but to one side until close upon it, then,
turning his horse, he went down at the same moment,
seized the plume of the hat, regained his upright
attitude, and came smiling back, though the horse,
not accustomed to such performances, was snorting
and bounding like a deer.

All hands were delighted, and Grace shot out to
Sedgwick such a look of pride and love that his heart
beat a tattoo for a quarter of an hour.

The officer who owned the saddle was most profuse in his expressions of delight. " Give up America, my friend," he said ; "come and be an Englishman and join my regiment. We will get you a commission, and supply every chance for promotion."

Sedgwick thanked him, and assured him that he would duly consider the offer.

The old English Colonel took a great fancy to Sedgwick. After dinner, the day of the ride, he sought him out, and they conversed together for two or three hours ; or, rather, the Colonel talked and Sedgwick listened. The Colonel had been sent on many a service by his government ; he was a keen observer, had good descriptive powers, and was an interesting talker. Moreover, he liked to hear himself converse.

Having visited South Africa a few months before, he described the country minutely, its topography, its flora and fauna, its geological presentations, and expatiated upon its promising future. Sedgwick was very greatly interested, and with his retentive memory the facts were fixed upon his mind.

As they were about separating, Sedgwick said : " You ask me to leave my native land and make this my country. I understand you, and appreciate the offer, but you do not comprehend the Great Republic at all. England, at the beginning of this century, was well-nigh the anchor of civilization. By the end of the next century England will be in cap and slippers, and her children across the sea will have to be her protector. The American who gives up his native land for any other is a renegade son."

CHAPTER XII.

Next morning Jack and Rose went out for a walk along the beach. Out in the little bay a man and a woman were sailing and enjoying themselves, for the sound of their laughter came across the water to the shore. Jack was just remarking to Rose that they in the boat were carrying a good deal of sail, when a sudden squall upset the boat. The man was not a swimmer, but as he came to the surface he managed to seize upon the overturned boat and support himself.

When the accident happened, Browning shouted to some boatmen farther up the beach to come with a boat quickly, and, throwing off coat, vest and shoes, he plunged in and swam toward where the boat capsized. Rose was left on the beach, wringing her hands and crying. The accident was not far from shore, and Jack was a strong swimmer. He reached the spot in time to grasp the arm of the woman as she came to the surface. She was half smothered by the water, and completely rattled, for the fear of death was full upon her, so she madly clung to Browning. He made the best struggle that he could, but the woman carried him under before the boat arrived. As the two rose to the surface, the boatmen managed to seize them and draw them into the boat, but the woman was senseless, and Browning was almost so, and fearfully exhausted.

As the boat was rowed to the shore and Rose saw Browning lying limp and helpless in it, she went off in a dead faint, and was so upset and nervous that it was determined to return to London that evening. When out of sight of the place and of the sea, she rapidly recovered, and was soon her old self, but she reproached Jack, and with an adorable smile told him she never would have believed that he would, on the very first opportunity, go off, half kill himself for another woman, and compel her to make such a spectacle of herself down on the beach before all those villagers.

The old days began again in London; Browning and Rose were all in all to each other, and Sedgwick and Grace were likewise in the seventh heaven of love's ecstasy.

In Nevada parlance, Sedgwick would have wagered two to one with Browning, on the measure of their respective happiness.

The happy couples visited every point of interest in and about London.

One day they went through Westminster Abbey. Sedgwick hardly spoke during the visit, and as they entered the carriage to return home, Rose said : " Mr. Sedgwick, I am disappointed ; I thought our great national chamber of death would greatly interest you."

" So did I," said Browning, " but I suppose a foreigner cannot understand just how English-born people feel toward that spot."

Sedgwick smiled faintly, and said : "You mistake me, Miss Rose, and you too, Jack. That Abbey is the only thing I have seen in England that I am jealous or envious of. I see your great works and say to myself, 'We will rival all that.' I read your best books and say of myself, 'they are a part of our inheritance as well as yours.' But that Abbey is a monument, sufficient to itself, it seems to me, to make every Englishman afraid to ever falter in manhood or to fail in honor. It is filled with lessons of splendor. There slumber great kings and princes, and queens who were beautiful in life, but there under the seal of death a higher royalty is recognized—the royalty of great hearts and brains ; the royalty that comes to the soldier when in the face of death he saves his country ; the royalty of the statesman who turns aside the sword and opens new paths and possibilities to his countrymen ; the royalty of the poet when he sets immortal thoughts to words, which once spoken, go sounding down the ages in music forever. And these should have their final couches spread beside the couches of kings, for each when called can answer, 'I, too, was royal.'

"And when other nations dispute for recognition with Englishmen, your countrymen have but to point to that consecrated spot and say : 'There is our country's record. It is chiseled there by the old sculptor, Death ; go and study it ; it will carry you through thirty generations of men ; from it you will learn how Englishmen were strong enough, while subduing the world, to subdue themselves ; to create

to themselves laws and a literature of their own, until
they at last held aloft the banners of civilization when
nearly all the world beside was dark ; there is
the record of England's soldiers, statesmen, poets,
scholars ; read the immortal list, and then if you will,
come back and renew the argument.'

"That pile ought to be enough to make every
Englishman a true man, a brave man, a gentleman,
for to me the names there make the most august
scroll ever written.

"Listening within those walls, it seemed to me I
could hear mingling all the voices of the mighty
dead ; the battle-cry of soldiers, the appeals of statesmen ; the edicts of kings ; the hymns of churchmen,
the rhythm of immortal numbers as from poets'
harps they were flung off ; the glory of a thousand
years shone before my eyes ; the splendor of almost
everything that is immortal in English history was
before me.

" That place ought to impress all who visit it with
what mortals must do, if they would embalm their
memories upon the world.

" You are right to reverence and to feel a solemn
joy at that place ; it is one of the few real splendors
of this old world."

" Forgive me, Mr. Sedgwick," said Rose ; " I
should have known your thoughts."   While she was
speaking, Grace, under the laprobe, pressed her
lover's hand.

CHAPTER XIII.

TWO KINDS OF SORROW.

But as June wore away, one day when Jack visited the office of his stepfather, he found Stetson there, and was informed by him that some evil-disposed persons were 'bearing' the stock of the Wedge of Gold Company, which was most unfortunate, as it interfered with the arrangements in progress for building the mill.

Browning did not know enough about stocks to see through the deception, but bluntly asked what could be done to stop the injury. "The true way," said Stetson, "would be to go on the market and take all the stock offered until the bear movement should be broken."

Browning had heard about Captain Kelly "bearing" the bonanza stocks, and how the bonanza firm had taken all he offered, so he said: "Why do you not go out and put a stopper on the beggars?" Stetson explained that he had not the money. "Why, we can fix that," said Jack. So he wrote a note to the —————— Bank to honor the orders of Jenvie & Hamlin until furthur instructions, turned the check over to Hamlin and told him to manage it. The days went by. There was an excursion of the young people to Wales, and another to Scotland, and besides Jack had gone down to Devonshire, bonded the place he liked, paid £1,000 down, and was to meet the remainder of the obligation—£9,000—when the titles were all looked up and transferred to him. Meanwhile, June and the better part of July were gone when one morning Jack went to the bank and drew a check for a few pounds which he needed for spending money. The cashier as he paid the check, informed Browning that the directors would be glad to see him in the private office of the bank. A messenger showed him the way, and he was there informed that the house of Jenvie & Hamlin had been drawing so heavily upon his order that only some £12,000 remained to his credit. The news was a paralyzer, but Jack was a game man and said: "That is all right," talked pleasantly for a few minutes, then withdrew, and going directly to his stepfather's office, demanded an explanation.

The old men informed him that they had tried to hold up the stock of the "Wedge of Gold," but their efforts had proved of no use. The shares had run down to almost nothing. They had even used the reserve fund intended for the building of the mill, and it looked, they said, as though they could never realize enough to get even.

"Has the stock recently bought been placed to my credit?" asked Jack. He was told that it had been. "And how much is it?" he demanded. They informed him that it amounted to 83,000 shares, which, with the 50,000 shares first bought by him, gave him 133,000 shares, or the entire stock except 17,000 shares.

Jack was lost in thought a few minutes, then said : " I want all the papers except the 17,000 shares, and I want with them your own and Stetson's resignation as officers of the company."

The papers were given him, and taking the bundle he carried it to his own bank and deposited it, then went home.

He repaired directly to Jim's apartment, found him, and said : " Jim, my heart is broken. You have stood by me so far, help me now to arrange things so that I can say good-bye to Rose"—here he broke down and sobbed—"and then go back to America."

" Why, old friend," said Sedgwick, " if you and Rose are all right, what can so upset you ? "

" Why, bless my soul, Jim, I'm ruined ; my fortune is nearly all gone," he answered.

Then Sedgwick drew from him all the dismal story.

When he had finished, Sedgwick said : " Get me that prospectus, Jack ; I want to see it before I make up my mind." Jack complied, and Sedgwick read it carefully through. The statement of the mine, the description of its development, and of the value of the ore, had been prepared by an expert so eminent that he could not afford to sell his name to bolster up a fraud.

When Sedgwich had finished reading he sat in thought for a few minutes, and then said : " Jack, go and find the man from whom this property was purchased, get all the facts that you can, even if you have to get him drunk ; then come to me to-morrow, and by that time we will think something out. By the way,

first run over to Rose, tell her you have been called
away on business and may not be home until late, so
that she will not expect you."

Jack left his friend and met Rose in the hall. She
had just come in to visit Grace. He caught her up
as men sometimes do children, kissed her and said
gaily · " Don't look for me to-night, sweetheart. I'm
going to be engaged until late."

She twined both her arms around one of his arms
and said teasingly : " Are not you and I engaged,
and is not ours a prior engagement ? "

" O, yes," he said, " but this other engagement is
with a man."

" So is mine," she said.

" And sometimes I think he is not much of a man,
either," said Jack.

" Don't you dare to slander him," said Rose. " I
know him better than he knows himself, and I will
not permit one word to be breathed against him."

" He ought to be most proud of so lovely a cham-
pion. He must be the most blessed man of all the
earth," said Jack, looking fondly down upon her.
Then he added : " Are you very sure that nothing
could ever come between his love and you ? "

" Why, Jack, how serious you are," the fair girl
said. " Nothing, nothing, can ever come to break
my admiration for him. Death itself can but sus-
pend life for a little while. My Jack and myself will
be loving each other when this world shall be worn
out and be floating in space, as does a dead swan
upon a lake."

Browning bent and kissed her again, said softly "Amen," and went out.

The day wore away, and when dinner was announced, Browning had not returned. Sedgwick went with Grace to the sitting room and remained for a few minutes. Grace chided him upon being moody, and with all her caressing ways tried to exorcise the evil spirit that was upon him, but with poor success. Finally he asked her to excuse him, telling her he was absorbed in a little matter not strictly his own, which he would tell her all about after awhile.

She listened, and when he had finished, she put her arms around his neck, and said :

"You see when confidence is withheld from me, I become violently angry, and punish the culprit by going away." Then she kissed him, arose, backed to the door, reached behind her, opened it, passed out, then kissing her hand to him, closed the door.

Sedgwick went out, and at once repaired to the hotel where Jordan stopped when in the city. He had been out of town following some whim, and Sedgwick had not seen him since Derby Day.

Reaching the hotel, he learned that Jordan had returned, and soon found him.

Jordan met him joyfully, explained why he had been away, that he was thinking all the way home from the Derby that if he remained he might be a burden to Sedgwick and his new friends ; that the best thing to do was to take no chances, and so he had been making the tour of Ireland.

Of that country he had much to say. "Yo' oughter go thar, Jim," he said. "Thar's a people wot ken look poverty in ther face 'nd laff it ter scorn; whar three squar meals a day ken be made on hope; whar wit grows on ther bushes; whar ther air ez filled with songs 'nd full hearts fill ther vacancy made by empty stomachs. It's ther most pathetic spot on earth, Jim. A race lives ther filled with energy and hope, a race as is generous and brave, 'nd warm-hearted, holdin' within 'em vitality enough ter found a dozen empires, but chained by poverty 'nd superstition, 'nd hate of the bruiser on this side of ther channel; nussin' impossible dreams 'ev a nationality which ther kentry couldn't support ef once obtained; proud ez Lucifer of a past which hez little in it 'cept wrong 'nd tyranny 'nd sufferin'; all ther exertions confined in a narrer groove, all ther work of no avail because uv indirection; clingin' ter homes which keeps 'em helpless 'nd only accomplishin' somethin' when transplanted to other fields, 'nd then carryin' on ther world's work, fiten' ther world's battles, sailin' ther world's ships, workin' ther world's mines, subduen' ther world's wildernesses, runnin' ther world's primaries, 'nd bein' ther world's perlicemen. I tell yo', Jim, it war pitiful.

"When I told 'em I war an American, they opened ther arms ter me ter once, 'nd took me in. What questions they asked! And when I told 'em about ther broad acres in Texas, how they cud go thar and each in a few months or years own his own farm half a mile squar, how ther eyes flashed 'nd ther faces

glowed!   It teched my heart, Jim, ter see 'em, 'nd
made a old fool uv me in one place, shore.

"I stopped in a house one night whar ther war ther
old man 'nd woman, a grown-up son 'nd a girl who
war, maybe, eighteen year old.   Thet girl, Jim, war
fine. . Blue eyes 'nd har that war the color which
ware 'twixt a brown and a flaxen, with er blush rose
shadin'; a clear-cut face like that of a Greek stater;
dainty form 'nd limbs ; the roundest arms yo' ever
seen 'nd a hand like Aferdites.   I noticed, too—ax-
identally in course, that ther thick brogans on her
feet were little 'nd shapely ef ther war thick brogans.
But, finest of all war her complexion.   Ther warm air
as blows over the Gulf Stream are good ter all com-
plexions in Ireland, but it had done extra fur thet
girl.   It war perfect.

"Then, over all, she hed a proud, shy, dainty way
'bout her which war exquisite.

"We had a jolly evenin' together.   I told 'em 'bout
America ; they told me all 'bout Ireland from ther
time of ther Irish kings.   They fired jokes at each
other that would sell for forty dollars apiece in Texas,
and they war ez thick ez though jokes growed on
trees.

"At last ther boy wanted his sister to sing, but she
got rosy red, 'nd told him ter be quiet.   I told her
ef she'd sing I'd make her a present, 'nd finally she
giv in.   Her brother played ther flute, 'nd she sung
'Tara's Harp,' not scientific, but jest nateral 'nd
sweet as iver a bobolink sang.

" When she finished I gin her a new guinea. She
didn't want ter take it, but I flung it inter her lap, 'nd
then it war passed from hand ter hand ez a curiosity.
Ther mother war last. She looked it over and then
sed : 'It's a beauty, shore, 'nd now, Nora, give it
back ter ther gentleman.' I sed : 'I don't want it.
I want Nora ter have it.'

" 'Shore nuff ?' sed ther mother.

" 'Shore,' sed I.

" 'Then, Nora,' sed ther mother, 'kiss the gentleman for the gift.' Would yer believe it, Jim, thet shy
girl come and put her arms around my neck and
kissed me.

" Blast me, but it took me back, but I rallied 'nd
said :

" ' Nora, I'd give another guinea for another kiss
like thet,' 'nd then she come back agin a-sayin' : 'Yo
ken hev another without any mo' guinea,' 'nd kissed
me agin, 'nd ther whole family laffed.

" Next mornin' when I come outer my room I found
Nora alone. Ther father and brother hed gone ter
ther field, and ther mother war cookin' my breakfast.

" Nora greeted me cordial like, 'nd I sed: ' Nora,ef
I war young agin I'd camp right here 'nd make love
ter yo'.'

" 'Out wid yer,' she answered. 'It's a cousin I hev
in America, 'nd she writes me how foine the land war,
but says ivery American is a mortal liar when he
talks ter ther girls.'

" ' The cousin slanders us,' said I.

" ' She does not,' said Nora

" ' And how can I prove it ? ' said I.

" ' Yez might make love ter me,' she said

" ' I'm too old, Nora,' I answered.

" ' Couldn't yez wait and let me tell yez thet ? ' she asked.

" ' I'd rether own it then ter hev yo' tell me,' I answered.

" ' O, it's makin' fun of me yez are,' said she. ' I know how far away yez are from the loikes of me and will forgit me to-morry, but I'm glad yez come, for it gave me a breath of the joy of the great world outside.   Here hearts be breaking continually, for our lives are narrowed down to a mere fight for food. It's jist slavery from the cradle ter ther grave, and slavery over which there shines no star of hope.'

" Jest then ther mother called us to breakfast. After breakfast I went ter my room and put ten £10 notes in a envelope, wrote a line thet it war to take the whole family ter America ; told 'em ter go ter Texas, and find the old neighbors, given' 'em a lot 'o names; told 'em not ter stay a minit in ther cities ; then went out and handin' Nora the letter ez I bid her good-bye, told her it war a real love letter, shore nuff, which she must not read till I war out o' sight ; thet she might give me ther answer when I cum back, and then I started straight for England.

I kep thinkin' all thet day, it war sich a girl as thet who after awhile become the mother of Pat Cleburne or may be Phil Sheridan."

" A moment later he looked up and said :

"But I wanted ter see yo', Jim, to tell yo' all the boys remember yo', and all allow yo' were the doldurndest tenderfoot thet ever crossed a hoss or fired a rope or a gun."

"Where can we find a quiet place, Jordan?" Sedgwick asked.

"I know a boss ranch," said Jordan, "whar we can have a private room and talk all we wanter, only a few steps away."

They found it a drinking house with private rooms in the rear.

When seated there, Sedgwick soon learned that Jordan had sold everything in Texas—stock and land—and had converted all into money in bank—some $35,000—and was, to use his own words, "makin' a tower."

"But how came yo' here, Jim?" asked Jordan.

Then Sedgwick told him of his life since the day he left Texas; how he formed a friendship for Browning; how the deal in stocks originated, and how it resulted.

The Texan went into raptures. "Yo' don't tell me?" he said: "Half a milliun! dod rot it, but thet's good; thet's immense! how it would tickle ther boys out thar to know it! And yo' give the ole man a cool $100,000? What did they think of yo' then? Har, waiter, give us a quart of y'r—whatyer call it? O, yes, Widder Clicko (Cliquot); durned if we don't sellerbrate."

They drank their wine, lighted their cigars, and settled down for a talk.

All the old times in Texas had been discussed
when Sedgwick said : " Jordan, I thought you were
prosperous and happy, and much loved by all who
knew you in Texas.   What possessed you to sell out
and leave?"

" I war prosperous," said Jordan, " doin' fust-class;
war contented, and I don't believe I hed a enemy in
the hull State.

" I hed ther ranch, ther cattle, ther mustangs; didn't
owe a dollar, and hed money in ther bank.   I hed
been doin' right pert, and the property war a-raisin'
every day.   Do yo' know the blamed igiots was
a-talkin' o' sendin' me to ther Legislature.   But after
awhile something happened.   A lot o' ther boys cum
in one day and said : ' Jordan, it's a blasted shame
the way the childer is growin' up yere.   We orter 'av
a school.'   ' All right,' says I, ' school goes.'   So they
agreed ter build a school house and ter hire a teacher
for six months.   I flung in more'n my shere, and
then ther question was whar to build ther school
house.   I spoke up and I says : ' Why not put it
down in the angle of my best section ?'   Yo' know
whar ther section lines cross thar.   It leaves a corner
in ther field which is a sharp pint in ther road, and
broadens as it runs back.   ' Well,' they said, ' but
whar'll the teacher board ?'

" Well, yo' know it's only six hundred yards up ter
my place ; so I says : ' I han't chick or child, but I'm
bound ter stay by ther school ; send ther teacher up
yere.   He can do chores enough for his board, if he
is techy at all on that pint.'

" The school house went up in short order, and one
of the Kinsley boys came by on a Saturday, and he
says, says he : 'Jordan, ther school'll be open Monday mornin',' and the teacher'll be down for supper on
Monday night.' 'Send him 'long,' says I. I thought
he gin a queer kind o' a igiotic laugh, but he said,
'All right,' and rid along. I went in through ther
kitchen and told Aunt Sue—yo' remember our old un-
bleached cook — that ther school master war a-comin'
to board on Monday night, and she must spread
herself.

" Her nose went up inter ther air, and she said :
'H'm, guess what we gets every day's good 'nuff for
one o' doze poor white trash teachurs.'

" Well, 'long 'bout five o'clock Monday evenin' I war
readin' ther paper, when I hearn a knock at ther door,
and same time I hearn Bolus—thet's the big collie, yo'
remember—kinder whinin' as though he war glad,
and bangin the door with his tail. I thought maybe
some of ther boys is cum back ; maybe it's Jim Sedgwick, and I gets up and goes and throws ther door
open, and was jest openin' my mouth to say 'Hello !'
when I got paralyzed.

" Thar war standin thar a little woman in a black
frock thet fitted her like a prayer on a nun's lips.
She had on a white collar, and when she looked up at
me yo' never seen sich a majestical pair o' eyes, and
I said ter myself, 'Blast my broad horns, but I never
seen so takin' a face in all my life.'

" Jest pale sorter, barrin' a little flush that creeped
up over her face, as yo' might expect would cum ter

thet stater—whatyer call it in ther play ?—Gal—, O, yes, Galerteer, thet's it—when weakenen' to thet feller's pleadin', she shakes ther stone and begins ter warm up ter his prayer. She had sorrerful eyes ter look inter, 'cept when she smiled, and then, Jim, hed yer seen thet smile once you'd never sarched fur no more bernanzers.

" Her nose was straight ez a blood hoss's fore-arm, teeth perfect, and white as ther starlight ; her har war between yaller and tawny, and lots of it. Jest then ther sun shone agin it, and my thot war, ' A smoked topaz ez big ez a dinner bucket war fused' and then spun inter threads ter make thet har.'

" And when she looked up and said, inquirin' like, ' Mr. Jordan ?' her voice war sweeter'n yo' ever hearn a turtle dove when callin' her mate ter breakfast.

" ' Thet's me,' sez I.'

" She held out her hand thet war soft an' white an' shapely, an' warm, and sed :

" ' I am Mrs. Margaret Hazleton, ther teacher in ther school, and I was directed here.'

" I thot I should o' drop through ther floo', but I braced up—waiter, another bottle—ez I war sayin', I braced up and said, ' Bless me, madam, I war expectin' ther teacher'd be a man ; but walk right in, we'll do ther best we ken for yer.'

" I called Aunt Sue, and told her to show ther lady whar ter dump her fixins,' and der yo' believe it, thet dog Bolus, thet war generally mighty questionin' 'bout strangers, set down 'nd thumped ther floo' like he war tickled ter death.

" Aunt Sue had cooked prairie chickens, pertaters, hed made hot bread 'n coffee, 'n fried bernanners, and opened can fruit, and brot out ther honey 'nd two kinds o' pickles, an' ther supper war fine.

" Ther little woman praised it, gentle like, jest enough an' not o'erdoin' it, till Aunt Sue's face war bigger'n a full mune, and filled with satisfaction ter ther very corners.

" All ther time ther lady kep talkin' 'bout Texas, askin' questions, 'bout ther sile, ther climate, and ther productions, and in course I talked and did my best a-entertainin' o' her till nine o'clock, when she got up and sed she'd bid me good-night.

" Aunt Sue give her the best room, in course—thet one beyond ther parlor. Yo' know I hed it furnished up kinder gorgus with a carpet from Shreveport, and spring bed and wash-stand and picters from Galveston, and I felt more satisfaction thinkin' mout be she'd be comfortable, than I ever hed before since I'd fixed it up.

" When she war gone, I sed : ' Boys, but we is in fur it,' but Aunt Sue spoke up, and says she : ' Der am white folks and white folks ; but dis one's a born lady, sho.'

" And the cowboys said, ' Shore,' and I was shore myself.

" She war up and out d'rectly in the mornin', fixed her own lunchen, talked clever a few words to Aunt Sue, petted ther dog a little, and asked him questions as though he'd been a kid ; stopped on the way out ter tie up a rose bush, 'nd so she came and went ev'ry

day, and though I didn't realize it then, ther house war
brighter when she war ther, and darker when she war
gone.

"Once Aunt Sue hed fever from Friday ter Sunday
night, and without any fuss thet thar woman did the
cookin', and doctored Sue as tho' cookin' 'nd doctorin'
war her regular perfession.

"We found out after a little thet she war a widder,
husband dead two year.

"After 'bout a week Aunt Sue says ter me one day:
'Mr. Jordan, yo' jest cum har!' I followed her ter
the woman's room. Der yer believe it, she'd downed
all ther flash picters that ther impenitent thief at Galveston hed coaxed me inter buyin', and in place hed
hung up some small engravins, not gaudy-like, but
jest catchin'; hed taken' off all the sassy trimmin's
from ther curtains, and the hull room war changed,
just ez tho' er benediction had been pernounced thar.
It war all kinder toned down, ez tho' a woman hed
slipped a gray ulster over a red frock.

"It made me feel kinder cheap like, and I sed ter
myself, says I : 'Thet's good taste!' I knowed it in er
minit, tho' I'd never seen it afore.

"Next Sunday in church we found out she could
sing, and after thet she sung for us o' nites, playing a
gitaw same time. Then arter awhile she got ter
readin' ter us. Yo' remember how yo' read, Jim?
Well, yer readin' war like a grand organ, hern were
like ther blendin' o' flutes and harps.

"Well, ther weeks went by, and sech a feelin' cum
over me ez I'd never 'sperienced afore. I thot first

'twar hay fever comin' on.   I couldn't eat, couldn't sleep.   I war restless when thet woman war gone.   I war skeery like when she war round ; and war given to havin' little hot spells and then chills, and I said, ' I know it's ther blasted malarier.'

So I took k'neen and juniper tea, and fancied I hed night sweats—jest the cussedest time, Jim, thet yo' ever seen.

"One day when I war a-sittin' in ther house and a-mopin', Aunt Sue cum in and looked hard at me, and says she : ' Mr. Jordan, does yo' know what's der matter wid ye ?'

' I told her I didn't ; thet I'd give a band o' cattle ter find out.

"' Laws,' says she, ' I'd tell cheaper'n dat, only yo'd think I is sassy.'

" I said: ' Aunty, yo' goahead.   If yo's sassy, I's too sick to care.'

"' Why, bless yo' soul, honey,' says she, ' yo's jest ded in lub wid the schoolma'm, Mrs. Margaret.   I noze.   I's been dar myself.'

"' O, git out,' says I.

" She went out laffin', but at ther door she stopped a second and says :   •

"' Dat's it, sho, Mr. Jordan,' and after ther door closed I hearn her ha-hain'.

" Then I did some thinkin' for the next half hour, and I said ter myself, ' It's thet, sho nuff.'

" The school term war ter close next day, and ther teacher had made her 'rangements ter leave right away for her home up No'th—Ierway, I b'lieve.   The

contract war for $100 er month, but when we met ter
fix up ther money I told ther trustees that some o'
ther neighbors hed been thet pleased with ther school
thet they had put up a little extry puss o' money,
enough ter pay ther teacher's board and give her
$150 extry.   It war a bald-headed pervarication, Jim,
but I thot it jestifiable under the sarcumstances,
inasmuch as I put up ther hull money myself.

I war fur gone. She closed ther school next
evenin' ; cum up ter ther house; wus goin' ter remain
till the train cum by fur ther No'th at 11:15 next day.
We hed supper and breakfast as usual. After breakfast ther boys all went off ter ther wo'k, and Aunt Sue
went ter a neighbor's to borrer some bakin' powder.
I was sittin' on ther verandy when the schoolma'm
cum out, and walkin' close up, says she : 'Mr. Jordan'—waiter, bring me a brandy smash—'Mr Jordan,' says she, 'I want to thank you for all your
gentle and generous kindness to me. Except for
your thoughtful consideration I should have had a
much harder time here. I thank you with all my
heart.' "

Sedgwick noticed that he had repeated the exact
words without a mistake in pronunciation. They had
evidently been burned into his very soul.

He drank the brandy, and then with a husky
voice went on :

" ' Yo' break me all up, Mrs. Hazelton,' says I.
' We is such rough folks down har. Yo' have been
er providence ter ther place.'

" She blushed a little at that, and said : ' You are too kind.'

" ' Not a blamed bit,' says I, and then realizin' it war my only chance, I blurted out : ' I'll be mighty sor-- rerful when yo' is gone. I don't know how others as knows how does it, but I want ter tell yer thet because of yer the flowers is brighter, the birds sing sweeter, the sunshine is clearer, the sky more smilin', and I cud get down and crawl on the ground yo' has walked over, that bad do I worship yer. And if yo' cud stay and marry me and civilize me, I'd try to brush up and be a decenter man than I ever war ; least- ways, I'd clar ev'ry rock and thorn outer yer path.'

" Do yo' b'lieve it, Jim, I wus perspirin' wus'n ther buckskin stallion did when yo' got thro' with him that fust mornin', and was tremblin' like a sick gal.

" She looked down compassionate like, got white about ther lips, 'nd her voice shook er little as she sed :

" ' I can't do that, Mr. Jordan ; there's much that I cannot tell, why I cannot, no måtter ; but I thank you with all my heart and soul, not only for your kindness to me, but for this last most generous offer.'

" Then she went on and talked, and cud yo' 'av hearn her, it would ha' made yo' think she war the prettiest and sweetest, and most compassionate woman as ever a-come ter bless ther world. She seemed ter me like a fur off priestess ministerin' to a sinner.

" After awhile I said :

" ' Mrs. Hazelton, o' course yo' is pore, or yo' wouldn't a-come down yere a-teachin' school among

these barbarians ; thet is, pore ez fur **ez** money goes.
I've been lucky.   I've $4,000 in ther bank which I've
no need of.   If you'll let me give you thet, no one'd
ever know it, and the reckerlection uv it, 'nd ther
thot thet it may be doin'. yo' some good'll give me
heaps more pleasure than keepin' of it would.'

"You see, Jim, I war fur gone.   But. she wouldn't
hev it, tho' ther tears jumped ter her eyes when I
offered it, and she remarked she b'lieved I war the
best man in ther world.   I told her if she ever needed
a friend and didn't send fer me, I should feel
slighted.

"Then I hitched up and druv her down ter the station.   She sat side o' me, Jim—waiter, more brandy
—in course.   Lookin' down, I cud see her smooth
cheek and clear-cut profile, and thinkin' I war takin'
my last looks, thar was sich a feelin' of all-goneative-
ness cum over me thet, do yo' know, if I cud ha' got
outer one side, I b'lieve I would a-bawled like er
hungry calf.

"We shook hands at ther station, and, not mindin'
ther crowd, she reached up both her arms, put 'em
around my neck, drew my head down 'nd kissed me
squar on the mouth.

"It perty nigh smothered me, and I said in a low
voice : 'Mrs. Hazleton, let me give yer ther money.
I positively has no use in the world fur it.'   .

"She give me a sad smile, shook her head and
jumped on ther train.   As it pulled out uv ther
station she nodded, wavin' her hankerchiv 'nd

dropped it axidently. I picked it up. I've got it till yet. I'll allers hev it.

"Thet war ther end. Bolus wouldn't eat fur three days, then he cut me dead and went off ter a neighbor's whar ther war a white woman, and would niver cum back.

"I stood it three months. I thot I should die uv the blues.

"One day a man from ther No'th stopped off at ther ranch fur the night. After supper he said he war a-lookin fur a stock ranch fur his son. I said, 'Why not buy mine ?'

"Then he asked all 'er 'bout it; how many acres; how much stock; 'bout the water, and what my price war.

"I told him $30,000   In the mornin' he gits a hoss, rode round with ther boys, and when he cum back, went down inter his pocket, drew out er wallet, and counted out thirty $1,000 gold notes, saying : ' I will take ther place.'

"It's a go,' says I.

"We went ter town and hed ther papers fixed up. That war last February. Then I started out, went slow round ter New York, then over here; I've been up to Scotland, over to Wales; been to France once; jest cum over from Ireland, and ev'ry day I ride 'bout twenty miles in this 'ere town, and I've never found any end to it yet, 'cept when I went on ther keers' 'nd thet day I went ter ther races. I believe it's bigger'n all Texas, and its very size worries me."

"What have you marked out for the future?" asked Sedgwick.

"Not a blamed thing," was the response.

"How would you like to take a trip with me?" asked Sedgwick.

"I'll go ter any place yo' say, Jim; I don't keer how fur," said the candid man.

"Do not promise too quickly," said Sedgwck. "I am thinking of starting for South Africa in two or three days."

"South Africa goes, if yo' say so," said Jordan; "I'my ours truly,blast my broad-horned heart if I ain't."

"Well, old friend, it is growing late. If you will be here to-morrow morning at eight I will tell you all that is on my mind," said Sedgwick, rising.

"I'll be har," said Jordan.

Sedgwick stopped to settle the bill, but Jordan pushed him aside, saying, "Not to any particular extent, if we knows ourself." He tossed a tip to the waiter, paid the bill, and was going to add a shilling for the young woman who was the cashier, when, glancing up at her, he changed his mind and made it a guinea, because, as he explained, "Her hand war sunthin' like Maggie's."

The friends separated at the door.

It was eleven p. m. when Sedgwick reached the Hamlin house. He would not have gone at that hour, except that he had been given a pass-key on the first day he was there, with a request never to fail to come in, no matter how late he might be detained. Moreover, he wanted to see Jack.

Before he could open the door, it was swung back by Grace. She explained that she was on the watch so that she might form an idea of what hours Sedgwick was in the habit of keeping, and to tell him how very angry she still was. Then she gave him a smile such as an angel might, and was gone.

Sedgwick went at once to Browning's room, but he was still out. He crossed over to his own, threw off his coat, put on a smoking-jacket and slippers, and lighting a cigar, sat down to think.

Before very long Browning came in. " I found him," he said. " He was shy about giving me the facts, but I ginned him up to the confessional point. He told me all the truth at last.

" He received but £2,000 for the mine, and he does not believe that a share of it was ever sold to any one but me. He was paid the £2,000 on the day I bought the first 50,000 shares. My money paid for the mine ; then I bought it over again. I furnished the purchase money, and then bought it again, paying an advance of 500 per cent. And the job was put up by the old duffers ; Stetson was only let in to clear the old chaps when the truth should be known. And then Stetson wants to marry my Rose.

" But the man told me that the mine was just as described, only a nasty road would have to be built to it that would probably cost £80,000 or £100,000, and the mill would have to be built. It looks to me like a total loss, Jim ; but the swindle is so manifest that I believe we can make the conspirators disgorge at least the last half that they robbed me of."

The room was still for many minutes. Then Sedg-wick said : " Jack, I thought those old men meant mischief to you when I first saw them. It was because of that—at least, in part that—that I remained. But one is your stepfather—another the stepfather of your affianced bride, and the other a mere stool-pigeon. There must be no scandal if we can help it. I believe the object on the part of Jenvie was to keep you from marrying Rose ; what your step-father means I cannot understand. But anyway, if we can help it, there must be no scandal. We shared alike in Nevada. I have as much money left as both of us need. We share alike still. But no matter about that.'

" But I have been a hopeless idiot to let these men rob me," said Jack, "and except for Rose, I would pull out for America to-morrow. I would, by Jove !"

" Your mistake was entirely natural," said Sedg-wick. " Had my father wanted all my money, he could have got it for the asking. Do not talk about going to America ; that would be ' conduct unbecom-ing an officer and a gentleman '; it would be a cow-ardly desertion in the face of the enemy. Then, you have never been very well since your ducking down on the Sussex coast; and, besides, you have entered into obligations here so sacred that you must not permit a little whim, or even a great disappointment, to lead you to think about trying to break them. Let us go to sleep now. To-morrow we will talk over this matter more fully. I want a few more hours to think and to make up my mind what is best to do." Jack returned to his room, and the lights were put out.

CHAPTER XIV.

TEARS AND ORANGE FLOWERS.

In the morning Sedgwick got a cup of coffee early, and was just going out, when Grace came running up to him in the hall.

"I believe you were running away," she said gaily, and, seizing his arm, declared that he was her prisoner,

He told her that it was true he was running away, but would be back before very long, and would then, he thought, explain everything.

"Then I am still very angry," said she. "I am going to my room to make a calculation how much I am being slighted, and to consult the fates as to what penalties shall be prescribed before you can possibly hope for forgiveness." Then she smiled, stretched out her hand to be kissed by him, then opened the door and said softly, "Do not be too long away."

Sedgwick went again to Jordan's hotel; found him and told him briefly all that had happened; all about Browning, the love affairs of both, and how Jack had been taken in on the mine; ran over the prospectus of the "Wedge of Gold," and explained that he meant to visit the property; that if it could be made available with the means he had, he intended to improve it and bring Jack's shares up to cost; that no one but his Grace and her mother was to know when he went away, that he was not going to America, and that he wanted some one with him who understood gold quartz.

Jordan listened with increasing interest as the story was told, interrupting only when Sedgwick spoke of his love for Grace Meredith, and when he explained how Jack had been swindled.

To the first he joyfully responded: "I am glad, old boy, blast my broad-horned heart if I aint! She's a daisy; she's a real woman; and I thank God she found yo' and tuk pity on yo'."

To the other he said: "Well, the dod-durned, Newgate, Rotten Row, British thieves! How I would like to 'ave 'em in Texas for one short quarter of a hour!"

His enthusiasm was at its height at the close of Sedgwick's story. He cried out:

"It'll be glorious, Jim. Ef the mine can be worked up, we'll make it, sho'." Then after a pause, he said slowly as to himself, in a low tone: "It'll take me outer myself, maybe; that'll be wo'th mo' to me than a gold mine."

"But it is a tough time of year," said Sedgwick. "The Red Sea and the ocean beyond will be like furnaces at this season."

"Red Sea, ocean, furnace, everything, goes," said Jordan. "I enlist fo' ther wah."

Another meeting was arranged for that afternoon, and Sedgwick returned to the Hamlin home.

He went direct to Browning's room, tapped on Jack's door, and then walked in. Jack was leaning upon the table, thinking, and was so engrossed that he did not hear the tap or the opening of the door.

He started up as Sedgwick laid his hand on his shoulder, and said : " I don't believe, Jim, that I heard you come in."

" That's all right," said Sedgwick, " but, Jack, you must hear me now." Then sitting down close beside his friend, Sedgwick went on :

" I have thought this business all out, Jack. I believe the prime motive for this swindle was to separate you and Rose, and prevent your marriage. The first thing to do then, is to secure that matter. You must see Rose, and if she is willing, you must be married to-morrow. I think she will consent, and that her mother will approve it when she shall have been told the truth. This must be, Jack ; first, because those old scoundrels will continue to plot against the marriage until they know it is of no more use ; and second, I want to go away to-morrow evening."

" It cannot be," said Browning. "They took all my money. They left me but a beggarly £12,500.

" How much did you keep thinking through so long a time would be sufficient to accumulate before you could come back and ' try to steal Rose Jenvie ?'" asked Sedgwick.

" O yes, I know," said Browning ; " but then it was different."

"What have you told Rose about your money matters ?" asked Sedgwick.

" Not one word," was the reply.

" Do you think she expects a no-account boy to go off to America, and with nothing but his head and his hands to accumulate more than £12,500 in three or four years?" asked Sedgwick. " But this is all foolishness, old boy," he continued. " The last half of the money those old men obtained from you can be recovered easily, if not all ; if that, after awhile, proves to be the best thing to do. And, moreover, I tell you that we are partners in this, and that we still have as much money as you and I can very well handle. I must have my way about this, old friend."

" But if you are going away, why cannot I go with you ?" asked Browning.

" For several reasons," replied Sedgwick. " If you remain here, or go down on your farm in Devonshire, the conclusion of Jenvie and Hamlin will be, that with your money mostly gone, all I could do was to return to America.

" Again, no one knows how much more money you have. You must remain. Be generous at the club, move among men, keep the prestige that you have won since you came here ; be entirely independent ; keep your eye on the man the mine was bought from, even if you have to pay him a salary to insure his remaining here, and so be in a position to help through any line of action we may agree upon. More, you must restrain yourself and have no trouble with young Stetson. He is as much fool as knave.

" Another reason is, that Rose has already waited years for you, and it would be a wicked and cruel thing to disappoint her again. It would kill her and unman you. No, no, you must be married to-morrow. But Jack, if I were you, I would never take my wife back under the Jenvie roof until full reparation should be made. See her, and gain her consent to an immediate marriage ; then go and hire a house or make arrangements at a hotel to live, and I want you to promise that you will not, after I shall have gone, bring any suit or make any sign that you have suffered a loss, or bother yourself much about business until I come back, or you receive word of me. I will fix money matters before I go, so that you will not be troubled. And now, think it over."

When Jack aroused himself, Sedgwick had disappeared. He sat in silence for a few minutes, then rose, went out, secured a conveyance, called and asked Rose to go out for a drive.

On the road he explained to Rose all that had happened ; how rich he was when he came home ; how his confidence had been betrayed ; how little he had left, and then asked if the dear girl was still willing to be his wife, and if she would consent to become his wife next day.

She laid her hand on his, and said : " Dear Jack ! it was to be for all time ; your home to be my home ; your God my God. I will be ready when you come for me. I will go exultingly to become your wife ; my joy will be the deeper, for it will be chilled with no fear of the future, which it might have been had I known you possessed £100,000. What you have is enough for us. But, Jack, let me begin to influence you.   Do not take a shilling of your friend's money unless you know that we can some time return it."

Later, Jack found a lovely furnished house, the owner of which desired to vacate for a year ; hired it, paid a year's rent in advance, engaged the servants of the family, and explained that he would bring his wife on the succeeding day.

On that same day, Sedgwick sought Grace, and made clear to her the situation, explaining how Jack had been wronged, what he had advised to do him, and unfolded his own plan to leave the next day, so soon as Browning and Miss Jenvie should be married— with Jordan for South Africa, to see if it was worth while to try to bring out the property, explaining that if the mine gave no strong promise he would be back in two or three months.   If, on the other hand, he and Jordan decided it was good, he might be absent for a year, and asked her if she would keep the secret of where he had gone, and if she were sure enough of her own heart to undertake to wait for him.

Grace had grown very white and still while Sedg-wick was speaking.   When he ceased she continued silent for a moment, and then said :

"I agree to it all, my king, all but one thing."

"And what is that, sweet ?" asked Sedgwick

She leaned over, put her arm around her lover's neck, laid her cheek against his, and said : "If Jack and Rose are to be married to-morrow, we should be married also."

"But I am going away, my child," said Sedgwick.

" I know," was her response, " but one object of my father in trying to break off the match between Jack and Rose was to try to have Jack marry me. We should complete the work. Then, should you need me, or could you send for me, I could go better as your wife than any other way ; then, when I gave my heart to you I gave it entirely, and should we never meet, I would, while I lived, want to keep in thought that you were my husband ; that I was your wife ; that all glory had come to me."

By this time the tears were flowing fast down her cheeks, and with tears in his own eyes, Sedgwick said:

" I wanted to ask you, dearest, to become my wife before I went away, but thought it a shame to so involve you, with a future so clouded as mine is to be for the coming months."

"You forget," she replied, " that it is my right in your absence to think of you as my husband."

So it was settled that on the next day, just before noon, they should be married ; that they should separate at the church, she to return with her mother, Sedgwick to start with Jordan on their long journey.

Then Grace called her mother. The matter was explained to her, and she readily consented to the marriage, saying to Sedgwick: "You know I asked you, in case Grace returned your affection, that the mattert might for the present be held a secret. My reason was that I felt that.something sinister, which I could not understand, was at work. I think you and Grace have a right to belong to each other ; that if you must

go away Grace is right in wishing that when you
are gone she can think of you as her husband."

So arranged, Sedgwick went to find Jordan. A
steamer had sailed the previous day from Southampton for Port Natal, via the Suez Canal, and Sedgwick's plan was to join that ship at Port Said.

He found Jordan, told him of the change in the
arrangements ; fixed with him to have all needed
baggage at the Dover depot, to meet him at the
church at 11:30 next day, and after the ceremony to
start with him from the church on their long journey.

" I'll be thar, old friend," said Jordan. " Thet's ther
sensible business. Make ther splendid girl yo'r wife,
and pervide for her so thet if anything happens she'll
be safe agin the petty cares that break women's
hearts."

Then Sedgwick returned to the Hamin house, and
went straight to Jack's room.

Browning greeted him with a smile, and said,
" Jim, old pard, it's all right. The marriage goes,
even as you planned, and I have found and secured a
nest for my bird."

"Good," said Sedgwick ; " but the arrangements
have been changed a little ; or, I might say, enlarged
upon a little. As I understand it now, you, with
Rose and her mother, will be at the church at
11:30 to-morrow. I will be there with Mrs. Hamlin
and Grace. We will be the witnesses of your marriage, and then, Jack, old man, you and Mrs. Browning must be witnesses for Grace and me."

Jack sprang from his chair, and cried : "Are you and Grace fond of each other?

" Well, somewhat, I trust," said Sedgwick.

" And you are really engaged ? " cried Jack.

" For all this life, at least," said Sedgwick ; then added gravely, " and heaven itself would be a cold and cheerless place to me without my saving Grace."

Then Browning wrung the hand of Sedgwick, embraced him, danced around the room ; then shook hands again, crying: " This is superb! this is glorious, by Jove! Why, of course it would be all wrong any other way. O, Jim, bless my soul, how glad I am !"

Then Sedgwick said : " Browning, we have not much time. You understand I will leave my wife "— his voice trembled—" at the church door. I am going away—where, no matter—with a thought in my mind which, please, do not ask me. I may be gone two months, maybe six months.

" Here is my will. Grace will keep it. Here is a check for her, which will secure her comfort, so far as money is concerned. Here is a check for £10,000 for you and Rose. Grace will return from the church to this house. If our marriage cause any friction here, she will go and live with you and Rose. I am glad you have secured a house. If I were you, I repeat, I would never take Rose under the roof of her stepfather until I received full restitution from him. Do not discuss this money part of the business any more ; it will do you no good. And when I am gone, do not get low spirited. Make life happy for Rose, and "—he halted a moment—" for Grace."

The dinner was not a happy one that day. A cloud was on the Hamlin house. As soon as possible the head of the house went out. He was quickly followed by Browning.

The eyes of Grace and Sedgwick met. They both rose from the table and passed into the hall. Grace twined her arms around one of his and led him into the parlor. She swung around an easy chair, made him sit down, then seated herself on an ottoman at his feet, and said: " It's going to be awfully hard to bear, my love ; but I have thought it all over, and I do not believe I should ever be quite satisfied if you should not perform what you have marked out as your duty. Of course, if the property will not bear examination, you will, if nothing wrong happens you, be back in two or three months. If it will justify further exertion, I understand it will be likely to keep you away for a year, and that will be fearful."

The tears filled her eyes.

" But that will be duty, and then if you conclude to remain, maybe you will send for me. It will not matter how I live. I would go now, but I know I would be a trouble to you. I should interfere with your work. To-day you would want to go here ; to-night, there; to-morrow you would want to be off on the mountains ; and while I do not imagine you would think me a burden, nevertheless your very best energies could not be exerted, and this time they must be."

She seemed very resolute as she spoke, though her face was sadder than Sedgwick had ever seen it. She continued:

" I shall be brave when the hour comes, my love.
I shall not vex you with a tear when we separate.
You shall carry a smile as my last gift away with
you."

Sedgwick was enchanted. He thought her the
grandest, noblest woman on earth, and thanked God
for his treasure.

After awhile he told her of Jordan, and all that he
had learned from him. When he rehearsed Jordan's
love episode, she kept exclaiming : " Poor, true man !
Poor, honest fellow !" But when it was finished, she
said : " Why, love, he is a ninny; that woman would
never have left him had he but had more faith in himself, and pressed his suit a little. I am glad he is
going with you. You will be a comfort to him, and
his mind will have an object to work upon. Poor
fellow !" she added with a sad smile. " You men are
very brave and bright. You tear down mountains,
exalt valleys, fight battles, navigate great ships, tame
wild horses and lasso wild oxen, but you do not—the
majority of you—know any more about a woman's
heart than a Fiji islander does of Sanscrit."

To all of which Sedgwick responded by calling her
an angel.

Then the matter of their marriage was talked over,
and Sedgwick advised that in case her stepfather
should be angry upon learning of the event, she
should take up her home with Jack and Rose.

" My father will not show much vexation," she
said. " If he begins that way, I will remind him of
the fortune he has taken from your friend, his own

step-son, and explain that it was his and Jenvie's work
that made necessary what we shall have done."

But it was agreed that all letters to her should be
sent to a private box in the postoffice, to which Sedgwick gave her the key.   It was agreed, moreover,
that even Jack should not know he had not gone to
America, because, as he explained, if Jack once suspected he was going to Africa, he, too, would insist
upon going, which would break Rose's heart, who had
already waited for years ; and then his going would
be altogether unnecessary, as he and Jordan could do
as well as three could.   Moreover, to go would be to
lose what he had advanced on the Devonshire estate.

They both tried to be cheerful, but it was a sad
night.   When they came to separate, Grace broke
down, but through her tears promised to be brave
when the final trial came.

Next morning, from half past nine to half past ten,
Sedgwick and Grace were saying their final good-
byes.   It was an hour never to be forgotten by them.
Grace did not attempt to restrain her tears.   In both
their hearts was the feeling that one has when the
last look is being taken of the face of a much-loved
one who has gone to the final rest.   There were kisses
and embraces and broken words, but there was no
faltering on either side.   Both were supported by the
thought that a duty had been presented and must not
be avoided.

At 10:30 they retired to their respective apartments.
Sedgwick dressed himself in a business suit of a dark

texture. Grace attired herself in a traveling suit and hat. The baggage of Sedgwick was sent off at 11:15, and both were ready when the carriage came. The carriage with Mrs. Jenvie, Rose and Browning came up almost immediately, and the two vehicles proceeded to the church. Quite a little company had gathered, drawn by curiosity, when the church doors were opened.

Jordan was present, radiant in a new suit, with a flower in his coat lapel, and he answered the smile and nod that each couple gave him as they passed up the aisle.

As stated before, Grace was in a traveling suit, but Rose was radiant in robe and train and orange wreath, and a buzz of admiration at her exquisite beauty followed her all the way to her place before the altar.

The ceremony proceeded in the usual order, The mothers gave the brides away; the last prayer was finished, the kisses given, the papers duly signed and witnessed, the certificates filled out and given to the respective brides, and the company turned to leave the church.

Then Jordan came forward. Sedgwick presented the two elder ladies to him, and all greeted him most cordially. In response he said :

" It's the whitest kind uv a day. I'm glad ter know yo' all ; glad ter congratulate yo', and I wanter say ter Mrs. Sedgwick—Grace grew rosy red on hearing the appellation—that I've know'd her husband a long time, and he's true blue, sho' ; there's not a better or a braver man on either side o' ther ocean."

With that he drew a package from his pocket, and tendered it to Grace, saying : "I wanter give yo' a little keepsake fo' yo' husband's sake."

It was a jewel case and contained a diamond cross worth £300.

At the church door the good-byes were spoken. Browning and his bride entered one carriage and were driven away to Jack's home. The two elder ladies and Sedgwick's bride entered the other carriage.

True to her promise, Grace gave to her husband, who stood near, a smiling good-bye, but when the carriage was driven away, she broke into uncontroleable sobs, wrung her hands piteously, and not until she reached home did the paroxysm of grief subside. She went to her room, laid by all her bright dresses and ornaments, robed herself in simple black—" in mourning," she said, " for my lost honey-moon."

Sedgwick and Jordan entered a carriage, and from it boarded the Dover train. Not a word was spoken until the train had passed beyond the great city's outermost limit, when at last Jordan said :

"Cum, Jim, brace up. It'll be all the sweeter when this accursed bitter cup shall be passed."

And Sedgwick answered : "You are right, old friend, but the dear girl will suffer. That last smile was such as is given when hearts break."

CHAPTER XV.

When the old men, Jenvie and Hamlin, reached their homes that evening and learned what had transpired during the day, they were dumfounded. Hardly tasting any dinner, Hamlin arose from the table and sought the house of Jenvie. He met Jenvie at the door who was just going out to find Hamlin. They went at once to Jenvie's library, and when Jenvie motioned Hamlin to a seat and took another himself, it was a long time before either spoke.

At last Hamlin said: " A bad business, Jenvie."

" I do not see how it could be worse," was the reply.

" I am too confused to think," said Hamlin.

" We got Jack's money from him, and yet he and Rose are married, and it seems with Rose's mother's full consent," said Jenvie.

" And a stranger of whom we know almost nothing has married Grace and left her at the church door, and it was with her mother's full consent, also," said Hamlin.

" And neither you nor myself is in a position to complain; I have not the courage to even storm about it," said Jenvie.

" Nor have I," responded Hamlin. " I did not intend to keep Jack's money. I wanted to break off

his engagement, and then offer him a little fortune if
he would marry Grace."

"I was determined that he should not marry Rose,
even if I had to rob him to prevent it. Curses on
him! He knocked me senseless while he was yet a
mere boy. And now he has given me a harder blow.
He has stolen Rose from under my spectacles, married
her, pauper that he is, and gone to housekeeping."

"What shall we do?" asked Hamlin.

"Look here," said Jenvie, "this move is that
American's who has married your daughter. He is
more subtle than Jack. He has engineered this
business. But I cannot fathom it. Why should he
have left his bride at the church door and gone off to
America?"

"I think I can understand that," said Hamlin.
"While Jack has made his £100,000, Sedgwick made
a little more than £20,000. He left that with his
father to buy a farm in the States, and came with Jack
merely as a lark.

"I think he has gone for as much of that as may
be left, and that before a month he will return, and
will back Jack in a suit to recover from us Jack's
money."

"Why, what can they hope to recover by a suit?"
asked Jenvie. "If mining stocks are offered to a
man and he buys them, and they do not turn out
well, whose loss ought it to be? Then we sold nothing. It was Stetson who did the business."

"But," said Hamlin, "if a man is induced by false
representations to buy wild-cat shares, and he seeks

recourse through our English courts, will he not recover ? "

" I made no special representations," said Jenvie.

" That will not answer," said Hamlin. " You made enough representations ; so did I. It was a direct swindle, and I did my part intending to make restitution. This business has practically destroyed the peace of our own homes. My wife never gave me a look of thorough contempt until to-day."

" Neither did mine," said Jenvie. Then there was a long silence.

At last Jenvie said: " Hamlin, there is but one thing to do. We must go to Jack to-morrow, good-naturedly chide him and Rose for being married without our knowledge, each carry a present, and as soon as possible settle with Jack, and get his receipt in full, before the return of that American devil that tumbles bulls, and might trip two old John Bulls like you and me."

" I agree to that," Hamlin responded. " We can tell him that bad news from the mine has decided us not to go on with the mill building ; that we will help bear the loss of the first investment, and tender him back £25,000. He will not only be glad to settle with us for that, but will feel grateful to us."

So it was agreed that they should go at noon of the succeeding day.

They each next morning purchased a valuable present, and repaired to Jack's house.

They were shown in, and their cards sent to Browning.

The servant returned in a moment and said : " Mr.
Browning is engaged, and declines seeing the gentlemen."

They went out incensed, but with such a mixed
feeling of anger, chagrin,' self-abasement, and appre-
hension as they had never experienced before.

A day or two later Hamlin met Mrs. Browning
face to face on the street.   He rushed up to her with
a joyful cry of " O Rose ! " whereupon she drew her
skirts around her so that they would not touch him,
and walked by. '

Not long after, Jenvie met Browning and addressed
him joyously.   Jack looked him steadily in the face
for a moment and then walked on.

These were unhappy days for the old men.   Something had fallen on their homes worse than a funeral,
and in their souls the fear of the coming of Sedgwick became a perpetual haunting specter before
their eyes.   Stetson joined in their apprehensions,
and then he realized besides that if he had ruined
Jack, still Jack had married Rose.

But as the days grew into weeks, they began to
have hope. They made two or three investments
that gave them quick returns and large profits.   Success begets confidence.   The men on change began
to look upon them as rising bankers ; deposits increased heavily, and so many enterprises were offered
them to promote, that, without using a dollar of their
own means, their commissions began to be enormous.

" We are on the rising tide," said Jenvie.

" Indeed we are, " said Hamlin. " If the suit comes now, we can settle without any business or domestic scandal."

" It is nothing to make money when a man once gets a start," said Jenvie, "but I would be glad to be fully reconciled with my wife and child,"

CHAPTER XVI.

Sedgwick and Jordan, with only now and then a few words of conversation, reached the coast and embarked on the channel steamer. A fresh wind was blowing, and the craft was shamefully unsteady.

"It must uv been heah, Jim, whar ther original mustang learned his cussedness," said Jordan. "See how ther steam devil performs, startin' up ez tho' it meant to climb a wave and then without er provercation rollin' half way over and all ther time shakin hisself an' makin' things thet uncomfortable thet ther man aboard, while sayin' nothin', wishes all ther time he'd never tackled ther brute. Didn't ther useter call ther sea, 'Mare?' I know why, she were a mustang shor."

Sedgwick's face kindled with the ghost of a laugh, and he agreed that Jordan's theory was not a bad one.

"But, Jim," said Jordan, "this war er famous old place after all."

"Yes," said Sedgwick; "history has compiled some of its wonderful pages right here. We are where the **Great Armada** sailed, the souls of those on board believing they were going to make the conquest of England. Here is where Howard gave that fleet its first blow; here is where Howard and Drake sent their fire ships to play havoc with the hostile fleet. A great place indeed! But it was only 300 years ago that Howard and Drake performed their part; before their day many a fleet swept over this watery way; the Crusaders crossed here; before them, a thousand years, the great Julius came and invaded England; before him, a hundred savage nations worked their rude boats in these turbulent seas. When the light of civilization well-nigh went out in the land where it was first kindled, it was re-lighted on these shores, and though it burned slowly for a long time it never quite went out; rather, it grew brighter and brighter until its sheen began to fill the world. Bright souls have peopled both sides of this channel; both are lands of fair women and brave men; their literature has made the world gentler and higher; their laws dominate mankind; their power is a controlling force among the nations; they make the center of the world's wealth; they are each examples of how much men may accomplish on small areas of land, provided they possess sovereign hearts and brains and souls."

The ship scraped against the pier while Sedgwick was talking, and the travelers hurried on their way. At Paris they were detained several hours, and Jordan hiring a carriage, they took in as much of the beautiful city as possible.

Jordan all the time exerted himself to talk, and by asking questions to compel Sedgwick to think of something besides the sad-browed bride whom he had left in London.

" What war the special charm 'bout Paris, Jim ?
I feel it, but blamed ef I can splain it even ter
myself," said he.

" I do not know," replied his friend, " but I suspect,
Tom,   it is the culmination of something which has
for a thousand years been maturing.   Long ago, a
full thousand years, there was an Emperor here who
was in advance of his generation. He believed that a
perfect education meant the full enlightenment of the
mortal, that his hands and eyes as well as his mind
must be disciplined, that every useful attribute must
be trained.   So he built cathedrals to improve the
taste of the people, established free drawing schools,
had the people taught the secret of fusing worthless   material   with acute brains   and   making
something valuable—something which the rich are
glad to give their gold in exchange for.   That emperor died, but his work continued to live and increase
until France became a nation of artisans and artists,
and that art has now become second nature, and
therein lies the charm.   See how yonder lady picks
up her drapery to cross the street ; not ten women in
England could do that little thing as she does.   Do
you know the reason why ? She caught the art
originally from old Charlemagne.   That is, thirty
generations ago, the old Emperor established the
schools which made possible the perfection of the
present, and the graceful art of that lady is in truth a
graceful compliment to the old soldier-Emperor
who more than a thousand years ago fell back to dust."

" I reckon yo' are right, Jim," said Jordan.   " When

I was heah afore, I put up at er tavern whar ther war
young women as waited on ther table. I jest had
plain food, in course, but when one o' them young
women brot me ther bill, she would hand et out in sech
er way thet tho' I knowed she war a-robbin' me, I never
thot o' pertestin'; rather, she war shor ter git er tip in
addition. Talk er high art,them girls war daisies, shor.
One time thar war a row. A dapper feller disputed
er bill. He thumped his heart, waved his arms,
and made er speech like er politician. Ther perprieter
cum in, then both made speeches. I thot ther would
be shootin' or cuttin', sartin, but finally one rushed
out, and I tho't in course hed gone for a gun. While
waitin' ter see ther fun, I seen over at er table a feller
smilin' like, and I tho't by his face he war a Yankee,
so I went over, and sez I : 'parler vouse Fronsa ?'
Then he laffed and said: 'Yes, a little, but I understand English better.' Then I shuk his hand 'nd
axed him wot ther row war, an 'nd ef he tho't that thar
man hed gone fur a wepin. He smiled sort o' quiet-
like, and said : 'No, it war jest a difficulty about an
overcharge of five sous, and it's all settled.' 'All that
row for five sous ?' I asked. 'Yes,' he answered.
Then I said, ' My God, suppose it hed a-been five
francs, it would uv been ez good ez er play.' Yo'
see, that old trick thet they got from big Charlie,
they overplay sometimes."

Sedgwick smiled faintly, and Jordan continued :

" But are they not er light-hearted, joyus race,
tho ' ? How they can sing 'nd dance 'nd play hades !
When I war heah they hed a review uv ther soldiers,

'nd how ther hull town turned out 'nd yelled 'nd yelled
'nd sung ther Marseilles, 'nd yet ther scars and humilit-
ation uv ther mighty defeat war still fresh upon them.
They'r ez hopeful ez ther Irish, same time they is a
great deal closer traders.   Ther stranger pays fur eny
bow they make, for any smile they give.   Still, they is
country-loving ; every one uv 'em 'r ready ter die fur
there beautiful France,'nd ther women ez jest ez'thuse-
astic ez ther men.   If I war young 'nd cud round up
ther language a little, I'd camp heah fur six months."

   " The place is worth a longer visit," said Sedgwick,
" just to study its past, to go over the spots made
sacred in history, to study the monuments, to visit
galleries ; to dream of all the events which transpired
to round the present city into form ; to trace the
city's career through wars, revolutions, uprisings,
victories and defeats; to learn the processes, and
count the throes which were necessary before the
manhood of the people asserted its superiority over
the manhood of kings.

   " Think ! It is but sixty years since the great
Corsican led his army out of here to his last cam-
paign.   One can picture him now in thought, moving
up this very street, the old familiar sovereign face,
eyes straining towards the star that even then had
become a fallen star, his ears thrilled with the plaudits
of shouting armies and shouting people, his soul imper-
turbable in its dream of conquest.   Then the man was
everything, the people nothing ; now the people are
everything, the man—he is asleep and his heart is not
colder in the grave than it was in life."

CHAPTER XVII.

But at last the hour for leaving came, and Sedg-wick and Jordan took the train and proceeded without delay to Marseilles, where one of the steamers of the French Imperial Messenger Line was about to sail for Port Said. They at once secured transportation, went on board, and a few hours later the ship proceeded to sea. The weather was fair on the Mediterranean, and putting aside any personal sorrows, Jordan exerted himself to be cheerful for Sedgwick's sake.

"This are ther water on which men fust learned ter be sailors, arn't it, Jim?" he asked. "I mean whar they fust got inter ther notion of venturin' out whar ther old shore-shaker could git a good hold on 'em?"

"Yes," replied Sedgwick. "This and the Red Sea. The Egyptians, the Carthagenians, the Phœ-nicians, the Syrians, the Greeks, the Romans, and a dozen other nations; later, the Venetians and Spaniards, and no one knows how many other nations, all learned how to build, navigate, and fight ships on these waters. Think of it, Jordan, there were sea fights here almost seven hundred years before the Christ came. On this sea floated the fighting Biremes, Triremes, and Quinquiremes of the Greeks, Carthagenians, and Romans; and here the Egyp-

tians and Phœnicians trained their ships three thousand years before the crucifixion.

" Could this sea give up its dead—its dead men and
its dead ships ; could they all come back as they
looked the moment before they sank, they would
make a panorama of the ages, and would show the
progress of the world for five thousand years. Every
mile square of this sea must be paved with things
which were once glorious in life and power. Maybe
below where we are sailing here, helmeted Roman
soldiers, being transported to some point of contem-
plated conquest, went down. Here pirate craft have
roamed ; here lumbering wheat ships have ploughed
their way ; here the watches have been set by the
crews of a hundred nations ; here sailors have been
cursed in a thousand tongues. Along these shores
ship-building had its birth ; from these shores the
ships sailed out over these waters, engaging in foreign
commerce, and the camel-owner on the land learned
to hate the thing which on the water could carry the
burden of many camels. One could sit all day and
conjure up the ghosts that these blue waters are
peopled with."

" Go ahead, Jim," said Jordan. " Thet sounds as it
useter when yo' read to us in ther old house thar in
Texas. What war thet book that told all 'bout Lissis
and Ajax, the hoss-tamer Diamed, and the boss fighters, Killes and Hector, and ther pretty gal Helen,
that raised all the hel-lo, and Dromine, the squar
woman thet war Hector's wife, and hed the kid thet
war afeerd of the old man's headgear ? "

THE WEDGE OF GOLD.

"That was the Iliad, Jordan," said Sedgwick, "the first book that we read. The story was the siege of Troy, That was a city over on the east shore of this very sea, and the Greeks went over there in their boats and besieged it for nine years before they captured it."

"How long ago war that, Jim?" asked Jordan.

"Three thousand years," was the reply.

"But they were fighters, them fellers?" said Jordan.

"Yes, great fighters," said Sedgwick.

"And their hosses war thoroughbreds, every one? Isn't thet so, Jim?" said Jordan.

"They were great horses, indeed," said Sedgwick.

"Powerful," said Jordan, "good for fo' mile heats, sho'? And thet other chap, Nais, didn't he settle round here somewhar?"

"You mean Æneas, Jordan. It was in Virgil that we read that. Æneas was of the family of that Priam who was king of Troy when the siege was on. He got away in a ship and finally landed and settled in southern Italy, off here to our left, and the legend goes that his descendants founded Rome."

"Yo' don't mean ter say he wur ther 'riginater uv ther Dagoes?" said Jordan.

"Well," said Sedgwick, with a laugh, "you know at that time there were wild tribes in Italy. Then there came in Greek colonies, and all races fused and assimilated, even as did the Romans and Sabines when the former captured a company of the women of the latter and made them their wives. Out of it all arose the mighty Roman nation."

" They inbred with mustangs, so ter speak," said Jordan, "and these common Dagoes is whar they has bred back showin' bad stock in ther dam."

" May-be," said Sedgwick.

" Half-breeds is no good, as a rule, but that Nais war a good one."

" A good one, I guess," said Sedgwick.

" He's ther feller that Queen—what's her name ?— O, yes, Queen Dido got soft on ?" queried Jordan.

" Yes, Queen Dido," was the response.

" And she got looney-like when he cum away, and uv nights would go down on ther shore and watch for him to cum back ?" said Jordan.

" So the legend has come down, and by the way," added Sedgwick, " her country was on this sea also, farther east and south, off to the right. It was called Carthage."

" Say, Jim," said Jordan, " them folks was a good deal like we is, after all, wuzn't they ? They'd fight for most nuthin'; they'd get gone on wimmen ; liked good hosses ; they'd trade and work tryin' ter get rich ; and ef they hed hearn of a gold mine, they'd gone ter Arizony for it."

" I guess you are right, Jordan," said Sedgwick. " you always are. The world changes its methods, but the original man is about what he has always been."

" Wurn't it from thet place Carthage that ther black feller cum what held ther Dagoes so level fur so long ?" asked Jordan.

" Hannibal, do you mean ?" asked Sedgwick.

"Ther same," replied Jordan.

"Yes," replied Sedgwick, "and a marvelous soldier and leader of men he was, to be sure."

"Indeed, he wur; but say, Jim, what do yo' calcerlate his pedigree wur?"

"Why, he came from a family of kings and fighting men," answered Sedgwick.

"Yes, I know; but I mean what breed war he? War he one of them ere Ethiopians?" said Jordan.

"No, I think not," answered his friend. "He was dark like an Arab or a Moor, but he belonged to a race that built cities and ships, tamed horses, and fought scientific battles."

"'Zactly," said Jordan. "And he wur a fighter from way back?"

"Yes," responded Sedgwick, "when the few great captains in the world are thought of, he is about third or fourth in the list."

"Thay ain't much in men, Jim. Thar's everything in a man," said Jordan.

"That is what Napoleon used to say," was Sedgwick's answer.

"Did Napoleon say thet?" asked Jordan. "He war a brighter man than I thought, but it is true, don't yo' think, Jim?"

"I think I understand, but am not quite sure," said Sedgwick.

"I mean this," he answered, and then paused a moment. "Well, yo' see," he continued, "I wur at Chickamauga in Hill's division, I wur in thur ranks, and wur a boy; but I hed a general idee how things wur. I knowed whar all our men war; how your army war 'ranged, and when we went in shoutin', and all your right and left melted away like a fog as comes up from the gulf melts when the sun comes up in ther mornin', I sed to Ned Sykes, who wur next me in ther ranks, 'Ned, we's got 'em,' and Ned answered back, 'we's got 'em, sho'.'

" Well, it wur a clar field, 'ceptin' your center war still solid, and they fell back all but a thin line. We charged up onto thet and broke it, killed lot's uf 'em, and gobbled up lots more, but it tuk us a right smart time, fur them was stubborn chaps 'nd they fought desperate.

" Then when I looked up, I seen the hull business. Thet line hed been flung out ter hold us till ther rest cud fall back on better ground. Thar they wuz fixed, and when our lines wuz dressed and other charge ordered, and we went in again shoutin' jest like the fust time, they laid down flat and they 'gin it ter us so hot we couldn't stand it and hed ter fall back.

" And they kept a-entertainin' of us thetway all ther evenin'. Other divisions wur called up and sent in, but what wur left uv 'em cum streamin' back, jest ez often ez it wur tried; a cavalry charge was ordered, but only a remnant cum back, and we hed made no more impression seemin'ly than ther waves thet bucks up agin a ledge uv rocks.

" Them wur no better soldiers than ther rest uv ther army, but thar war a man directin' 'em, and lookin' all ther time so kinder majistical and lofty and so fur away from all fear, and ez tho' he hedn't a thot of

failin', thet ther men, yo' see, tuk on ther same state
o' mind, and ter fight 'em war no use. If the fust
bullet we fired hed killed thet General, we would a-
scooped the hull army by four o'clock.   Thet's what
I mean when I say :   ' They ain't much in men, thar's
everything in a man ! ' "

" I understand you fully, and you are right, Jordan,"
said his friend.

Jordan continued " War it not 'round yere somewhar' thet ther Greeks lived ? "

"Yes, north of this sea, ahead of us, and to the left,"
said Sedgwick.

" They wur the ones that fit Marathon and Ther-
moperlee, and it wur from ther thet big Aleck cum ?"
asked Jordan.

" Yes," was the reply.   " It was only a little country,
but had many states,   The Spartans and Thespians,
mostly the Spartans, fought at Thermopylae.   Marathon was fought mostly by Athenians, and Alexander
was Phillip's son, of Macedonia."

" ' Zactly," said Jordan.   " Athens wur the boss
place, wur it not ?   It had ther best talkers, and best
public schools, and wur it not thar thet the woman
Frina kept house ? "

" Yes, Phryne was an Athenian, I believe, a woman
of a good model, but not a model woman," said Sedgwick, with a faint smile.

" I reckon yo' wur right, Jim," said Jordan, "but it
wur not singular she bested them fellers in her law-
suit.   Her showin' would ha' brought a Texas jury

every time, sho', in spite of any 'structions, no matter how savage, from ther court."

Then he continued, "Thar wur another bad one 'round here, somewhar. Don't yo' reclect readin' 'bout her and ther Roman? They got spoony on one another. He neglected his family and business, he wur thet fur gone; finally got hisself killed, and then she pizened herself with a sarpent, not a moccasin nor rattler, but a little short blue-brown scrub snake not a foot long."

"You mean Antony and Cleopatra," said Sedgwick.

"'Zactly, Cleopatra," said Jordan. "She wer ther one. I never liked her, not half so well as the one with yaller ha'r thet they called Helen. One wur bad on her own account; the other, as I calcerlate, wus bad jest because she hed er disposition to be entertainin' and agreeable. One wur naterally bad; t'other wur a lady by instinct but her edecation had been neglected."

Still he ran on: "Wur it not on this water thet old Solomon fitted out ships for ther Ophir diggings?"

"I do not know," was the reply. "It probably was, if, as is believed, a canal connected this sea with the Red Sea in his day."

"Which way are Jerusalem from here, Sedgwick?" he asked.

Sedgwick pointed in the direction.

"And Tyre and Venice and Egypt and ther Hellespont?" Jordan asked.

Sedgwick explained.

"The country 'round this sea made ther world once, didn't it ? " was Jordan's next exclamation.

" Very nearly," answered Sedgwick. "The cradle of civilization was rocked more on these shores than anywhere else. Egypt and Greece and Carthage and Phœnicia and Syria and Rome, and a score of other nations, grew into form on the shores of this sea. The arts had birth here ; arts, architecture, ship-building, sculpture, poetry, eloquence, law and learning, all began on these shores ; and Roman soldiers crucified the Savior a little beyond where the waves of this sea break against its eastern shore."

" Thet's good," said Jordan. " Big region this !"

And so the great-hearted man kept talking to try to lure Sedgwick's mind away from the thoughts that possessed him, and which made his heart heavy and his face grave.

The ship touched at several ports, and the changing of passengers, the different races, the varying scenes, kept the minds of both men diverted and their interest all the time awakened, and kept Jordan talking more than he had talked before for weeks.

"I'm glad I cum, Jim," he kept saying. " Why, we fellers out in Texas as never traveled don't know nuthin', so ter speak ; nuthin' 'bout the world outside, I mean. We useter think Texas wur almighty big. Tain't nuthin'."

Then after a pause he spoke again, and his next question was : " What did yo' call them ships thet ther old fellers sailed ? "

" They had many names. There were Galleys,

Biremes, Triremes. Quadquirimes, Quinquirimes and and so on, according to the number of their oars and the way they worked them," answered Sedgwick.

"This are a daisy ship thet we is on, don't you reckon?" said Jordan. "Suppose yo' and I cud uv cum along heah with this ship when they hed ther fightin' fleets out? Wouldn't we hev astonished them old-timers?"

"I think we would, indeed," said Sedgwick, "but, Tom, with the ships that they had, they did some fighting that gave the world such a thrill that men feel it still when the name of Actium or Salamis is mentioned. As long before the coming of the Savior as it has been since, the Phœnicians were scouring this sea with their craft, founding colonies, and it is said they ventured out upon the Atlantic and went as far north as England, while amid the ruins of Tyre models of boats have been found with lines as fine as any that any modern ship-builder can draw.

"Nothing of mechanical achievement to me compares with a ship like this that we are sailing on. Panoplied in steel, with heart of fire, with iron arms picking up the burden of ten thousand horses ; facing the storm and the night without a quiver except that which comes of its own great heart's throbbing, buoyant above the beating of the deep sea's solemn pulses, lighted by imitation sunlight, and making its voyages almost with the precision of the hours— what could be grander ?

"Standing on the deck, with the midnight black above and the ocean black below, feeling its regular pulse-beats and its onward plunges over its uneven path ; it is hard to shake off the impression that it is a grim Genie that has come to make ferries of the broad ocean, to draw the continents with their freights of nations closer together.

" But suppose, Tom, that the onward rush of this ship should bring us close beside three little ships, two with no decks and the larger one only ninety feet in length, we would look down upon them with a kind of pity, would we not?

" Still, with such vessels, the mystery of the sea was first cleared up ; with such vessels, the vail was pushed back from the frowning face of the ocean ; with such vessels, the New World was found.

" It was from over one of those open decks that the cry 'A Light!' rang out upon the night ; it was from one of those decks that the vision of the New World materialized before the eyes of the great Italian ; on one of those decks he knelt as the vision grew brighter in the dawn, and his soul was thrilled as souls are when they feel that a visible answer to prayer has been vouchsafed.

" But the man was there, Jordan ; the man who could charm the terrors from the hearts of a fear-stricken crew ; who could convert a meteor's fall into an augury of good instead of an omen of terror ; who could quell the mutinous spirit which was awakened by a varying needle and raging storms.

" It is not the great ship that counts, but the motives in the souls of those who build and navigate the ship.

" When on the shores of this sea men first built
boats and went forth on these waters, they were but
rude boats indeed.

" Who knows how many were lost, how many
brave souls were drowned ?

" But each calamity gave new thoughts to those who
escaped ; they kept on improving, building better and
better boats and making longer and longer voyages ;
they found islands and the shores of far-off mainlands ;
they carried back the products of those lands, and so
Commerce was born.

" They made at last their ships meet the caravans
from the East ; the ideas as well as the products of
the East and West were brought together ; manu-
factories were established, robes and dyed garments
and flashing blades were made that became immortal,
and those people made such an impression on the
world, as brave and capable and alert men of affairs,
that the impression still remains ; even as the strong
and true men of Venice renewed the impression
twenty-five hundred years later.

" The same spirit worked three thousand years ago
that has been at work in making the transformation
from the bungling ships that Nelson fought Trafalgar
with to this ship under our feet, from the carrying
up of ore from the deep mines on the heads of peons
to the hoisting engine and safety cage of to-day."

" That is good, Jim," said Jordan, " it is ther soul
of man, after all, soul of courage that counts 'nd all
ther advancement is only because we has better tools
ter work with than ther old-timers hed."

CHAPTER XVIII.

THE SOUL IN THE CLAY.

At Port Said the travelers left the French steamer to wait for the English ship which was on the way from Southampton. It came in on the evening of their arrival, and they went on board. They were glad to do so, for the few hours in Port Said convinced them that it was a tougher place than they had ever seen on the frontier.

At daylight next morning the ship proceeded on her way through the canal.

Our travelers were on the deck, watching the scenery.

Finally Jordan said : "This looks like Arizony, only more so. Arizony looks as though thar war a strike among the mechanics and it war never finished. This looks like it were finished once and then ther perprieter, not bein' satisfied with ther contractor's job, smashed it. They tell me ther mustang is ther blood-horse run down by starvation 'nd abuse, 'nd in-breedin', but mostly from in-breedin'. This country looks ez though it hed been ruined ther same way precisely. I shouldn't wonder but it wur true. Them old Faros wuz big fellers ; so war Sesostris and ther hull race of the old chaps from ther Shepherd Kings down, and they useter call this ' the granary of the world,' didn't they?

" And old Cambysis cum here on a robbin' expedition?

" Well, it's clear enough since then things has been goin' ter ther dogs heah.   I tell yo', Jim, civilization gone to seed is wuss than 'riginal barbarism.

" Them chaps as bilt the pyramids and obelisks war powerful men.   They must er hed sum pride in the kentry or they wouldn't been so everlastin' perticelar 'bout their gravestunes, and this must uv been a different kentry from what it are now.   Yo've seen men as has lived too long.   It's so, I reckon, with patches of this old world.   Anyway, I ain't buyin' no sheers in Egypt, leastways not on the showin' these croppin's make."

When the ship passed into the Gulf of Suez the temperature was something fearful.

"This wur the water that divided, wur it not?" asked Jordan.

"Yes," said Sedgwick, "this is the water, I believe."

Jordan was silent for several minutes.   At last he said : " No mistake 'bout thet story, Jim? "

" Why do you ask? " was Sedgwick's response.

" Nothin' much," said Jordan, "only hain't yo' noticed ther newspapers don't hardly ever git things right?"

Sedgwick acknowledged that he had known them to make mistakes.

" Hain't it jest posserble," said Jordan, "thet what war really the fact war thet the Gipshins war drowned jest ter git 'em outer ther misery in this cussed place, and ther Jews war saved jest ter punish 'em? "

"I never thought of that," said Sedgwick. "But if the weather then was anything like it is now, the theory is not improbable."

"'Zactly," said Jordan. "From ther other side over there ther Israelites started for Canaan, didn't they?"

"I believe so," was Sedgwick's reply.

"It must uv been like goin' from Tuscon to Fort Yuma in August, don't yo' think, Jim?" said Jordan.

"Very like, I believe," said Sedgwick.

After a pause Jordan spoke up again: "Jim, it ain't for me ter try ter understand much, but ther kentry 'round heah and ther people we has seen kinder breaks me up. They tell us over ther to ther right, man fust cum outer his wild state; ez yo' has it, that 'ther cradle of civilization war fust rocked.' For five thousand year, they has been a-tryin'. Look at 'em now! Then over on the other side, the chosen people of God pulled out; they flourished; they killed their enemies, built cities and temples; hed big talkers and writers and fiters; fixed up language thet thrills a man's soul jest ter read it now; made a starter thet the world's been a-follerin' ever since, and right and left ther whole world are blasted, and no one wud ever think thet God's smile once lit this region. If this showin' makes ther balance sheet fur five thousand years, what's ther use in tryin'?"

"True," said Sedgwick. "In everything, the ancient man was the equal, if not the superior, of any men who live to-day. As soldiers, orators, and writers, the utmost men hope for is to emulate them,

never to excel them. A famous English orator not
long ago said that he had often been called upon to
address boisterous men who had gathered in mobs
for mischief, and that the only time he had ever suc-
ceeded in quelling such a gathering and turning
them completely over to the side of order and peace,
was when he had repeated to them his own translation of one of the impassioned orations that Demos-
thenes had flung with all the majesty and power of his
eloquence at an Athenian mob twenty-two hundred
years ago. No modern sculpture equals the ancient ;
no modern song or eloquence ; and then there have
come down to us lessons in patriotism, devotion to
duty, self-abnegation and valor, which will thrill great
hearts as long as civilization shall last.

"Only in one thing that I can note does the modern
man excel his ancient brother. The world is more
merciful than of old. Prisoners of war are no longer
sold into slavery or killed ; woman has ceased to be
first a plaything and then a slave ; in exalting woman,
man has been exalted, and the perfect modern home
had no parallel in the ancient world. The influence
that the Cross gave out is still spreading and softening
the hearts of men."

"May be," said Jordan, " but, Jim, it's a mighty big
undertakin' to civilize men. Here's all Africa over
here ter the right whar only the old rule prevails; man
is a monstrous brute ; woman is wuss nor a slave."

"That is true, Tom," said Sedgwick. "The cruel-
ties practiced there are almost enough to make one
doubt the divinity of man and the mercy of God."

"Yet who knows?" said Jordan. "What are a few thousand years ter God? Thar must be somethin' behind, or men wouldn't hev been born. Ther other day in London thar war a man carryin' a flag on a short staff thet hed a glitterin' p'int. He war preachin' on ther street corners thet men hed no souls ; thet ther man ez sed he hed a soul war a fool, 'nd he asked whar ther souls war, 'nd ef any surgeon hed ever cum upon a soul when dissectin' a body, or on ther place whar ther soul hed lodged in ther man's lifetime.

'I wur listenin' 'nd thinkin'. After awhile he finished 'nd then a gentle, kind-faced man stepped outer ther crowd 'nd sed he: 'What are thet bright metal on ther end of y'r flag-staff?' Ther man sed it war aluminum. Then the kind-faced man asked what aluminum cum from. Ther other answered : 'Clay.' 'Jest common clay?' asked ther man. 'Jest common clay,' said ther other. 'How long since ther beautiful metal war discovered?' asked ther kind-faced man. 'It war within ther last half century,' war the answer. Then the kind faced man made a discourse sunthin' like this :

"'Yo' want a wisible proof thet man hez a soul. Ef yo' hed lived sixty year ago 'nd men hed told yo' ther wur in common clay a metal ez bright ez silver, ez ductile ez gold, with almost ther tensile strength uv steel ; sunthin' thet could be worked inter eny form, indestructible under ther usual destructive agents of ther world, yo' wouldn't ha' believed it, would yo'? Yet it war thar all ther time. Fur thousands of

years, men delved in clay. Ther wheels of ages
ground it inter powder, which ther winds blew away ;
when men died, other men sed, 'They is turned ter
clay,' which signefied ther utter degrerdation o' death ;
but ther men what bilt ther Bable Tower, hed they
but known ther secret, mighter from thet same material
have bilt a dome higher nor St. Paul's, thet would uv
shone like burnished silver 'nd would hev retained all
its strength 'nd splendor, notwithstandin' ther erosion
uv time 'nd ther abrashin' uv ther ages, even till now,
tho' since then two hundred generations uv men has
lived and died.

"Still, yo' think thet ther power thet put thet
imperishable, indestructible, stainless soul in ther
clay at our feet, war less thoughtful, less wise, less
merciful when he created man in His own sublime
image ? Ther chemist found this property in clay
after er thousand nations hed spurned it under ther
feet ; this soul in clay, which will not tarnish, which
can be drawn out inter finest wires and thinnest leaves;
hev yo' ther audacity ter proclaim thet ther subtle
chemistry of death cannot reveal anything bright and
indestructible fur man, when these pore mortal senses
shall have spent ther energies; when this pore body
shall uv fallen back ter dust 'nd ther clearer light
shell 'ave dawned."

" It war a great sermon. The unbeliever shambled
shamefaced away, 'nd I've been er thinkin' uv it ever
since."

" It must be true," said Sedgwick. " Somewhere
must be kept the records of the hearts that break in

silence, of the eyes that grow dim in straining at signals on heights beyond the vision of mortal man, of hands that lose their hold on immortality, because of the merciless buffetings of the world.

"This looks like a wrecked world around us, but there was a splendor here once. Here the alphabet of the stars was first traced out, and the order of their shining processions made known ; here barbarism was first beaten back ; the first code was made here ; here were originated the sciences of architecture and of war ; here the arts of agriculture and mechanics were born ; and here was lighted and kept bright the flame of knowledge until it became a beacon to the world, that, before that light was kindled, was altogether dark.

" The tides of the sea advance and recede. It may be so with nations. The earth was made habitable by convulsions that rent its crust, the storms that beat upon it, and by the grinding of glaciers; the pressure necessary to create the rocks and coal measures was brought to bear ; the continents were upheaved ; the seas were beaten back ; the world was loaded for a limitless voyage, before the vapors were rolled back, the full dawn was born.

" We cannot see far, but if this life is all there is to us, then, indeed, it is a pitiful failure. If our thoughts and longings are bounded by this little span of life, then there is no balance-sheet for mortality. The gift of life is then not worth the expense of supporting it.

" But, if, like the earth, the beatings and upheavals and sorrows are but the preparation for the perfect

dawn, with peace in its coming, with the increase of
immortal flowers in its air ; if there are to be a time
and place where there is to be full fruition, then
it is different, and we can afford to smile as the frosts
of disappointment chill us, as the salt spray of misfortune is dashed in our faces.

"Tom, with such gifts as are given us, we must do
the best we can for ourselves and our fellow-men ;
must do it with faith and courage, do it with gentle-
ness and in truth, and with a purpose so high that
we shall never fear anything except to do the wrong.

"And all the rest we may leave to God."

It was hot and calm all the voyage through the Red
Sea, the straits, and Gulf of Aden, till, when round-
ing the stormy cape of Guardafui and the ship swept
out upon the broader ocean, the barometer dropped
rapidly and a furious storm came on. It was really
a mighty gale, and the heavily-laden ship labored exceedingly.

At its height, Sedgwick and Jordan stood watching
the majesty of the forces exhausting their fury around
them, when Jordan said :

"Jim, I needed this. Yo' know how grand ther
other ship wur ; yo' know how great and strong this
ship are. Well, watchin' both, a senseless kind uv
pride cum over me, and I sed ter myself over and over,
' This ere ship cud outride any gale whatever blow'd.'
Look now ! It's only a toy on ther water when God's
wind goes out ter battle with God's everlastin' seas.

"Cumin' over, I stopped and tuk a look at Niagry.
It wur grand, but a dozen Niagrys wouldn't make one

hurrycane out ter sea. I can't explain what I wanter, but I mean as how God's majesty is nowhar else revealed as when his hurrycanes is sent ter paint a picter on ther face of a mad ocean. Nowhar else did I ever feel thet small as when watchin', as we is now, all these forces that is makin' the commotion 'round us. They all show us what pitiful weak creaters we is, and ther man who ever watched one storm at sea and ever arter dares to hev one feelin' uv pride or scornfulness, that thar man are weak somewhar and makes a spectacle of hisself."

But the storm was weathered safely; the temperature grew cooler as the ship stretched away to the South, and after a generally prosperous voyage the steamer dropped anchor in Port Natal roadstead.

CHAPTER XIX.

THE WEDGE OF GOLD.

The voyagers were glad enough to stand once more on the solid earth. It had been twenty-one days since they had left London.

Quickly as they could they made arrangements for a journey inland. They chartered conveyances to go to the end of the road and sent forward to the capital to charter a train of riding and pack animals, with a full corps of attendants, to meet them where they had to take the trail. They employed, moreover, a civil engineer and a half-dozen frontiersmen, Boers and Kaffirs, who knew the country well.

Studying their maps and the description supplied them by the former owner of the mine, they calculated the mine was distant some 250 miles, and that it would require some thirty-five days to make the examination and return to D'Umber, the town on Port Natal Roadstead.

·Sedgwick had written daily to his bride, sending the letters from every port called at.

Now he wrote her that it would probably be forty days before he could forward her another letter.

When everything was ready they started on their trip. The men were all Boers and Kaffirs, except the engineer ; all strong, good-natured men, but the least bit suspicious of their employers. They had come in an English ship, wore English clothing, and if their

English accent was not quite up to the standard the natives could not make the distinction.

They examined Jordan's saddle with a great deal of curiosity, as it was, with the rest of the luggage, put upon the wagon. One of them, in broken English, asked about it; where in England he found it.

He laughingly answered that they could not make any such saddle in England; that it was a Mexican saddle. Then the Boer wanted to know if he were a Mexican.

"Not by a blamed sight," said Jordan. "Do I look like er greaser?"

The Boer looked at him helplessly.

"Did you never har of ther United States?" asked Jordan.

The Boer shook his head. "Never har of America and Americans?" Jordan asked.

The Boer smiled. He had heard of Americans, and asked eagerly if Jordan and his friend came from America.

"Yo' may bet yo'r everlastin' broken Dutch diaphram that we did," said Jordan, at which the Boer hurried to tell his companions that the two strangers were not English, notwithstanding their clothing.

The first eight days of the journey, the travelers found excellent roads, and averaged twenty-seven miles a day. They did not go by the capital, but turned off to the left.

The first day the road lay mostly over the coast mountains. Toward night they entered upon the table-lands of Natal, which were generally level, except where, here and there, a low mountain spur nad to be crossed. It was a grassy country, sparsely dotted with palms, with here and there timber in sight up ravines that ran down from the hills, and occasionally they ran upon clusters of heath-flowers. Indeed, the whole country was covered with flowers of rare beauty, but mostly odorless. It was all new and strange, and was noted with keen interest by the two Americans. It was the rainy season, and the road was soft in places, and some of the streams were pretty high. But they got along without serious trouble. One had been in Nevada, the other in Arizona, and both in Texas.

The first night they camped by a little stream, ate their supper, and spread their beds by some willows on the grass. It was a perfectly calm night, and in that clear air the stars shone magnificently.

As they were smoking their pipes after supper Sedgwick pointed out to Jordan the constellation of the Southern Cross as a sight which their friends in the North-land could never see unless they crossed the equator.

Jordan looked at the stars some time in silence, and then said: "Them stars is been shinin' thar allus, and yit, Jim, they wuz outer sight o' us. To see 'em we had ter cross ther line. Who can tell. Jim, what new stars'll shine on us when thet other line, thet men call death, shall be crossed, and our eyes shall be given ther new light beyond?"

He paused a moment, and then went on: "I'z been prospered. When I war a boy I went to ther wah. I war in many a fight. Men as loved life mightily wuz killed all 'round me ; many another brave feller tuk sick and died. Not a scratch cum ter me.

"I made er stake easy-like in ther mines. I've dun well 'nuff ; and yit, Jim, if thar should cum ther summons ternight, and I knowd I'd got ter go, I wouldn't hev a sorrer 'cept thet we haven't passed on ther mine yit."

Then Sedgwick realized that in the selfishness of his own loneliness at leaving his bride, he had forgotten his friend, and that he had all the time been concealing a deeper grief and trying to cheer him.

"Dear old Tom," he said humbly. "I have been absorbed and selfish since we left England. I did not realize my own selfishness. We have found new stars in the sky. Let us trust that no sorrows will come to us that will not be cheered by stars behind them, and let us nurse the hope that this journey is but a discord in our lives that will make the music of them sweeter when it shall be passed."

"Shore enuff," was Jordan's answer. "I war once down at the bottom of ther Colorado Cañon. It war terrible. I never seen a place so desolate and wild ; but, Jim, I looked up along the walls hundreds of feet overhead, and thar in ther daylight, away off in ther infinite sky, some stars war shinin'."

So there, in the starlight, on that lonely table-land in South Africa, the two true men clasped hands in silence, and their hearts drew nearer to each other than they had ever been drawn before.

The second day, the road in places skirted a forest in which the yellow tree and the great beech were the most prominent trees; creepers grew around them, and vines trailed over their branches; marvelously tinted flowers mingled with them, and the scene was enchanting.

More than once a band of antelope was seen scudding away in the distance; here and there a zebra fled from before them, and once a pair of giraffes were discerned afar off over the plain. Though it was the beginning of winter, the tsetse fly bothered their stock a good deal, but the Boers cut branches from the trees and covered the animals with them when the sun was hottest and the insects most troublesome.

After the fourth day the road began to ascend, and at last the point was reached where the vehicles had to be given up, and the saddle and pack animals from the capital had to be brought into use. The real hills had been reached. The trail ran over a succession of sharp mountain ridges, and narrow valleys. It was not a well-made trail on the ridges, and the flanks of the ridges were so abrupt and rocky that progress was very slow; moreover, it was clear that to build a road on the line of the trail, over which heavy loads could be hauled, would be a most expensive, almost impossible, undertaking.

It required three days to make the trip of forty miles.

Finally, though, the last summit was crossed, and after a heavy descent, there spread out another valley, and on a ridge beyond, from the mountain side, could be seen something like a dump, with rock piled upon it. The two friends recognized the spot at the same moment and stopped their animals in the trail, to take in the surroundings. They estimated that the mountains must be a spur of the Drakenberg Range, that they were within the basin drained by the head waters of the Vaal River, and that they were in the Southwestern Transvaal. The mountains of that point had a general course northeast and southwest, and it was clear that the mine was practically over the range in approaching from the direction of Port Natal.

" It's all right," said Jordan, " 'cept it seems to me like we orter uv cum down on ther other side of Africa, and cum in from ther West. From this way it would need a pack train of bald eagles ter bring in supplies, while ter get a mill in—Good Lord ! "

"I fear you are right, as usual, Tom," said Sedgwick, " but if, as I suspect, the mine is of no account, it will not matter much."

" ' Zactly," said Jordan. " Thar's no use tryin' ter put up collateral on which ter borrer trouble 'fore we know anythin' 'bout ther mine."

So they pressed on and made their camp that night near a great spring that the miners had lived by while opening the mine. Next morning both Americans were up early, and, the breakfast disposed of, they went to the mine with buckets of watera nd hammers.

They kept their natives pounding rock all day, while they washed the samples. They took the ore from

every part of the dump. The result was most satis-
factory. " It will assay more than $30," said Jordan.
"I believe it will work up to $30 by mill process, for
it's perfectly free gold ore and not too fine."

The next day the inclines were all explored, and
samples taken, step by step—taken and marked, as
they proceeded. The ore body where practically
exposed was carefully measured, and where any change
was discernible it was noted and special samples taken.
The floor of the lowest level reached was not only
sampled, but a hole a couple of feet below the lowest
excavation was dug, and the samples were saved.

The vein was a contact between slate and granite,
and was very regular in size, and apparently in quality.
The vein was exposed for probably 600 feet, and
thence up the hill it was covered with debris. It was
almost night when the camp was reached, and the
men were very tired.

Next morning the samples taken the previous day
were crushed and carefully washed.

When all was finished, Jordan said: " Jim, it's a
honest mine. Ther only drawback is ther place. I've
no idee what er road would cost, but it would take a
power o' money, sho."

It was decided to try to explore the slope of the
range they were on, up and down, to see if a break in
it could not somewhere be found. They tried it to
the north, and soon found themselves in a mighty
gorge, with great mountains closing them in from
every direction except the one from which they had
come. They returned to camp, and one more day

was gone. The next morning they started early to the south, and toiled until eleven o'clock, to find themselves once more ambuscaded by the precipitous hills. Again they made their way back to camp, without comfort, except that they had passed through a great forest of beech and yellow wood sufficient for fuel and mine timbers for years.

Next morning when they had finished breakfast, Sedgwick asked Jordan what his idea was by that time as to the best course to proceed.

Jordan shook his head, and said : " I'm afeerd we must try to build ther road or invent a berloon."

From the spring there ran a considerable stream off at right angles from the mine, and in exactly the opposite direction from whence they had come.

Sedgwick said : "Tom, that stream, unless it sinks, finds its way to the sea after awhile. We are in for it ; a day or two more will not count. Suppose for awhile we follow that stream and see where it leads us."

" Agreed—a good idee," said Jordan. Taking with them two Boers, the engineer, and a pack animal with food and some blankets, they bade the rest keep the camp, as they might be absent two or three days. They started down the stream. It flowed in a general course to the west. After a mile or more from the camp, the banks widened out into a wooded valley, several hundred yards across, but when six or seven miles had been traveled the valley narrowed down again, and the mountains closing in, made what, at a little distance, seemed a solid wall in front. " Headed off once more, I fear," said Sedgwick.

"The stream keeps up a full head. It must git through ther hills somewhar," said Jordan.

"True enough," said Sedgwick. They followed it to the very base of the hill, to find that there it made a bend at right angles to the south and flowed through a cleft of the mountain not much wider than the stream itself. Into this they entered, and pursued their way for about 600 yards, when the stream again turned through another mighty fissure to the west, and ran a quarter of a mile farther, when another large valley opened out which was some five miles across. In this valley the stream sank in the sands and was lost. The travelers skirted the valley, keeping close to the hills where the ground was hard. Reaching the other side they found a narrow opening through which the stream had once flowed. They followed a winding way for two or three miles, the chasm bearing a little west of south, emerging at last into an open country. A fringe of willows was seen low on the southern horizon. The Boers said they knew the stream, the course of which was marked by the willows; that it was a big creek, along which their people had stock farms. They marked the obscure opening through which they had traced their way out of the mountains and started for the creek and possible ranches. The Boers said that farmers' roads ran from these ranches out to the main road over the range to the east, the road which they had come up on from Port Natal. They pressed on another seven or eight miles, and a rude house, half dug-out, came in view, distant a couple of miles.

They approached it, and from the people living there the Boers learned that it was seventeen miles out to the main road, over a good farmers' road all the way. They camped at the house, or near the house, all night. One of the residents brought in a fine young antelope, which they bought and cooked, and they suppered royally on antelope, hard tack and coffee. Next morning they returned to the mine, reaching there early in the afternoon. They had been out from Port Natal seventeen days, had found and sampled the mine, and explored a natural pass for a road.

How to proceed was the next question. Sedgwick's idea was that both should return to the seashore, proceed to England, and order a mill from San Francisco, because they knew that there were no good patterns for quartz mill machinery on the continent; and both agreed that should the mill be built in England and shipped thence to South Africa, the fact would be published and all their plans would be interfered with.

Jordan was silent for awhile ; at last he said: " Jim, I ken understand thet ther thot uv goin' back ter London ez mighty enchantin' ter yo'. But thet's a game girl, thet thar young wife o' yourn ; she listed fo' this wah ez well ez yo,' er she'd never let yo' cum away. Yo' must go by ther straightest track fer San Francisco and bring ther mill. I'll stay and hev some rock ready for crushin' when ther mill cums."

" But, dear old friend," said Sedgwick, " it will take a year, perhaps, to get a mill here from San

Francisco. To leave you here—you would die of the horrors with no company but these Boers."

" How d' yer know but I'd make a pretty good Boer or Kaffir my own self with er little practice?" asked Jordan. " We'll stay over termorrer and git some work goin' ; then I'll go with yer ter the coast and get some men and things I need. I'll cum back ; you'll go ter Frisco, and everything 'll be lovely."

" No," said Sedgwick, " you go to San Francisco, and I will stay and work the mine. It was I who proposed this thing ; of right I should meet the heaviest sacrifices." But Jordan was obstinate, declaring that he would enjoy himself at the mine, and after a long discussion his programme was agreed to. In the morning Jordan took the engineer and three natives to the top of the hill, where the mine was covered with debris ; walked along to where the mountain, as it sloped to the west, was very abrupt, and there set the Boers to making an open surface cut.

They went to work, and Jordan and the engineer went to measuring to see where, down the hill, a tunnel would have to be started to tap the lode 500 feet deep. It was so sharp a hillside that the tunnel site would be only 1,260 feet horizontally from a point 500 feet below the open cut. Jordan engaged the engineer to remain with all the men who would stay, and begin that work if the indications on the hill would justify, and also to build a rude stone house at the spring, large enough to accommodate a dozen people.

Then they climbed the hill again and found the croppings of the ledge uncovered in the cut. Being tested, these croppings were found richer than the ore on the dump lower down, where the vein had been opened.

Next morning, with two saddle animals, one pack animal and one Boer to ride another horse and lead the pack horse, the two Americans started back for Port Natal. They followed over the route they had traced out two days before to the ranch, then took a road traveled by the stockmen, and on the second night from the mine came to a house on the main road to Port Natal, which was six or seven miles nearer their destination than the point where they had left the road and taken the trail for the mine.

They hired a Boer to go up and bring back their wagons. They came next morning. The best rig was selected, and the two friends started for the seashore. In eight days they were back at Port Natal, having made the round trip in twenty-eight or twenty-nine days. On arriving at the seashore they found that no steamer was in port bound North, but there was a fine steamer in the roadstead that was to sail next day for Melbourne, Australia.

Sedgwick's plan had been to go back to London, take his wife and go thence, via New York, to San Francisco. But no ship was awaiting him, and the agent of the Northern Line did not know when a ship would sail. It would have to come first, and might return soon, or might lie in port fifteen or twenty days. So, talking the matter over with Jordan, both concluded that the best thing was to try the voyage via Australia. Again Sedgwick begged

Jordan to go, yet he kindly, but firmly refused, saying, " I must hev my way this time, Jim."

Accordingly, Sedgwick engaged passage to Melbourne, then wrote his wife what they had found; that he had decided it was best to go by Australia to San Francisco ; that, if prosperous, he hoped to reach that port in forty-eight or fifty days ; that he would be detained there probably sixty days, and would then return to Africa via England, hoping to be with her in one hundred and twenty days, and to be able to remain with her for a month.

Jordan found six English miners and engaged them to go with him, bought as full an outfit as possible, through a trader ordered more, including a portable saw-mill from England, made an arrangement with Sedgwick how to send and receive news, and the two tired men lay down to take their last night's rest together for, as they calculated, at least six or seven months, perhaps a full year.

It was a memorable night to both, and the confidences they exchanged and the sacred trusts they each assumed, they never forgot.

In the morning Jordan started back for the mountains and their solitudes ; Sedgwick boarded the steamer, which later in the day started on its voyage, and the sea for Sedgwick was a counterpart of the solitude which the mountains held for Jordan, except that at Port Natal he had received from his Grace the greetings which her soul had given his soul through the mornings and evenings of the first twenty days of her married life. They were to be his balm through all the days of his imprisonment on board ship, and he felt that they would be sufficient. But it grieved him to think that poor, brave, sorrowing, but cheerful and clear-brained Jordan had no such comforters.

" It is very lonely, my glorified one," she wrote ; " the roar of the great city seems to me an echo of the voice of the ocean, of the wilderness that surrounds you ; but I would not have it different, for I kept saying to myself : ' He is doing his duty, and beyond the horizon that bounds our eyes now, I know that higher joy awaits us which comes of a consciousness of a great trust bravely executed.' Be of good cheer, my love ; it will be all right in the end, for the heavens themselves bend to be the stay of steadfast souls when with a holy patience they struggle for the right, as God gives them to see the right.

" I will wait for you, and in thinking what you have undertaken, and of the persistence required to carry your work through, will try to catch your own grand spirit, try to exalt myself by imitating your patience and faith, and thus be more worthy of you when once more it is given me to clasp your dear hands, and to gaze into your true eyes, which are my light. "

As Sedgwick read, his eyes became suffused until he could not see the page before him because of his tears.

" See," he said to himself ; " a man's love is selfish ; it is a woman's life and light, and yet my beautiful wife loses sight of herself, and all her words are but an inspiration for me to go on and conquer if I can. Thank God for the treasure that has been given me ! And may God comfort her and comfort brave and true Jordan !"

CHAPTER XX.

The ship was twenty-four days in reaching Melbourne. It caught a gale crossing the stormy Bight, and for two days no progress was made. It was all that the men in charge could do to hold the plunging craft up into the face of the storm and meet the big seas as they rolled, furious, up against her stem. But the winds were laid at last, the ship was put upon her course and her natural speed resumed. On the afternoon of the twenty-fourth day the ship passed between the heads of Port Philip, and two hours later came to anchor before Sandridge, three miles below Melbourne. Going ashore, Sedgwick cabled to his wife his arrival on his way to San Francisco, " as first letters from Port Natal would explain," and added : " Hope to be with you in one hundred days. Write, care Occidental Hotel, San Francisco." Then he took the night train for Sidney, and arrived there the next night about nine o'clock.

Going to a hotel, he found that the first steamer for San Francisco would sail on the next day but one.

He then sought his first sleep in a comfortable house, with modern improvements, that he had found since he left London.

Next morning he went early and secured transportation on the steamer, then returned and wrote a long letter to his girl-bride ; then engaging a rig took in

as much of Sidney as he could.   Next morning he
cabled his wife that he was just going to sea again,
and boarded the steamer early.   The ship sailed
promptly at mid-day, and as it passed out of the
beautiful harbor the islands and shores beyond were
just putting on the vestments of spring.   Sedgwick
had never before seen spring approaching in October;
never before had he heard the love-calls of mating birds
at that season, and apparently had never before realized so keenly that he was on the other side of the world
from those whom he loved and knew.   After dinner
he went on deck.   He knew no one on board, and
he was nearer being homesick than he had ever been
before. It was a balmy night.   The sea was tumbling
a little from the effects of a far-off storm, but the ship
was riding the waves superbly and making rapid progress, and the stars were all out and sweeping grandly
on in their never-ending, stately processions.

In the midst of his thoughts, when he was fast
giving way to a mighty fit of the blues, he happened
to glance upward. *Corona Australis* was blazing
with unwonted brilliancy, and, it seemed to him, the
constellation was making signs to him from its signal
station in the heavens.   Instantly he thought of the
night that he and Jordan had particularly noticed
it, and of what the great-hearted man had said.   Then
he thought of his friend; how unselfishly he had turned
his face away from the ship that would have carried
him to a pleasanter country, and had voluntarily gone
back into that profound wilderness to work out
a trust which would require months of time ; and he

said to himself : " What a selfish creature I am to repine, when I have been so blessed; when in England an angel is waiting for me ; when in the depths of Africa a brave soul by his every act is teaching me lessons of self-abnegation."

A moment later another thought came to him which was a delight, and that was that with every revolution of the screw he was drawing nearer to his Grace. When an hour later he retired to his stateroom he hummed a song as he went, and the throbbing of the machinery and the wash of the seas against the ship's beam made his lullaby, as the long roll of the steamer rocked him to sleep.

As before stated, Sedgwick had written his wife fully at Port Natal. Two days after he left, the steamer from the North came in. It remained five days, and then started North again. Its mails were eighteen days in reaching London.

Grace was looking for a letter from Port Natal, when Sedgwick's cable from Melbourne reached her. She could not quite comprehend the matter until, a day later, his letter came, and the next day his second cable, announcing that he was just about to sail for San Francisco. That day she did what she had not done since she left school—got a map of the world and studied it until she put her finger on a spot between Sidney and New Zealand, and said : " He is there now," and bent and kissed the place on the map.

That evening she went over from her home to call upon Jack and Rose. There she found a gentleman who, with his wife and daughter, were going to sail two days later for Australia, via New York and San Francisco. Their names were Hobart. Grace had known them ever since her father had moved to London. They were talking of their proposed journey, when the young lady said gaily : " Mrs. Sedgwick, come along with us as far as New York, or San Francisco at least." At this the father and mother together seconded the invitation.

" Do you really mean it ? " said Grace.

" Indeed we do," said all three.

" And when do you sail ? " asked Grace.

" Early, day after to-morrow. That is, we leave here early and sail at noon," said Mr. Hobart. " We have two full staterooms engaged. You can room with Lottie "—the young lady's name—" and be companion for us all."

" I will be ready day after to-morrow morning," said Grace, seriously.

" Not in earnest ? " said Rose.

" In sober earnest," said Grace.

" To New York ? " said Browning.

" To New York, and may be farther," was the reply.

" As far as Ohio, I guess," said Jack.

" May be as far as Ohio," said Grace, and she smiled as she spoke.

The Hobarts were delighted, but Jack and Rose looked serious.

" It is a long way, Gracie," said Jack.

" A fearfully long way," said Rose.

"Suppose, Rose, that Jack was as far away, would you think it a long way to go to see him?" asked Grace.

"O, Gracie! No, no," said Rose.

"When did you hear last from your husband?" asked Hobart.

"This afternoon," said Grace.

"And how long, Grace, before he will be in England?" asked Jack.

It was the first time any question had been asked of her more than the question if she had heard, and if he was well.

"About one hundred days, I think," said Grace; "that is," she added, "if I go and find him and bring him home."

Next day Grace made all her arrangements and was ready to leave early on the following morning. Parting with her mother was her great sorrow, but the mother approved of her going, and the good-byes were not so sad as though they did not expect to be soon again reunited.

They made the voyage to New York in nine days. Remaining one day in that city, they started West; stopped one day in Chicago, and reached San Francisco seventeen days from Liverpool.

Hobart had been in San Francisco before, and wanted to stop at the Lick House, but Grace insisted that her friends liked the Occidental best; so they went to the Occidental.

Four days after reaching San Fracisco, the Hobarts sailed for Australia. They urged Grace to accompany them, but she declined, saying, with a smile, that she believed for the present she preferred the solid earth to the unstable sea. She saw her friends aboard the steamer; then returning to the hotel, sent for the manager, Major H.; explained that she expected her husband by the first steamer from Australia ; that he did not expect to find her ; so she wished to surprise him, and desired the finest apartments in the hotel, including a private dining-room ; and requested that when it was known that the ship was coming up the harbor, the rooms should be elaborately dressed with flowers. She also stipulated that her husband, on his coming, should be conducted to his apartments without any knowledge that any one was waiting for him.

Major H., captivated by the little English lady, entered into the full spirit of the programme and promised that he would personally attend to the matter.

Grace was transferred to the new rooms, and thereafter had her meals served in her own dining-room.

Three days later, about one p. m., a message came that the Australian steamer had at noon been sighted outside the Heads, and was then entering the Golden Gate.

The flowers were forthcoming; the apartments were swiftly decorated ; then Grace, with the utmost painstaking, robed herself in her richest costume and seated herself in the private dining-room, with the sliding doors slightly ajar so that she could look through into the parlor of the suite without being seen.

The suspense was fearful to her for half an hour. Would he really come? Separating in London, and he traveling east, would she by coming west find him? Would he be well? Had he really escaped the African fever and all the dangers that lurked in the weary stretches of treacherous billows?

Those were a few of the questions she was asking herself, when, in the hall, a well-known voice rang out which made her heart bound. It was saying: "There must be an oversight somewhere. I surely ought to have had some letters awaiting me."

The door opened, and the hearty voice of Major H. was heard by the listener. "These are your apartments, Mr. Sedgwick," he said, "and I trust you will find them pleasant."

Then the other occupant said: "But I do not care for any such rich rooms as these; any little corner will suffice for me."

"Oh no," said the Major. "Try these quarters for a day or two, and if by that time you wish to exchange them for others, we will see to it. We try to please our Australian friends, for we hope for more and more of them throughout all the years to come."

With that he closed the door.

"Australia!" Grace heard her husband say. "I'm no Australian; I'm a full-blooded African, a regular Boer or Kaffir, and no mistake. But, bless my soul, this is a fairy spot! A way-up place, surely! From the depths of Africa and the society of Boers and Kaffirs to an enchanted palace! This must be the bridal chamber of the establishment. I believe they have made a mistake and think me the King of the Pearl and Opal Islands.   I wish dear old Jordan could see this.   I wish, O God, I wish my Grace, my queen, could see this, that I might first crown her with flowers, and then fall down and worship her !"

She could bear the tension no longer.   Pushing the doors back quickly, she stood pale, but radiant, for an instant, before the astonished man; then stretching out her divine arms, said, " O, my darling ! "

CHAPTER XXI.

SHIPPING A QUARTZ MILL.

That evening Major H. met Sedgwick in the office, and, with a twinkle of the eye, asked him if he was really anxious to take cheaper apartments.

The young man smiled and said he rather thought, as he would probably only remain two or three months, it would not be worth while to change.

Next morning Sedgwick ordered a forty-stamp gold quartz mill complete, with two rock-breakers, the batteries to be of five-stamp each and low mortars, with a single pan for cleaning up—a free gold quartz mill. Instead of one heavy engine, he ordered two, each of forty-horse power to work on the same shaft, to be supplied by six thirty-horse-power boilers to be set in two batteries. He ordered also one six-inch and one four-inch steam pump, with the necessary boilers, and besides, a donkey hoisting engine, good for an eight-hundred hoist. The order included all the needed attachments, belting, retorts, duplicates of all parts subject to breakage or wear, a forge, and shoes and dies enough to last two years.

He stipulated, too, that the wood-work of the battery should be gotten out, exactly framed and marked, and that all the pulleys, bolts, etc., should be included.

In two days the specifications were gotten ready, and the contract signed, which included a clause that the whole should be ready in sixty days, or less, from that date.

Then Sedgwick wrote fully to Jordan, giving him the account of what he had done, and sending him a draft of the ground plan of the mill, and full details as to the grading, hoping he would receive the letter and have the rocks hauled, the battery blocks gotten out, and the grading done.

This work under way, the exultant man devoted all his time to Grace, except that every day, when in the city, he would make a run two or three times to the foundry to mark the progress of the work.

Meanwhile, the happy pair visited every point of interest in and about San Francisco. They frequented the theatres, drove to the Park and the Cliff House, and both declared that San Francisco was the most delightful spot on earth.

They were all the world to each other. In the happiness that filled their hearts their eyes were softened, so that everything they looked at took on roseate hues—the world had become a throne to them, over which had been drawn a cover of cloth of gold.

Once they made a journey to Virginia City, and descended the Gould and Curry shaft, and Sedgwick showed his bride where he and Jack first discussed the probability of trying to make a little raise in stocks. They went and looked at the lodging-house on the Divide where Jack and Sedgwick roomed so long; visited the mills, saw crude bullion cast into bars, and watched the procession of a miner's funeral, and in their rambles Sedgwick stopped many a miner whom he had known, and presented his bride.

Returning, they got off at Sacramento and waited over one day. There Sedgwick ordered four seven-ton wagons, with four trail wagons of five tons each, and four more of three tons each, and twelve sets of team harness, a dozen of yokes and no end of chains; also a strong, covered spring wagon with harness to match.

After forty days, Sedgwick was informed that everything would be ready in ten days. His idea had been to charter a brig or bark, and send the machinery to Port Natal by a sailing craft; but in crossing the bay in visits to Oakland, Saucelito and San Rafael, he had noticed anchored, out in the stream, a small iron bark-rigged steamer which carried the British flag, and had read thereon the name "Pallas." One day he asked some men on the wharf what ship it was and why it lay so long in the harbor.

The answer was that it was an English tramp steamer that some months previously came in loaded with wines and brandies from Bordeaux.

The men also gave the information that, though a tramp steamer, it was thought to be a very strong craft, fully bulk-headed, with first-class machinery, and was commanded by the owner, a Scotchman named McGregor, who, when not on his ship, stopped at the Occidental Hotel.

Sedgwick had already made his acquaintance at the hotel, so when he met him that evening he asked him how long he expected to remain in the city. McGregor replied that he was waiting to secure a cargo for his ship.

Then Sedgwick drew him out and learned that his steamer was of six hundred tons, built with all care for a gentleman's yacht; that after awhile the owner tired of his plaything and sold it to him at a mighty discount on its first cost ; and that he was seeing the world in it, and trying at the same time to make the craft pay its own expenses. He said also he had a picked crew and private surgeon, and added: "When I secure a cargo, if you and the madam will become my guests, I will adopt you both as long as you please to follow the seas."

Sedgwick declined with thanks, but said : " You want to see the world ; how would you like to make a run to the coast of Africa ?"

" I would not object," he replied. " I have had the ' Pallas ' overhauled since we came into port. She is in first-class trim, good for a year if no unusual misfortune overtakes her. I would as soon go to Africa as any other place."

The result was the " Pallas " was chartered to carry out the machinery, some mill-wrights, a couple of engineers, a couple of mill workers, an assayer, and any miscellaneous freight that Sedgwick might desire to send.

The ship was hauled into the wharf next day, and the loading of what was ready was begun. Sedgwick got on board his wagons and trappings from Sacramento. He ordered also a great quantity of drill steel, picks and shovels, quicksilver, some giant powder and caps, some blankets, mattresses, canned

fruits, pickles, boots and brogans, and a whole world
of other supplies such as miners use.

In fifteen days the ship was loaded, and the craft
put to sea, as was understood and published, with a
mixed cargo for Australia.

Sedgwick had insured the cargo; had paid the
owner in advance the freight, and McGregor estimated that, if prosperous, he could, running slow to
save coal, and stopping a week or ten days in Australia for coal and fresh supplies, make Port Natal in
eighty days.

In the meantime Sedgwick and his wife had made
the acquaintance of an English gentleman and his
wife, named Forbes, who a few days previous had
started for England, but who had promised to visit
some English friends in Indianapolis, Indiana, until
Sedgwick and Grace should overtake them, that they
might sail on the same ship from New York.

The day after the " Pallas" sailed, Sedgwick and
his bride took the overland train for the East.

CHAPTER XXII.

A LOST TRAIL DISCOVERED.

They reached Indianapolis in due time ; stopped at a hotel, and Sedgwick had no difficulty in finding the Forbeses. He was presented to their friends, the Brunswicks, and Mrs. Brunswick insisted that Sedgwick should go straight to the hotel and bring his wife to her house.

He thanked the old lady warmly, but begged to be excused, saying they could visit without that.

"Very well," said the old lady, " but I will certainly have my way in another thing. You must go right off and tell your wife that an old English woman up the street says she must waive ceremony and come right here for dinner."

This was agreed to, and Sedgwick proceeded to do the errand.

The Sedgwicks were shown into the drawing-room of the Brunswicks, and had been for a few minutes conversing when the door opened and a lady entered.

A glance was enough to show that she was exceedingly beautiful. She was perhaps twenty-six or twenty-seven years of age, not too tall, rounded into full maturity, with a most strong but winsome face. Her eyes were blue, her hair a golden brown and glossy, and when she spoke, her teeth were revealed, perfect and white.

She was presented to the strangers as Mrs. Hazleton.

Dinner was shortly after announced, and after dinner, when the gentlemen had returned to the drawing-room, Mrs. Brunswick asked Mrs. Hazleton to sing. She did not say " Mrs. Hazleton," but just " Margaret."

Without making any excuses she went to the piano and asked Mrs. Brunswick if she desired any particular piece. She answered:

" No, my dear, sing anything you feel like singing; only have it old-fashioned and sweet, rather than scientific."

Strangely enough, she struck a few wailing chords on the instrument, and then with a pathos and tenderness most touching, sang the old song beginning :

"Could you come back to me, Douglas."

The effect was great on all the company, but to Sedgwick and his bride it was intensely thrilling.

The eyes of Grace filled with tears, and Sedgwick, who was near, unobserved by the rest, took and pressed her hand.

The company separated early, with an agreement for the ensuing day, which was to fill it with rides, luncheon, a matinee for the ladies, and dinner afterward.

So soon as Sedgwick and his bride were by themselves, Grace said : "Love, did you ever hear anything half as sweet as that singing ?"

" Yes," said Sedgwick, "I heard that same song once, more sacredly sung."

"O James!" Grace replied, and a celestial glow
warmed her face.

"But that lady has a secret grief, certain," said
Grace. "There was real sorrow in her tones, and
there is a sorrow in her face, despite its superb seren-
ity."

"Well, she is a widow," said Sedgwick.

"Yes, I know," was the answer; "but there is more
than sorrow; she gives me the idea that her thought
is that something priceless has been lost which she
might have saved."

"Now I think, little one, that 'you have struck it,'
as the miners say," said Sedgwick.

"How do you mean?" asked Grace.

"Some one who would have made her his wife and
worshiped her has gone, and she is miserable," said
Sedgwick.

"What makes you say that, dearest?" asked Grace·

"Because," replied Sedgwick, "I know it, and I
know where he has gone, and she does not."

"Why, what do you know of her? Did you ever
meet her before?" asked Grace.

"No, I have never met her, but I have met some
one who has," said Sedgwick.

"O, tell me all about it!" said Grace.

"Why, child," Sedgwick said, "that is the lady
who went to Texas and taught school one season, who
set the honest heart of Tom Jordan on fire, and
burned it half to ashes, made him sell his home because he was so wretched, and finally, with my help,
or through my fault, set him to running a tunnel to a

mine in Southern Africa, among the Boers and Kaffirs."

"Do you believe that can be true?" asked Grace.

"I know it," said the confident man. "The description and the singing tally, and the name is the same. Tom says her singing would make a lark, out of envy, 'fall outer a tree'."

"Upon my soul!" said Grace, and then lapsed into silence.

"What are you thinking of, sweet?" asked Sedgwick, after a pause.

"I was thinking what accidents our lives hang upon," she said. "O, love, suppose you had not fancied me at all, what would have become of me?"

"And suppose you had, when I did fancy you and you knew my heart was in the dust at your feet, that the touch of the hem of your robe upon me thrilled me like old wine; suppose then I had pleaded for your love, and though you felt it was mine and intended to give it to me, still had refused me; might you not be singing, Could you come back to me, Douglas, in tones to break any one's heart who might hear you?"

Grace thought a moment, and then said: "There's more than all that to this, love; you men do not know much when it comes to the hearts of women. She had some other and good reason when she refused the true-souled man."

"I believe now that you are right, my little sorceress," said Sedgwick, "and I believe that the reason has since been removed, and her great grief now is in thinking of Jordan's sorrow and than she cannot find him."

" I will tell you what," said Grace ; " I will get as near her to-morrow as I can, and will try to coax her, hire her—if needs be—to accompany us to England."

" A capital thought, my wise little wife !" said Sedgwick. " Then when you gain her confidence, if you think it best, we will try and help her find the great-hearted man."

" I believe you are an angel," said Grace.

" I know you are," said Sedgwick, and involuntarily they kissed each other.

CHAPTER XXIII.

Before the Sedgwicks left Indianapolis, Grace found her opportunity and said: "Mrs. Hazleton, soon after we reach England my husband will go away for four or five months. I shall be awfully lonesome. You have never been across the sea. Take pity upon me and be my guest for a few months until you weary of me."

The lady was startled by the proposition, waited a moment, and then said:

"I do not know how to thank you, but I came here to teach music. I have several pupils, and have a contract to sing in the choir of one of the churches. I need the little revenue that I receive, but if I could get released from my obligations I would most gladly go, for I do covet a change exceedingly."

"Then," said Grace, "if I can get that release, and will pay you as much as you receive here, and all your expenses out and back, will you go?"

"Indeed, I will," she answered, "and will be grateful to you all my life."

The arrangement was easily made, and the further arrangement that Sedgwick and his bride should go to Ohio, visit Sedgwick's family for three or four days; then should join the Forbeses and Mrs. Hazleton at a certain hotel in New York, and all would embark on the steamer that would sail on the next week Saturday—ten days from that day.

Then Sedgwick and Grace started for the Miami Valley.

What a welcome was there! The old house had been repaired, modernized, refurnished and repainted. A new house had been built on the other farm. It was in the first days of February. That year there was good sleighing, and the whole town seemed to turn out to celebrate the occasion of Jim Sedgwick's bringing home his bride. Four days passed in a whirl of pleasure. The first morning after their arrival, Sedgwick asked his brother for his trotting team, his new cutter, and the bells, to give Grace her first sleigh-ride. The steppers were of the 2:30 class, the roads good, and the fair English girl-wife was in ecstacies. They drove past the Jasper farm on the hill, and Sedgwick told Grace that it was his dream for years to accumulate $30,000 to release the mortage from his father's farm and to buy the Jasper farm.

" Then what would I have done?" asked Grace.

" Married some English banker, or may be some 'My Lord Fitzdoodle,' probably," said Sedgwick.

" But, then, suppose a year later I had seen you, what would become of me?" she said.

" We should have been very formal and polite, and then have gone our several ways," said Sedgwick.

"Yes, because you are a man of principle, and I hope my pride of womanhood would have sustained me, but my heart would have broken, for with me it was a mad passion which absorbed my life before I had been in your presence half an hour," said Grace ; and then added : " I do not any more wonder at the crimes which come of mismated marriages."

Then Sedgwick told her how,when he left her side the first time, he took that ride and asked cabbie how much they would charge at Newgate to hang him.

And they both laughed, but there were tears in the eyes of Grace even while she smiled. But she rallied in a moment and said :

" Why not buy the place still? Except to leave my mother, I would be on that farm with you as happy a wife as ever lived. I would rather live upon that hill than in our great modern Babel, London."

Just then the cutter went in and out of a "Thank-ee-mom"—a hollow between two snowdrifts—and Sedgwick bent and kissed his wife.

" Thanks," said Grace.

" That was a kiss on principle. That was a pure duty," said Sedgwick. Then he explained how venerable was the custom, and elaborated upon the respect due it because of its age and its usefulness to bashful lovers, because a youth must kiss the girl who goes sleighing with him whenever he comes to a " Thank-ee-mom " among the drifts.

" What a poor old country England is," said Grace.

" Why so ?" asked Sedgwick.

" Why, had we but had snowdrifts and 'Thank-ee-moms,' I would have made you kiss me three weeks sooner than you did," said Grace.

" Did you want me to kiss you sooner than I did ? "
asked Sedgwick.

" O, you blind darling!" said Grace. "When I
read of your exploit before the church in Devonshire, I told Jack and Rose that I would like to
kiss that man. Then he told me who the man
was, and after all I had to wait so long I
began to fear he would never give me a chance to
carry out my desire."

" Is that true, Gracie ? " asked Sedgwick.

" Indeed it is," she replied, and then she quickly
continued, " Does it drift badly along here ? "

" Pretty badly," answered Sedgwick.

" Then, love," answered Grace, "buy the farm by
all means and at all hazards."

" I believe I will," said Sedgwick. " I believe we
need it in our business. If when we get back to England it shall be known that we have bought a home in
America, and are having a house built, it will take all
suspicions about a possible African enterprise away."

And that day he bought the farm, and the next
one to it, and told his brother he would send from
England plans for a house to be built in the spring.

Next day came the parting from the old home.
Sedgwick promised to return before many months and
stay longer, and he and his wife started for New
York.

They rested over one train at Niagara, and took in
its splendor as seen in winter-time, and arrived in
New York on Wednesday. Forbes had purchased
the tickets, and secured the rooms on the ship for the

whole party. Thursday and Friday were devoted to taking in as much as possible of the great city. On Saturday they sailed.

The voyage was generally uneventful, except that one day they were treated to a beautiful spectacle of rescuing a crew from a water-logged craft. The wind was fresh, and there was an uneasy sea on, when a signal of distress was noted off across the water. The steamer was headed for it, and in half an hour came up to it. It was a little old lumber schooner. The sea was washing its deck with every wave. In the meantime, the second officer, with six seamen, had taken their places in a boat. The boat had been swung out over the water. The sailors were standing by, holding the tackle by which a boat is lowered ; the commander was on the bridge, and when in hailing distance of the craft he dropped his hand and the engines stopped. He shouted through his trumpet, asking what was wanted. " To come aboard," a voice came back. The commander dropped his hand again, and down ran the boat and pulled away for the wreck. It would mount a wave, and then sink out of sight of those on the ship's high deck ; then climb again. It returned in twenty minutes, and it was the commander of the great ship that took the hand of the schooner's rough skipper as the boat was hoisted, and for the remainder of the voyage the shipwrecked skipper had a state-room by himself, and his seat at the table was at the commander's right hand.

They reached Liverpool on the tenth day—Monday—and went up to London the same afternoon.

Reaching the city, Sedgwick sent a message to Mrs. Hamlin to meet them at the house of Jack and Rose, for he would not go to the Hamlin house.

Sedgwick, with his wife and Mrs. Hazleton, went at once to the home of the Brownings.

Rose was wild with delight at their coming. She hugged Grace, kissed her and cried over her ; kissed Sedgwick, and welcomed Mrs. Hazleton so cordially that the lady was sure it was sincere.

Then Mrs. Hamlin came, and the whole business had to be done over again, the elder lady reproaching Grace and her husband for not coming to her, and scolding even as she embraced them.

Then matters quieted down enough to talk. Rose explained that she was a deserted wife; that Jack six weeks before had come home one night and told her that he was going to sail for South America next day ; that she could not go along, but must be good and not be lonesome for six or eight weeks.

Then she continued : "That is the kind of monsters these men are. They beg and tease and protest until we women take pity on them and marry them, and then when the woman's chances for getting a good man are all spoiled, they rush off on the slightest provocation to America, or India, or Australia, or China, or some other barbarous place, and all a woman can do is to mope and threaten that next time she will know better."

And then she laughed, and then as suddenly cried and said : "Poor dear old Jack! May the seas be merciful, and may the good ship bring him safely back and be quick about it !"

And sure enough, a week later a step was heard outside, someone with a night key opened the door, and Rose flew into Jack's arms and cried so hysterically that it took Jack a long time to calm her.

Browning explained to Sedgwick that he had been earning a commission by going out and reporting on a mine in Venezuela, just over the border from British Guiana. He brought to Rose a world of tropical and marine curiosities. He was in superb health and seemed to be in good spirits.

It was understood that Sedgwick would have to go away again in a month, and it was his wish and that of Grace to find a house and have an establishment of their own.

Jack and Rose insisted that during Sedgwick's absence Grace and Mrs. Hazleton should be their guests, but Sedgwick said with a laugh : "O, Mrs. Browning, you and Jack are good, but you both know that no house is big enough for two families." And quietly Jack and Rose and Mrs. Hamlin were enjoined never in Mrs. Hazleton's presence to mention Jordan's name.

However, the difficulty was finally settled. The house Jack lived in was a double house. The other half was occupied by a gentleman, his wife and one child. The lady was delicate, and the doctors, baffled by her case, ordered her—as usual—to try a change of climate. So Sedgwick hired the house as Browning had his ; the servants remained, and permission

was obtained to cut a doorway in the partition walls
that divided the two halls, so that Rose could visit
Grace in the morning and Grace could visit Rose in
the evening.

Sedgwick and Browning were almost inseparable
during the day-time. Sedgwick assured Browning
that things were working well, begging him not to
disturb either old man Hamlin, or Jenvie, or Stetson,
but to "rig some purchase" after he should be gone,
to get the remaining shares in 'The Wedge of Gold'
from them, and also to be sure to keep the former
owner of that mine in the country, even if he had to
raise his salary.

He told him also that he expected next time to be
absent four or five months.

One morning about thirty-five days after his arrival
in London he received a cable from McGregor
announcing the arrival of the "Pallas" at Melbourne
and saying he would sail again in four days. Then
Sedgwick made his final preparations for departure.
He sent full plans for a house to his brother, with
directions where to build. He obtained a promise
from Mrs. Hazleton that she would not desert Grace
during his absence, and from Jack that he would not
try any prosecutions to obtain his money from the old
men until his return, explaining that he had made his
arrangements in America, and was then going to see
that African mine and work it if it would do.

His wife knew where he was going; the others
except Jack, believed he meant to return to the

United States.   He told them he had a little business
in Paris and would this time take a French steamer.

Grace worried more over the second parting than
she had over the first.   She cried a good deal and
was much distressed.   But it was over at last, and
Sedgwick was gone.   He did stop over a few hours in
Paris, made an arrangement which he desired to with
the Bank of France, then speeded on to Marseilles,
caught the Imperial steamer, sailed over the same
route as before to Port Said, and there embarked on
exactly the same steamer that he and Jordan sailed
for Port Natal in seven months before.

He was twenty days from London to Port Natal.
Jordan was at D'Umber waiting his coming, and the
joy of the meeting was immeasurable.   When they
became calm, Jordan said: "It war a good while, old
friend, but I knowed as how y'd cum."

CHAPTER XXIV.

The presence of Sedgwick in London greatly excited and alarmed Jenvie, Hamlin and Stetson. That mysterious American had returned, and all confidently expected each day to be served with a notice of with a suit or a warrant of arrest.   But finally it leaked out that he had bought a home in Ohio and ordered a house built, sending the plans from London, and as day after day passed and no sign was given, they gained courage, and when Sedgwick once more left England, as they supposed for America, they grew jubilant again.   The firm was now Jenvie, Hamlin & Stetson.   Their business was prospering, and they all realized that the way to make money was to have money to use, and the prestige which the command of large means gives.

About a week after Sedgwick's departure they were seated in their private office one morning congratulating themselves, when the former owner of 'The Wedge of Gold' was announced.

" We cannot afford to snub the origin of our foi-tune," said Jenvie ; "show him in."   This man's name was Emanuel.   He was a Portugese.   On this morn-ing he presented a seedy and dissipated appearance, as though he had been enjoying his fortune too rapidly.

Once ushered in, he did not waste any time, but explained that he had very little money left, and had called to see, in case the gentlemen did not intend to develop 'The Wedge of Gold,' on what terms they would transfer back to him the mine, or any interest they might possess, and give him a chance to go over to Hamburg and try to work the capitalists of that city to buy a mine down among their second cousins in Boerland.

"How much could you afford to give for the property?" asked Hamlin.

"I sell him for £2,000. I would, for one speculation, buy him back if you could sell, and would give £1,000."

"But you always said it was a good mine," said Jenvie.

"Of course," he answered, "an excellent mine," but on ze best of ze mines there vos always one selling and then one buying price."

"If we were to sell to you, would you work the property?" asked Jenvie.

"Most certainly," he replied; "I would work it as I did before—on ze paper."

"We have sold the control," said Hamlin, "and have only left some shares of stock."

"I understand," said the man; "Mr. Browning has the control and is unloading the stock cheap. He three days ago tendered me some stock for one shilling per share. I said, ' No, but give me one bond at three pennies per share for four months, and I will consider ze matter, and try to help you close out

some unproductive property.'   He would not comply,
but he thought it over very much, and asked me to
call again.   One broker, Mr. Williams, offered to sell
me plenty for four pennies, but would not make one
bond."

"We do not care to bond ours," said Jenvie, "but
would sell for four pennies."

, "I will not give it," said Emanuel, rising to go.
"I would give you three pennies, but no more," and
he started for the door.

The three consulted in private for a moment, and
then Jenvie called to Emanuel, who was half out of
the door, that he might have the stock at three pennies for cash, but begged him not to mention that he
had purchased it.   Emanuel paid the money and took
the stock, and then said : "You ask me not to mention
this business.   Are you crazy ?   Suppose Mr. Browning by and by bonds me ten thousand shares less
than half he has got, with this in my pocket who will
then have ze control ?   I want you to promise to say
nothing about this sale for six months.   In the meantime I propose to become just so intimate with Mr.
Browning as possible."

Then he winked and walked out, and the conspirators looked in each other's faces and smiled.

Emanuel went directly to Browning and delivered
him the stock, but he lied about the price he had paid
for it, telling Browning he had given five pennies per
share for it.   But while Browning was sure the man
had lied, he was satisfied, for he then had all of the
stock of "The Wedge of Gold."

Browning had, as he told Sedgwick, gone to South America on a commission. It was known in London that he was a miner who had made a success in America. An Englishman who had a bond on a mine in Venezuela had hired him to go over and make a report on it. He fulfilled the trust, but he heard while there of another mine in a district ten miles away. He went to see it and bought it for £2,000, hired a foreman and ten men; laid out the work for them for six months ahead, and left £1,000 in a local bank to pay them, with instructions to the foreman to send him a report and sample by every steamer.

The first mine was sold on his report, and besides his commission of £300, the happy man who had sold the mine called at his house one day when Browning was out, and left an envelope directed to him. The envelope contained a check for £3,000, and a note saying that the writer thought he was entitled to one-tenth of the proceeds of the sale, and that Browning must accept the money, for the writer intended that day to leave England. Browning turned the money over to Rose as her fee "as an expert."

A month later a steamer from Georgetown (British Guiana) brought news that the Browning mine was developing superbly, and still a month later the foreman estimated that he had five thousand tons of ore in sight which would average as well as the samples sent. Browning had the samples assayed, and they averaged £5 6s. in gold per ton.

He had a friend named Campbell, who was a broker: Campbell dropped in upon him as he was looking over the assays, and he told him all about the mine.

"What will you give me to sell that property for you, Browning ?" asked Campbell.

"Not a penny," said Browning, "but I will give you a bond on it for four months for an even £100,000, and you may make as much above that as your conscience will allow ; you may, by Jove."

"Will you make me a report and map ?" asked Campbell.

"I will write you a report, and make you a rough sketch," said Browning, "but my drawing lessons were neglected when I was young, and I am not a very reliable or finished map-maker."

The conversation closed with an agreement, and the bond and report were in due time finished.

CHAPTER XXV

A WEDGE OF GOLD INDEED.

Sedgwick and Jordan waited at Port Natal for the coming of the "Pallas." Sedgwick explained what the ship would bring, and told Jordan about Grace being in San Francisco to receive him, and how, while the mill was being built, he and his wife had raced around the country.

Jordan was delighted. " I told yo' she war a game girl," he said. " Think of her traveling six thousand mile to jine ther man who hed run away from her at ther meetin' house do'! But I'm mighty glad she did, all the same. It confirms my estermation of ther lady."

Then he explained that he put on eight-hour shifts to run the tunnel, two English miners on each shift to handle the drills and gads, and Boers and Kaffirs to carry back the debris; that the rock was most favorable, and rapid progress was made, averaging a little over ten feet per day; that he offered bribes and bounties to the shift that should make most progress; and that he had tapped the ledge and cross-cut it in four months, "because," he added naively, " we lost all reckonin' o' time, 'nd I'm afeerd we worked of er Sunday sometimes;" that the ore was quite up to the average, or a little better than what was on the dump; that so soon as the vein was struck he had started drifts up and down the ledge and an upraise, and had, when

he left, probably 1,000 tons of ore on the dump, and
that as the mine was further opened the daily output
was steadily increasing.   He had, moreover, got the
mill site graded, and the wall that the battery was to
be set in front of, built, comfortable quarters put up,
and the road through the cañon made so that it would
be good for heavy teams.

When he heard that Sedgwick had sent some heavy
wagons, yokes, harness and chains he was glad, saying : " I war afeerd you'd forget it," and at once went
about to select the stock and drivers for those wagons.

After they had waited eight days, the " Pallas "
made the port.

Captain McGregor reported a prosperous voyage,
and the next day the discharging of cargo into
lighters began and was rushed with all speed.   As
soon as the wagons were landed, the work of setting
them up began, and the training of the teams was
likewise inaugurated.

The first full loads were started for the mine in a
week.   The heavy machinery was loaded on the im-
ported wagons, native conveyances were secured for
the other freight, and in fourteen days everything was
in transit.

In the meantime another mail had arrived from
England, bringing letters from Grace to Sedgwick.
One had news of special interest.   It told that the
confidence of Mrs. Hazleton had been partly gained ;
that she had learned much of the lady's life ; how she
was left an orphan at thirteen in New Jersey ; how at
seventeen when at school she had run away and mar-

ried a wild youth ; how they left at once for the West;
how the wild boy settled down, and with a few hundred dollars which he had when they were married he
had made a few thousand and was doing well when he
suddenly sickened and died ; how then his relatives
came forward and made a contest for his property, setting up that she had never been married ; that the
showing was so fearful against her that the court in
Iowa refused her any support from the estate, and in
her shame and confusion she went away to Texas and
taught school for six months to earn money enough
to make her defense; that there she met an unlettered
and sensitive man, but at the same time one of the
clearest-brained, most generous and noble-hearted men
in the world, but in whom, from the fact he was so
sensitive and generous, she could not confide, lest she
might not be able to vindicate herself ; and if she
failed, she feared she would not only lose his confidence, but that it would make him believe there was ·
no truth in the world. How with the money she
earned, she was able to go to New Jersey, to find in
the papers of the old clergyman who had married her
(and who had in the meantime died), not only a full
record of the marriage, but the marriage certificate
with the names of the witnesses attached, which certificate had never been called for. By it, too, she was
able to find the witnesses of the marriage, and one of
those witnesses had known her all her life. So when
the case came on for hearing she was so completely
vindicated that her neighbors who had turned on her
a cold shoulder came back with every outward

demonstration of joy over her triumph. But she hated the place ; converted all she had into money ; bought a lot in a cemetery outside that State and had her husband's remains moved there, because she thought his sleep would be vexed in a community so mean ; and then wrote to her friend in Texas, merely asking if he was well, and if she might explain something to him.

In ten days the letter came back with the endorsement on it by the postmaster that her friend had sold his property at a sacrifice and disappeared, his nearest friends did not know where. Grace's letter added that she was worrying under the fear that perhaps if she had not gone to Texas the true man would never have made the sacrifice.

Grace declared that she was in love with the lady ; that she was a fine scholar, a finished elocutionist, a marvelous musician, and the comfort of her life in her husband's absence. The letter closed with an injunction that Sedgwick must bring Jordan safely home with him, and not be too long about it.

How Sedgwick wanted to show that letter to Jordan ! But he realized that if Mrs. Hazleton loved him it was for her to tell him so.

He racked his brain to invent a necessity for Jordan's return to London, but a little thought convinced him that all such expedients would be in vain, because Jordan had, as he said, " enlisted fo' the wah," and Sedgwick realized that if on any pretext he sent him away, the suspicion might arise in Jordan's mind that the object was a selfish one, now that the labor and anxiety of making the enterprise a success had well-nigh passed.

So he decided that the thing to do was to hurry the work in hand to culmination. The rainy season was pretty well over, and the material for the mill was pushed forward with reasonable dispatch. It was all on the ground, set up, and in motion in fifty days.

Sedgwick found on reaching the mine that Jordan had built the needed houses, and had the mill as nearly completed as it could be before the machinery was set in place.

The ore crushed easily, and the mill reduced two tons and a half per stamp readily in every twenty-four hours, in thirty days crushing 3,000 tons. It yielded in the mill $35 per ton, and at the end of thirty days there were bars of the value of $100,000 ready for shipment. Then Sedgwick said: "Come, Tom, our work is finished here, at least for the present; let us seek civilization."

"Agreed, old friend," said Jordan. "I'll get my trophies together and be ready ter start in ther morning."

"And what are your trophies?" asked Sedgwick,

"Why, didn't I tell yer?" was the reply. "It got kinder lonesome while yo' war away, so I went on a hunt. I've got ther finest pair o' leopard skins yo' ever seen, some elephant tusks, 'nd I migh'er brought a sarpent skin that war a daisy, but I drew ther line on snakes." But he war twenty-three feet long, and ther look outer his eyes war not reassurin' by a blamed sight. I migh'er got a giraff skin, too, but she hed her baby with her, and I'm not breakin' up no giraffe families."

It was understood that they were to leave in the morning ; were to go in the covered spring wagon, and were to carry the gold.

One of the English miners was made superintendent of the mine. The mill-men from San Francisco agreed to look after the mill for a year, and the civil engineer undertook to see to the books, to attend to the finances and send an express to the coast once a week.

So Sedgwick and Jordan, with one Boer, started early in the morning. It was in the last week in May; the weather was cold for that region, for it was the beginning of winter.

They drove out of the narrow valley, through the cañon, out upon the open table-land and down to the house or dug-out which they had first found when in search of a way out. They rested there, ate some luncheon, fed their horses, and after an hour and a half started on.

They had brought with them their repeating rifles and revolvers. Before getting into the wagon, Jordan had rolled up and fastened the curtains of the wagon, examined closely the guns, and then gave a long, sweeping look all around the horizon.

"What are you looking for, Jordan ?" asked Sedgwick.

"Nuthin' much," he answered. "Only, Jim, have yer gun whar yo' can reach it quick if wanted."

" Why ?" asked Sedgwick.

"Nuthin," said Jordan. "Only I never seen this place afore thet thar, war not a dozen cut-throat-lookin' scoundrels 'round, and they mighter mean mischief, knowin' as how we have ther treasure aboard."

They had driven on for perhaps a mile, when the road ran down close to the stream. All at once half a dozen shots rang out of the willows, and the Boer sprang from the wagon and ran for the bush.

Sedgwick was driving. Jordan in a second caught his gun, and springing over the seat, said:

"Drive on quick, Jim, and in ther meantime I'll try ter entertain ther varmints."

A Boer stepped out of the willows and raised his gun. He never fired it, but threw up his hands and fell on his face. A shot from Jordan's gun had changed his calculations.

Three or four more shots were fired from the bush, but they did no harm.

Sedgwick had urged the team into a run, and they had just begun to hope the ambuscade had been passed, when three more Boers sprang out of the willows nearly opposite them and fired.

Jordan killed two of them in a moment, but the third one fired again, and the bullet struck Jordan's left arm, disabling it and making a bad wound.

"Can you drive, think?" asked Sedgwick.

Jordan thought he could, and took the reins; Sedgwick picked up his gun.

Three more Boers just then appeared by the willows opposite. Sedgwick could shoot as rapidly and as accurately as Jordan, and he cleared the field in a moment.

The road bent away from the stream soon after, back upon the table-land, and they were safe. They stopped, and Sedgwick bound up Jordan's arm. The bone was not broken, and no great blood-vessel was seriously injured, but he had received a nasty flesh wound through the muscles of his forearm.

As they proceeded on their journey, Jordan said : " That black guard as I first got a crack at hed been working for us two months. He war at his work yesterday. He put up this business, but how we sprised him ! Ther devil that jumped from the wagon when ther scrimmage begun war his runnin' pard. Wur it not lucky neither hoss war hit ? "

They reached Port Natal in six days without further incident ; but despite all the care that Sedgwick could give it, Jordan's arm was badly inflamed and very painful when they reached the seashore.

No regular steamer was in port, but the " Pallas" was seen at anchor out in the roadstead.

Sedgwick engaged a boat, and with Jordan pulled out to the steamer.

McGregor was delighted at their coming, took them on board and said : " Now, boys, we will have a night of it."

But Sedgwick said : "First, Captain, I want your surgeon to look at Jordan's arm."

" Why, of course," said McGregor. The doctor was called. He examined the arm, then tested the man's temperature, and finally said :

" The wound is nothing in itself. Under normal conditions it would heal in a fortnight, but Mr. Jordan's system is run down. He has a low fever on him now, and needs immediate treatment and careful nursing."

This was a new situation, and one that troubled Sedgwick exceedingly. He was silent for a few seconds, and then looking up, said :

" Captain McGregor, where do you go next ?"

" I was just going to pull out for Calcutta, Hong Kong, Yokohama and San Francisco," he replied.

" And when do you sail ?" asked Sedgwick.

" I intended to put to sea to-morrow," was the answer; " everything is ready."

" Can I induce you for love and money to make the run at full speed to Naples or Marseilles ?" asked Sedgwick.

" Not for money, but for love, yes," was the reply.

"And can I have a room for Jordan right now ?" was the next question.

". You shall have the bridal chamber of my ship," said McGregor.

" Thanks, Captain," said Sedgwick, "and now let us get the dear old boy to bed."

Jordan insisted that he was not ill, but before they could get him undressed he was seized with a chill, and they worked upon him an hour before he rallied, grew warm and fell asleep.

In the meantime the night had come down, so Sedgwick got a little supper and then went back to his friend. The captain, steward, indeed all hands, were all attention, for they knew all about both men.

Next morning Jordan was comfortable, but the
fever was having its way.   Sedgwick went ashore,
got his own and Jordan's baggage and the bullion,
and when he returned the ship was at once got under
way for her northern voyage.

The attentions of Sedgwick to his sick friend were
simply incessant.   The ship's surgeon was also assid-
uous in his care.   Captain McGregor was all the
time most solicitous.   As they approached the equator, they fixed for Jordan a bed on deck where the
air, even if it was hot, was better in motion over him
than in the stifling state-room.

The ship rounded the great cape in ten days, and
reached the Red Sea on the twelfth day.   Then the
surgeon motioned Sedgwick aside, and said : " The
case of your friend makes me very anxious.   His
wound is not of itself serious.   He has a little fever,
but it would not be of a dangerous type in an ordinary
patient.   In this case the sick man acts like one who
has lost hope, and under the sorrow of his loss his
nerve power has ceased to exert its force, and the
man is liable to die simply because he will make no
effort to live."

" I know," said Sedgwick, " and I have been dread-
ing such a report as you have made me, for the last
seven days.   If you can keep his life from going out
until we can reach Naples, I believe we can then
find a tonic that will save him."

" I will try," was the answer, " but he is growing
weaker every day, and I am afraid.   However, the

temperature is growing cooler and it gives us a better chance."

Sedgwick tried by talking, by reading, and by drawing rosy pictures of what they would do in England and America, to rouse Jordan, but without much success.

He lay patient and still on his couch, and to all inquiries would answer : " I'm perfectly comfortable, dear friend. Do not worry about me ; everything is as it should be."

Then Sedgwick tried another experiment. He told the sick man that he must exert himself to be better ; that sickness was often influenced by the will of the patient, and added that the real work of trying to undo the wrong perpetrated upon Browning would have to be done when they reached England, and that he should then need the best counsel and help of his friend.

Jordan listened and said : " I'll do the best I ken, Jim, but it will be all right, I'm shor."

So the hours went by, and Captain McGregor told the engineer to crowd on all steam, and to bribe the fireman to give the ship all the speed possible.

At Suez, Sedgwick went ashore and cabled his wife that he was on the " Pallas;" to come at once to Naples ; to induce Jack and Rose to come also, and, if she thought best, to bring Mrs. Hazleton, for Jordan was ill, and he feared nothing but the cheer of friendly faces would arouse him and give him the strength to live. He added that she must use her woman's wits as to what she would tell Mrs. H., and that to outsiders it must all seem but as running over to the continent for a few days' outing.

When Grace Sedgwick, very early one morning, received and read that message, she held it for many minutes, lost in thought. She had grown very near to Mrs. Hazleton, but except when she had drawn from her the story of her life, she had never probed in the least to see if in her heart she was nursing a vast regret.

But she had noticed some things that led her to believe that the lady had an anxiety which she was trying to conceal. She was always ready to visit any point of interest that would naturally attract a stranger, or to attend any public assemblage that a stranger might be lured to. Again, she always approached such places with vivacity, and returned from them in silence.

As Mrs. Sedgwick sat with the dispatch doubled up in her closed hand, Mrs. Hazleton came into the room. Touching a chair by her side, Grace said: "Come and sit by me, Margaret. I want to talk with you."

She complied, merely saying: "What do you want to talk about, love?"

"Are you happy?" asked Grace.

"Indeed, yes. Why do you ask?" was the reply. "Have you not been making my life a bed of roses ever since your blessed eyes first rested on me?"

Grace looked at her intently for a moment, then said: "Is there some one whom you wish exceedingly to see?"

A rosy flush swept like a wave over her face, which
was followed by a quick pallor.   But she recovered
herself almost instantly, and said :   "Why, Mrs.
Sedgwick, do you ask me so strange a question ?"

Grace arose, then bending down, took her hand,
laid the dispatch upon the palm, closed the fingers
gently over it and said :

" My dear, there is a paper for you to read.   I am
going to Rose for a few minutes.   When I return,
you may tell me anything you please, or nothing at
all, as you please ; only let me tell you first that before my husband went to Nevada, he went to another
State, lived there with a great-hearted man for a year,
and that man was with him when he left me at the
church door on my wedding day, and they have been
together since, except when my husband left him to
go to America to buy machinery and came back this
way to join him again."   Then she suddenly bent and
kissed her friend and was gone.

She went through to Rose's side of the house, found
her, and asked where Mr. Browning was.

"He is in the library," said Rose; "he has not
yet gone out this morning."

" Then come with me," said Grace.   Once in the
library, she said : "I have news from my James
this morning.   He cabled me from Suez.   He is
coming home, and he wants us to meet him at Naples.
Mr. Jordan has been with him—is coming with him,
is ill, I fear very ill, and he wants us to meet him, I
believe chiefly on that dear man's account.   I shall
leave this afternoon ; can you go with me ?"

"I can," said Jack.

"I can," said Rose.

"I am so glad," said Grace. "And say, there must be nothing said to the servants, except that we have run over to the continent on a lark, for a few days. And now good-bye until we are ready."

With that she returned to her own sitting room. Mrs. Hazleton was gone, and it was a full half hour before she returned. When she did, she was very pale. A look of anxiety was on her face, but a radiant new light was in her eyes.

She came straight up to Grace, and in a low voice said : "When do you start?"

"To-day," said Grace; "by the first Dover train."

"O, thanks; pray God we be not too late," was the answer; and then the poor woman sank into a chair, covered her face with her hands, and broke into sobs that were almost hysterical.

Grace stood by her for a few minutes, then knelt down, put one arm around her, drew her toward her, gently drew down the hands and laid her cheek against the tear-dripping cheek of her friend, and said : "Now you must be brave, dear Margaret; it's going to be all well. I feel it in every fibre of my being. My husband is with him. He will supply him with the vitality to live until the vision of your face above his pillow will bring the stimulus that he needs."

The true woman recovered herself at length, and said : "O Mrs. Sedgwick, how did you discover my secret, and the great-hearted man whom I have sought for and prayed for so long ?"

"It was not I," said Grace. "It was my husband. He lived with Mr. Jordan a year in Texas. After he had made his little fortune in Nevada, he—thanks be to God—came home with Jack. He met his old friend here, who frankly told him how he loved you, and why he had sold his home and turned wanderer. Just then Jack had been induced by his step-father and mine, and the knave Stetson, to invest part of his fortune in a gold mine in South Africa ; and by a deception, nearly all that was left of his fortune was lured away into the same channel. Jack was well-nigh frantic. Rose had been waiting for him for four years and a half, so my husband insisted upon their marriage and determined to go and see if anything could be made out of the wreck, and asked me to wait until his return. I agreed, only stipulating that we, too, should be married before he went. I left him at the church. My husband was a silver miner ; Mr. Jordan was a gold miner—I do not know the difference, only the gold miner can test gold ore—and they together went to Africa. They found the mine good, and found a new road to it, over which the machinery could be transported. Then my husband sailed via Australia for San Francisco to buy the machinery ; Mr. Jordan remained to open the mine. My husband cabled me from Australia, and the next day I received his letter from South Africa, telling me that he would be two months in San Francisco, and then would come by London on his way back to the South Land. I took the first ship and reached San Francisco before his ship came in from Australia ; then when I knew the ship was coming up the bay, I had the apartments dressed in flowers, robed myself in attire such as I had meant should be my wedding garments, and waited his coming."

Then she paused a moment as the memory of that meeting swept over her, while the arms of her friend stole around her.

Continuing, she said : " When ready to start for England, we, as you know, made arrangements to stop a day or two with our friends in Indiana. When you were presented, my husband recognized you instantly by the name and description given of you by his friend. When you sang that first song, he guessed your secret and told me his thought, and helped me to work the stratagem to lure you here. When he reached Port Natal, he tried to invent some plausible reason to induce Mr. Jordan to come here, but he could not ; and so has hurried to get the mill working, and now both are on the way, and I must meet them. Jack and Rose are going with me ; will you ? "

The arms of Margaret Hazleton were clinging to Grace, and the tears were raining down her face. So soon as she could speak, she said :

" And so, while I thought you were my best friend, you have really been my guardian angel. I came with you because I hoped to find the noble man who had self-exiled himself, and all the time when I thought I was disguising my heart, your clear eyes have been reading it.   I remember now in Texas the boys were always talking of a famous Jim who had lived with them, but I never dreamed that he was your husband.

"My gratitude to you and your grand husband is bankrupt, but now no matter.   The first thing to do is to be on our way—only, do Mr. and Mrs. Browning also know my secret?"

"Not at all," said Grace.   "Until just now they did not even know that Mr. Jordan was with my husband, but I will tell Rose all that may be necessary."

All left that day, in due time reached Naples, and engaged ample quarters before the "Pallas" entered the bay.

CHAPTER XXVI.

FEVER VISIONS.

As the " Pallas " passed out of the canal upon the broad-breasted Mediterranean, Jordan noticed the change in the motion of the ship, and said to Sedgwick : " Jim, old friend, we is back agin on ther waters whar men first learned ter be sailors, aren't we ? "

" Yes," said Sedgwick, " and in three days more I hope to gladden your eyes with the faces of some dear friends."

" Yo's mighty kind, old friend," said the sick man ; " but, Jim, I wanter tell yo', if we should be diserpinted, yo'll find inside my trunk a little trunk, and in thet yo'll find things all fixed ter tell yer what ter do. I 'ranged it when yo' war away, not knowin' what mount be. Remember one thing mo': everything's all right 'nd goin' ter be right. I'll get well 'nd help yo' ef I ken; ef I don't, yo'll make it easy, nuff, without me."

" Indeed I cannot," said Sedgwick. " You must brace up and get well, for I tell you, dear old Tom, that I can see better than you, and I have worked out a plan which is. going to be a delight for you."

" Maybe so, Jim," said the sick man, and dozed off into a troubled sleep. The surgeon had been giving the patient some powerful medicine, and told Sedgwick it might make him flighty, but not to permit

that to alarm him ; that he thought he could promise
to hold the life in his friend for a few days more.

Jordan awoke after an hour's sleep, and said :
" Jim, I had a mighty quar dream, sho. I seen all
ther fleets ez hez ever sailed on these waters, havin'
er grand review. It war ther ghosts ev ther ships, I
reckon, but they looked mighty real. I seen ther
fleets ev Tyre with ther sails like calico mustangs ; I
seen ther Persian fleets thet ther Greeks done up et
Mycale 'nd Salamis; I seen ther fitin' ships uv Rome.
'nd Carthage, 'nd Egypt, 'nd Venice, down ter Nelson's fite on ther Nile. O, but it war a grand perses-
sion ! Thar war calls in a hundred tongues ; thar
war responses in a hundred mo' ; thar war decks filled
with armed men, with helmets, spears 'nd shields ;
thar war singin' 'nd · prayin' 'nd trumpet calls ;
thar war ther rattle ev arms, ther ring ev steel,
'nd ther harsh blast ev war-horns, 'nd ther sounds
changed from age to age, until thar came at last
ther roar uv hevy guns in regelar broadsides. All
ther echoes uv all ther battles uv all ther cen-
teries war in my ears. It war grand ; grander nor
Chatternooga. Thar sea gave up its ded fur me, so
fur ez this water goes. History held befo' me all its
pages, 'nd they wuz all 'luminated. Ez thet picter
swept befo' my eyes, 'nd all thar clamors filled my
ears, it war more thrillin' then anything yo' ever
dreamed of. I ken har ther calls, 'nd ther replies,
'nd ther beatin' uv oars, tho' thar oars war broken,
'nd ther calls growed still two 'nd three thousand
year ago. It war beautiful, Jim, even ef it war all

'lusion ter ther eyes 'nd ears.   Do yo' remember, yo' read me once 'Ther Midnight Review?'   Why, Jim, thet war nuthin'.   This uv mine war ther review ev all thar ages, er movin' picter uv ther world since befo' civilerzation begun."

Then the sick man dozed off into sleep again, and Sedgwick bathed his face, and hung over him as a mother watches when the life of her child wavers between this world and the next.

After awhile Jordan awoke again.   This time there was an eager, joyous look in his wan face, and he searched the room around with a most expectant gaze.

Sedgwick bent over him, and said softly :   " What is it, old friend ? "

"Why, Jim, old man," said he, "that war most singler.   I hearn *her* voice a-prayin', hearn it jest ez plain 'nd natral ez ever I hearn it afore, prayin' thet I might git well.   O, Jim, it war music, sho' nuff ! and ef eny angels war a-listenin', they'd intercede fur me jest outer courtesy."

" She was praying, dear friend," said Sedgwick. " I knew it, and her prayer is going to be answered. Her soul is trying to call to your soul to rouse itself, and you must heed the call."

" I'll try," said the sick man.   " But don't worry, old friend ; no matter what comes, it'll be all right. And, say, Jim, open my grip and put ther handkerchief you will see with dots upon it here next my heart."

For the twenty-four hours prior to reaching Naples

Jordan was delirious most of the time, and did not sleep at all. Finally the surgeon administered a powerful opiate, and when the ship came to anchor in the beautiful bay, the invalid was in a profound sleep.

Browning was on the lookout for the ship, and was soon upon its deck. He and Sedgwick clasped hands, and the first words of Sedgwick were: "Jack, are all well, and who is here?"

"All well," said Jack; "and your wife, my wife, and Mrs. Hazleton are waiting at the hotel for you. And how is your friend?"

"Desperately ill, but I have hopes of him now," said Sedgwick.

The surgeon was appealed to, and he said it would be better to take Jordan ashore while yet he slept.

"I must first send a message that we are coming, and that he is asleep under opiates, or we shall frighten those who are watching for us," said Sedgwick.

Captain McGregor volunteered to deliver the message as he was going ashore for a few minutes to report to the port officials that he brought no cargo to be discharged, except the baggage of two passengers. Sedgwick thanked him, took his arm, led him aside, and said to him: "Captain, when you find my wife, tell her privately that she must keep the other ladies from seeing us as we carry Jordan to the house. It would disturb and perhaps alarm them, for he is not only wan and poor, but the sleep upon him looks like the twin brother of Death."

"I will see to it all," said the captain, and at once went ashore.

Grace saw him and recognized him as he alighted at the hotel, and ran to the parlor to meet him alone. He explained to her the situation, and she undertook to see that the injunction should be carried out.

"How long before they will come?" asked Grace.

"Perhaps thirty minutes," was the answer.

"Then excuse me, captain," said Grace, "but come back later. I want to thank you for all your kindness, and have a visit with you. But now I must see to my two charges, that no mistake be made."

McGregor promised to return, shook hands, called Grace a "trump," and strode away.

So soon as he had gone, Grace rang, and when a servant came she sent for the manager of the hotel. To him she explained that in a few minutes a sick man would be brought to the house; that his illness was not at all contagious; that No. — of her apartments must be prepared for him, and he must be carried there at once.

He asked if she was sure there was no danger to guests from the sick man, and she answered that he must know that no sick man could be landed without a permit from the port surgeon.

He bowed and promised that her wishes should be carried out.

Then she went to find Mrs. Browning, and told her to propose to Mrs. Hazleton to go for a drive to kill time, and to be sure to drive in the opposite direction from the bay; to hurry up and to be absent for an hour or an hour and a quarter. She had before explained to Rose the real situation.

Rose complied. As the two ladies came from their rooms attired for the ride, Rose said :

"Grace, come and join us ; we are going to see Naples a little."

But Grace excused herself for that day, promising to go next morning.

She saw them driven away, and then took up her watch for the expected visitors.

She did not wait long. Four sailors were carrying the sick man ; while Jack, the ship's surgeon, and Sedgwick were walking near. The manager met them and directed the way to the room set aside for Jordan. Grace waited in the upper hall for the procession. Sedgwick sprang to her, but she put a finger on her lips, caught his hand, then circled his neck with her arms, swiftly kissed him, and then whispered : "O darling, we must see now to our poor dear sick friend," and tore herself away from him.

Jordan was put in bed still sleeping. Then Sedgwick, the surgeon and sailors came out. Sedgwick feed the sailors generously, though they did not want to accept anything. He then presented Surgeon Craig to his wife.

Grace greeted him and said : "Doctor, when the sick man awakens, will there be any danger to him if some one very dear to him shall be sitting by his couch ?"

"None at all," was the answer. "That is the medicine that he needs. If we could find the right friend,

I believe it would cure him ; if we cannot, I fear the result, for it is a sorrow more than the fever, I believe, that is killing him."

Half an hour later the ladies returned. Grace had Sedgwick take Browning from the sick room ; then explained to Mrs. Hazleton that Mr. Jordan was in the house very ill and sleeping, but that if she were strong enough she ought to be at his bedside when he awoke ; asked her if she could bear the ordeal, and if she thought she could, whether she would prefer to be alone or to have her with her.

"I am strong enough," was the answer, "and I would rather no one would be near."

Then Grace led her to the door and said : "Margaret, be brave, and keep in thought that you are going to restore your friend to health ; and see, this room is next to mine. I shall be waiting there; if you need me, tap softly upon the partition door." Then she opened noiselessly the door, kissed her friend, waited until she passed into the room, closed the door, and then ran to her husband, climbed upon his knees, embraced and kissed him, and cried with joy.

It was two hours before any sign came from the adjoining room. Then the door was softly opened ; Mrs. Hazleton came in without speaking, grasped Sedgwick's hand, pointed to the room where Jordan lay, and said in a whisper : "He wants you." And as Sedgwick passed from the apartment, the overwrought woman fell upon her knees, buried her face in the lap of Grace, and said : "Dear friend, help me to thank God."

Later Sedgwick reported that as he approached the bed, Jordan smiled, and in a feeble voice said : " Jim, old friend, I'ze mighty weak, but don't mind it ; I shall pull through easy now. But if I don't, I'll be even ; ther world's been thet kind ter me thet I'll keep thankin' God ter all eternity."

Then in his weakness he wept, but controlling himself at last, he continued : " I'ze too powerful weak ter make much noise, but if yo' think a loud invercation is heard sooner nor a weak one, thank God fur me in your loudest key."

Sedgwick took up his watch by Jordan for the night. He slept much of the night, and smiles stole over his face as he slept, but he was awfully prostrated with weakness.

After that, a regular order was prescribed. Sedgwick watched at night, and the others took turns by day.

Three nights after their arrival, the fever left Jordan. The doctor had anticipated it, and had told Sedgwick he would remain with him. The fever left him so utterly prostrated that it was all the doctor and Sedgwick could do to keep life in him for two or three hours. But the faintness finally passed, and the patient dropped into a peaceful sleep ; and the doctor, with a sigh of relief, said : " The crisis is passed, Sedgwick. He is going to pull through."

But it was a wearisome rally. It was several days before the anxiety was over. It was a week after the coming of Sedgwick before Sedgwick explained to Browning what he had done ; how Jordan was an old gold miner; and that the reason he had not told Browning much of what he was doing was because Jordan was the one to test the ore, and was anxious to go; he, Sedgwick, thought it was a shame to separate Jack and Rose; then he thought also if Jack knew he had gone to Africa he would worry over it. Then he told him of the mill, and finally that he had with him $100,000 in bullion, the result of the first month's run of the mill; had fixed matters so that the mill would be running right along, and that there was ore enough in the stopes to insure steady crushing for at least four or five years to come.

"And what now?" asked Jack.

"Now your work must come in," said Sedgwick. "You and your wife must go to England as soon as Tom is a little better. In your own way, make arrangements to have announced, so that Hamlin, Jenvie and Stetson will see it, that there is a good deal of movement in 'The Wedge of Gold'; have substantially the same report, only differently worded, as that contained in the prospectus which you were caught on; let it be known through what brokers the stock is being handled, and have copies of the reports in their hands, only fix the price at £1 per share. If the old men please to buy, let them have some of the stock. If they do not, we will try to make them sorry that they did not buy when they could. By the way, have you still your hand on Emanuel, and can you depend upon him?"

"I think I can," said Jack.

"Well, then," said Sedgwick, "if no news of the

mill has been received in England, and the conspirators think you are merely trying to unload some of
your stock on the old report, may be if they can be
handled right, they may be induced to sell some of
the stock short.   If they can, perhaps we can get
back some of the money from them."

"I understand," said Jack, "and I believe I can
work it."

"Especially if, when I get to England with the
bullion, we can call a meeting and declare a dividend," said Sedgwick.

"I see," said Browning.   "But, old boy, I wish you
had let me help you work this thing out.   I do, by
Jove."

Just then Grace and Rose came out on the veranda,
where the old friends were talking.

Rose bent over and put her arms around Jack's
neck, and said: "Dear old Jack, do you know what
day this is?"

"Why, little one?" asked Jack.

"O, you stupid!" said Rose.

"What is to-day?" asked Sedgwick.

"Another stupid!" said Rose.   "Two beautiful
and accomplished ladies go to church and give re-
spectability to two of the wild tribe of the West, by
marrying them, and they forget it in a little year."

"It was this day year, on my soul," said Jack.   "It
was, by Jove."

"Come here, sweet," said Sedgwick to Grace.
Then taking her in his arms he kissed her, and said:
"My days have been turned into nights of late, else

I would not have forgotten. Are you glad you are married, Grace?"

"Very glad," Grace whispered. "Are you glad?"

"Very," said Sedgwick, "even as is the ransomed soul when the symphonies of Summer Land first give their enchantment to the spirit ear."

"I will tell you why I forgot, Rose," said Jack. "My life did not count until you became a part of myself. I am really but a year old, and you do not chide one-year-old kids for being forgetful."

"What glorified prevaricators these men are, Grace, are they not?" said Rose.

"O, Rose!" said Grace. "The mission of woman is to suffer and be devoted in her suffering, and how could we carry out our mission if all men were good, and had good memories, and did not run away to Africa and Venezuela and Australia, and come home with fevers, and—and—." Then she kissed Sedgwick, and jumping up caught Rose by the arm, and said: "Let us punish them by running away from them."

As they walked away Sedgwick watched them, and when they turned a corner of the veranda, said: "Jack, would you give the year's happiness just past for all the gold in Africa?"

"No, indeed," was the reply; "but you had the strength to leave your bride on your marriage day for a chance of gaining a little of that gold."

"O, no, old friend," said Sedgwick "We had enough money left, but there was a principle at stake. I went to vindicate that principle if I could."

"Pardon me, Jim," said Jack. "But you were stronger than I could have been. I could not have left my bride then. I had waited so long, that to have parted then would have broken her heart and would have destroyed me."

"I realized all that, Jack," said his friend; "so did Grace, and we both sympathized with you both, and decided that the cup of bitterness must be turned from you."

"Of course," said Jack. "What you did was jolly grand; what you have done has been so splendid that I cannot express my thoughts of it yet; I can't, by Jove! And Gracie's part through all has been superb. I think, too, your sick friend has been pure gold through it all."

"Pure diamonds rather," said Sedgwick. "O Jack, you do not half comprehend the grandeur of that sterling man. When his heart was slowly shriveling up in his breast, he forgot himself and his sorrow to cheer me, and when it was necessary to go for the machinery, he insisted that I should go, and he, of his own accord, went back to the depths of that South Land wilderness and worked uncomplainingly for months. No grander man ever lived."

CHAPTER XXVII.

SELLING STOCK SHORT.

After a few days more Jack and Rose returned to England.

Soon after their return, one of the morning papers had an announcement that the banking house of Campbell & Co. (Limited), No. —— street, was promoting the "Wedge of Gold," a mining property in Southern Africa, near the border of the Transvaal, which was believed to be a most promising property.

The same day Emanuel dropped into the house of Jenvie, Hamlin & Stetson. He was seedy-looking, and seemed a good deal run down both in purse and spirits.

"What do you think of the 'Wedge of Gold' announcement?" asked Jenvie.

"What is it?" asked Emanuel. He was shown the paper.

"What do I think?" he said. "I think may be the young man needs a little money. The mails came in from Port Natal yesterday. Is there any news from the mine?"

"None at all that we can find," said Jenvie.

"I have no idea," said the Portugese, "but if it is more than three shillings per share, it is one good chance for a bear to sell it short and hug himself for his own act."

With this he went out. The three men were silent

for a good five minutes. Then Jenvie rang the bell, and when it was answered he said to the messenger : "Go to Campbell & Co.'s ; find out the price of 'Wedge of Gold' stock, and ask what data the house has from the property."

The clerk returned in half an hour, and reported that it was held at £1, and he produced a statement of the property.

This was eagerly run over by the three. "Why," said Jenvie, as he completed reading it, "this is but a rehash of the statement of a year ago ; the same depth is given, all the details just as they were. Jack must be making a desperate play for money."

"One pound per share !" said Hamlin. "Why, the man must be after some other Nevada miner who has more money than judgment."

"The 'Wedge of Gold' was our good fortune," said Stetson. "Through it we got a real start. We made a good bit out of it, which we have since doubled. Let us try another venture in the stock."

"What ! Buy it at £1 per share ?" asked Hamlin.

"No, no," said Jenvie. "Let us sell 20,000 shares to be delivered in three months at ten shillings. We can send Emanuel and get it at four or five shillings."

After weighing the matter in every way they decided to increase the amount and sell 30,000 shares.

The offer was taken, the money paid, and the contract to deliver the 30,000 shares in three months was signed by Jenvie, Hamlin & Co. Then each, unknown to the other, sold 10,000 shares more short.

The fact was wired to Sedgwick at once. He showed Grace the dispatch and said : " My enchantress, that will leave your mother's husband and Rose's mother's husband bankrupt if we wish it ; what shall we do?"

" How will it do so ? " asked Grace.

" In three months that stock will be worth £5 per share," said Sedgwick. "See what it will require to produce 60,000 shares to fulfill their contract."

" What did they obtain from Jack ?" asked Grace.

" Almost £90,000," said Sedgwick.

" Well," said Grace, " I know very little of business, but it seems to me if they would make that good with the year's interest, it would be about right, inasmuch as it is a family matter."

" You little bunch of wisdom and justice !" said Sedgwick. " To make them do just that thing was what I started to Africa for."

CHAPTER XXVIII.

CONVALESCENT.

The " Pallas " had been in port twenty days before Jordan began to sit up, a few minutes at a time. He was still very weak, but his face was transfigured by an almost divine light. It was reflected radiance from the eyes of Margaret Hazleton.

The doctor had thrown away his medicine, telling Jordan that all he needed was good nursing and as much food as his stomach could assimilate.

It was a happy little company. Jordan and Mrs. Hazleton, Sedgwick and his wife, the doctor and Captain McGregor—for the ship had been left with the first officer, and the captain had turned nurse to relieve Sedgwick.

A week later Jordan could sit up most of the day, and Captain McGregor had begun to absent himself two or three hours every afternoon. About this time Browning's dispatch was received.

Sedgwick was needed in London. What was best to do ?

He prepared a statement of the mine, signed it and got Jordan to sign it, and he shipped the bullion to a well-known Paris banking house.

Nothing held him back except Jordan's illness. He was growing anxious, and his wife, who watched his every mood, quickly discovered it. So soon as she did, she went to him, put an arm around one of his, and said.

"What is it, love? What is it that is troubling you?"

He explained that he ought to be in London, but Jordan was yet too weak to travel, and he could not leave him—not for twenty mines.

Grace thought the matter over for two or three minutes, and then said cheerfully:

"I have it, husband! We will get a nurse for the dear man. I will remain, and Margaret and myself and the nurse can see to him, and will follow you when he can travel."

Sedgwick looked at her fondly for a moment, and then said :

"You are a great little woman, sure enough ; but you are such a one that I would rather remain than go without you."

She put her hands upon his lips, and said :

"Duty, love. Hist, we must always be brave and self-forgetful enough to do our duty. I am going now to see Margaret." She walked a few steps, then turned back and said :

"Why would it not be the right thing for Mr. Jordan and Margaret to be married before you leave?"

"I believe it would," said Sedgwick, "only that I have planned that we would give them a great wedding in London."

"So had I," said Grace, "and we will."

Just as they were talking, Captain McGregor came from the direction of the harbor.

"I have news for you," he said. "I have sold the 'Pallas.' She will sail to-morrow, and now I propose to remain with you, and go with you to London when you go."

"You have sold the dear ship?" said Sedgwick. "And what of the doctor and the crew?"

"They will sail in her. The doctor will be up to make his adieus to-night. They wanted to charter the craft for a long voyage. I would not go, but offered to sell, and they bought, and re-engaged the officers, the surgeon and the crew."

"Let us go on board," said Sedgwick. "I want to bid those good men good-bye."

"So do I," said the captain. "I will be grateful if you will go with me."

"Wait a moment until I run down to the bank," said Sedgwick. "While I am gone, Grace, get your hat and wrap; and by the way, captain, how many men and officers are there?"

The captain replied: "Six officers, the surgeon and steward, three waiters, twelve seamen and sixteen men in the firing department."

The company soon set out, and went on board the "Pallas."

All hands were called on deck. Captain McGregor made them a little speech; told them that his chief regret in giving up the ship was in parting with them, and wished them all happiness and prosperity. They gave him three cheers, and all shook hands with him, wishing him long life and asking God's blessing for him.

Then Sedgwick stepped forward, and said:

"MY DEAR FRIENDS:—That I was able to bring one whom I love better than a brother to where he could find the strength to get well, I owe to you. He is yet too weak to be moved, or he would be here by my side to thank you. I was much absorbed on the voyage, but I saw how you, officers and seamen, worked to take advantage of every puff of wind and every current of the sea. I know how you others were working in the hell of the fire-room, and I shall be grateful to you as long as I live. I wish you all health, happiness and prosperity in the future.

You, with your grand captain, carried the machinery to Africa, which has made me a good deal of money. You brought home my friend when he was making an unequal fight for life. I want each of you to have a little souvenir of my gratitude."

With that he undid a package which he had been holding in his hand. It contained a bunch of envelopes. He handed one to each of the officers and men.

Those for the mates and engineers each contained bank notes of the value of £200. Those of the men each contained £50. The doctor's contained £1,000.

The men whispered eagerly among themselves for a moment; then the third mate said:

"Mr. Sedgwick, the lads want me to ask you how they can best thank you. They are not much talkers, and this gift of yours has about beached their tongues."

Sedgwick smiled and said: "No thanks are needed,

but I want to tell you that this is all due to the dearest woman in the world," putting his arm around Grace. "If you will each come and shake the hand of my wife, all the gratitude you feel will be receipted for."

They joyfully responded, and one old tar, more bold than the rest, said, as he took the fair little hand of Grace in the grasp of his own knotted hand: "Your mon is a mighty poor hand to save money, but he'll be richer nor Rothschild as long as you are spared to him."

They gave their old captain and his friend three cheers as they passed over the ship's side, and McGregor wiped his eyes all the way back to the hotel.

Grace went at once to the sick-room. Jordan was half reclining in an easy-chair. Margaret was sitting where he could see her, and was evidently reading to him, when Grace entered.

Jordan spoke: "Take a cheer, madam. Maggie wur readin' 'nd it's mighty comfortin'. It's like sipping old wine and hearin' music in thar next room same time."

"Don't you mind him, Grace," said Margaret. "He is still very weak, and all that he says is not as deep as it might be." But she smiled fondly him while she spoke.

"Don't yo' b'leve her, Mrs. Sedgwick," said Jordan. "We all has weak spots in our hearts; she's mine."

Grace put one hand on Jordan's hand, the other on Margaret's cheek, and said:

"Say all the pretty things of her that you please, Mr. Jordan, and do not mind her, for her heart has been starving for those same words from your lips for a long time."

Margaret was silent, but she smiled; and a great flush swept over her face as she smiled.

"Everything war right, after all," said Jordan. "Hed I not lost her, I mighter grown careless o' her like other men do sometimes uv those they luv, but no matter, we has a understandin'."

And again the happy woman smiled and blushed.

Then Grace explained how much her husband was needed in England; that she had determined to remain until Mr. Jordan could travel, and let her husband go; that Captain McGregor had sold the "Pallas," and she thought she would remain with them, and asked Jordan if he thought they, with a nurse, could take care of him.

Before he could answer, Mrs. Hazleton interposed and said:

"All this sickness and sorrow came through me. Henceforth my life is to be devoted to where it can do most good. We do not want any display. Why can we not be married? Then I will be his nurse, and he will need no other. You can go with your husband, and we will come when Tom is stronger. What say you, love?"

"Do not answer, Mr. Jordan," said Grace. "We have fixed it for you to be married where husband and myself—where Jack and Rose—were married. We will remain until you can travel."

" I'd be mighty glad ter call yo' 'wife' now, Maggie," said Jordan; " but I don't reckon it's squar for a man ter take advantage of his nuss." Then turning to Mrs. Sedgwick, he continued: "Tell Jim I'll be ready ter leave ter-morrer evenin'."

So next day they started by easy stages for London. Sedgwick engaged a special car to be stopped off at any point he might desire. They rested a day in Milan, another in Paris, and there Sedgwick arranged to have the bullion that might come from the 'Wedge of Gold' at all times at his immediate disposal. They reached London in six days; Jordan had gained so much that he walked to the carriage from the Dover depot, and with Sedgwick's and McGregor's support, walked up the steps of Sedgwick's house.

Rose had dinner waiting for them, and at dinner expressed the sentiments of all by saying: "I believe this is just now the happiest house in all England."

CHAPTER XXIX.

Sedgwick found waiting for him advices from the mine, all of which were favorable and the output for another month, less the expenses of mining and milling, which amounted in the aggregate to something over $90,000, had been forwarded to the Bank of France.

The Wedge of Gold Mining Company was reorganized. Browning was made president; Sedgwick, treasurer; McGregor, secretary; and all three, with Jordan, directors. A regular dividend of two shillings per share, and a special dividend of as much more was declared, aggregating in all £30,000. This was given to the *Times* for publication, and attached to it was the following note:

"The reporter of the *Times* was able to obtain the following particulars of this wonderful property from the secretary:

"'A forty-stamp mill has been in operation on the property since June last. The mill yielded in June, above expenses, £17,000 and 15 shillings; in July, £18,000 and 5 shillings. The ore already developed above the tunnel level is sufficient to insure the running of the present works to their full capacity for five years to come. The ore on the tunnel level is equal to any in the mine, and the ore chute has been demonstrated by exploration on the tunnel level to be

at least 630 feet in length, with an average width of
16 feet.   The tunnel cuts the mine at a depth of
500 feet.   The office of the company in London is
No. ——, —— Street.   The officers are John
Browning, president; James Sedgwick, treasurer;
Hugh McGregor, secretary; and these, with Thomas
Jordan, make up the directory of the company.' "

When, next morning, Jenvie,. Hamlin and Stetson
read the above in the *Times*, they were filled with
consternation.

" I feared that man Sedgwick from the first," said
Jenvie.   " Our first account of him, that ' he must be
a prize-fighter,' was true.   He has knocked us out,
and he has made no more noise about it than does a
bull-dog when he takes a pig by the ear."

" What are we to do ? " asked Hamlin.

" We must take in enough stock to cover our short-
age at once," said Jenvie, " even if we have to pay
£1 per share for it."

So a messenger was sent to the office of the broker
through which the stock had been shorted, to buy at
any price up to £1.

He returned with the information that the stock
could be had, but the price was £6 per share.

Then the three men realized for the first time the
trap which had been set for them, and how fatal had
been its spring.   The messenger was at once sent out
again, this time to the office of the company.   He
found the secretary, who referred him to the ——
Bank, from which the dividends were to be paid.

There he found stock for sale, but the price demanded was £6 per share.

He returned home and made his report. The three men gazed at each other with blank looks of despair.

"Thirty thousand shares at £6 will take all we have," said Hamlin.

"And I shorted 10,000 shares besides," said Jenvie.

"So did I," said Hamlin.

"So did I," said Stetson.

"It seems clear enough that we are absolutely ruined," said Hamlin.

"I wonder what has become of that Portuguese, Emanuel," said Hamlin.

At that moment he entered the office. He looked like the picture of despair. He broke out with : " It is awful ! I have just heard ze truth. It was that American who did it. When you thought last year that he had gone to America, he, with another American, had gone to Africa.

" They found ze mine. They found a way out from it by going in the opposite direction from which they came. Sedgwick went by Australia to San Francisco, and ordered a forty-stamp mill. The other American remained, and opened the mine by a tunnel. Sedgwick came back this way, and, left here to meet the mill at Port Natal.

" It has been running three months. Two months' proceeds are here, and pay dividends of four shillings, and it is good for two shillings per month for years ; with machinery doubled, good for four shillings per month for years to come. The stock has gone to £6 ;

it will go to £10 so soon as it is well understood.
And I lost it all, because I had not the sense to find
that way out from ze mine.   The road by the trail
would have cost £75,000 or £100,000, and I believed
only impassable mountains were to ze west."

"How did you find all this out?" asked Jenvie.

"From ze Secretary, McGregor.   He was master
of ze ship that carried the machinery from San Francisco, and he brought ze Americans from Port Natal.
One was very sick with the fever, and came near
dying.   He had, besides, one wound which he received
with ze Boers coming out to the coast from the mine.
They are two devils.   Ten or a dozen Boers attacked
them to get the first month's bullion, and they two
killed five of them, and drove ze rest away."

"I wish the Boers had killed them both," said
Jenvie.

"They are hard men to kill," said Emanuel.   "Mc-
Gregor says, when ashore one day at D'Umber, there
was a chicken-shooting match.   The chickens were
buried in the ground all but their heads, and the people
were shooting at ten paces when these men passed.
They asked about it, and asked if they might shoot
with their own pistols; and when permission was given,
they drew their weapons and killed six chickens each
in a minute, and were laughing all the time as though
it were nothing.   They are devils, shure enough."

"Do you think Browning knew all about this from
the first?" asked Hamlin.

"Not at all," said Emanuel.   "No one in London
knew where the Americans had gone, except his wife.

Browning thought he had gone back to America. His wife knew. She got a dispatch from Australia, and letters from Port Natal ze same day, saying he was going to San Francisco to order machinery, and would return this way and be with her in four months, and then she left at once and beat him a week into San Francisco.

"And I am ruined. My little stock is all gone. A mine worth £2,000,000 I sold for £2,000." And he went out.

"What can we do?" asked Jenvie. "I expect a notice every moment to call at the broker's and settle."

"Can we not assign our property?" asked Hamlin.

"We could," said Jenvie, "but to-morrow we should all be looking through the bars of a prison."

"And even Grace was in the conspiracy to rob us," said Hamlin, in an injured tone.

"She is a brave, true woman, I think," said Jenvie, "and as it looks to me, she is the only one to whom we can now appeal."

"May be so," said Hamlin. "Her husband worships her, I am told."

"Suppose we go to your house and persuade your wife to go and bring her home where we can see her," said Jenvie.

This was agreed to, and with heavy hearts the three men entered a carriage and were driven to the Hamlin house.

As they went up the steps, Grace Sedgwick herself opened the door. She had been to see her mother, and was just going out.

"Come back, Grace," said her stepfather; "we wish to see you particularly."

She returned with them, and her stepfather told her how they were involved—in what danger they were, not only of absolute ruin, but of a criminal prosecution, and begged her to see her husband and intercede with him.

"My husband needs no entreaties to do what is right," said Grace. "Suppose the case were reversed, what would you grant my husband?"

They all hung their heads. Grace looked at them and continued: "You robbed dear, confiding Jack of his fortune, which he had honestly acquired. You robbed him for the double purpose of making him a beggar, and of breaking his heart, though one of you was his stepfather, another the stepfather of the woman he loved better than his own life. It was that which set Jack's nearest friend to be your Nemesis. Our troth had just been plighted. It was like death to part us, but he who is my husband said to me : 'There must be no scandal, if we can help it, but this wrong must be righted. I must go to Africa, and if I can work out the dear boy's deliverance, it must be done.' And I consented to it. He moved secretly, but with the force and energy of his nature. He and the friend who went with him have performed a great work. They have taken what was unloaded upon Jack as worthless, and converted it into something richer than a little kingdom. It seems, too, that in the blindness of your avarice, you dared fate itself to make more money out of that wreck, and

now you are in the toils. Suppose my husband had
done by you as you have dealt with Jack, and you
had him where you now are, what mercy would you
show him ?"

They were silent. They had not even self-respect
to sustain them.

Grace waited a moment, and then went on : "But
he is of different material. There is no malice in his
nature. He cares nothing for the triumph which
comes through revenge.

"He knew when you dared to sell that stock short,
told me of it, and asked what would be right. I replied
that I thought if you would restore to Jack what he
had been robbed of, with interest on the money to
date, it would be fair; and his answer was that to
compel you to do that very thing was what caused
him to leave me and go to Africa.

"In that you can get an idea of him. He had
money enough for himself and Jack both; he had
no desire for revenge, but he was determined that
you should be made to do justice to his friend, whom
you had so greatly wronged, and that, if possible, it
should be done without any noise."

"Do you think he would settle that way?" asked
Jenvie.

"He has no settlement to make," said Grace; "but
I think he would recommend Jack to settle that way."

"And where could we meet Jack?" asked Jenvie.

"I do not know," said Grace, "nor is it necessary.
I think the broker with whom you dealt in the stocks
has authority to settle. That was a little trap set for

you. There is not a share of the stock that is not in the company's office at this moment."

"I did not mean to rob Jack," said Hamlin. "I wanted to break his engagement with Rose, hoping he would turn to you."

"We all understood that from the first," said Grace, "but we had made entirely different arrangements— arrangements worth two of that—which suited us all around." And bowing, the young wife left the room.

The three men found, upon visiting the broker, that he had received orders to settle with them on the terms outlined by Grace, and they complied by turning over what money they had and some outside property.

It left them with fair fortunes. But the story got out through Emanuel; their prestige was broken, and they closed up their business within a few days, and disappeared from the business walks of London. Two months later Jenvie died in a moment of apoplexy; the succeeding autumn Hamlin succumbed to typhoid fever, and Stetson sailed away to lose himself in the depths of Australia.

CHAPTER XXX.

GRAND OPERA.

Jordan improved rapidly, and soon began to take long drives to different points of interest. After a month it was one evening proposed that they should all attend the theater. It was agreed to, and it was left to Jordan to decide where to go. Queerly enough, he selected a theater where the opera of "Tannhauser" was to be performed.

"Did you ever attend a grand opera performance, Tom?" asked Sedgwick.

"No," was the response. "Thet's ther reason I wanter go."

He seemed greatly absorbed throughout the performance. The opera was put on with every splendor possible, and the strange man sat almost motionless through the mighty rendition, and was unusually silent all the way home.

Arriving there, Grace said : "Mr. Jordan, give us your idea of the opera."

"I reckon yo' might laugh at me ef I should," said Jordan.

"No, we will not," said Grace; "for when it comes to that, we are none of us quite up to the comprehension of the mystery of a grand opera—at least, none but Margaret."

"Well," said Jordan, "mystery are a good word ter use thar. If yo' jest occerpy yo'r eyes and ears, yo'

hear mostly only a ocean roar uv singin', a brayin' uv
trumpets, a clashin' uv cymbals, a beatin' uv drums,
with ther soft strains uv viols, harps 'nd flutes, and
not much music. Ef yo' set yo'r mind workin' ter
foller ther myths outer which ther story of the opera
war made, then ther tones become voices, 'nd ther
music only tells er story. But ef yo' give yo'r soul a
chance, then it's different. Ther music assumes forms
of its own; it materializes, as Jim would say, and each
man as listens understands in his own way its language. It brings ter ther human ear the tones uv
ther ocean when it sobs agin ther sands; it steals ther
echo of the melodies thet the winds wakes when they
touches ther arms uv ther great pines on ther mountain tops and makes 'em ther harps; it steals ther
babble from the brooks; it calls back all ther voices
of the woods when within 'em ther matin' birds is all
singin' in chorus; it borrers ther thunder from ther
storm; it sarches ther whole world for melodies, 'nd
blends 'em all for our use.

"Still, they all ter-night war, ter me, only compni-
ments. Underneath all wur a symphony which wur
thet of a higher soul singin' ter my soul—may be
'twere my mother's singin' ter my soul uv glories thet
we hasn't yet reached. It war a call fur men ter look
higher ter whar thar is melodies too solemn 'nd sweet
fur ther dull ears uv poor mortality ter hear, ter whar
ez picters too fair fur our darkened eyes ter see, but
which all august is a-waitin' fur us.

"When I war sick, I thot one night I hearn Margery

prayin' fur me; some uv thet music ter-night seemed like a rehearsal uv thet prayer."

"Why, Mr. Jordan, that is better than the opera itself," said Grace; and Margaret bent and kissed the brave man's hand, while he blushed like a girl, and said, "Sho'."

CHAPTER XXXI.

MARRIAGE BELLS.

A month more rolled by, and Jordan became himself again. Grace and Rose worked together to make such a wedding for him and Margaret as should be a joy in their memories as long as life should last.

The day before the wedding, so soon as breakfast was over, Sedgwick went out, telling Grace to tell Jack that he wanted to meet him and Tom at the "Wedge of Gold" office at 1 p. m.

Grace went to deliver the message, but learned from Rose that her husband had gone an hour before, leaving word for Sedgwick and Jordan to meet him at the same place at 12:30 p. m.

They all met there at about the appointed time.

A meeting of the directors of the "Wedge of Gold" Company was called to order, and a motion made and carried that another dividend of two shillings per share should be declared.

Then Sedgwick arose and said he had an important matter to lay before the company. He had received an offer of £7 per share for the property, and the proposition had been guaranteed by the Baring Brothers, and asked Browning what he thought it best to do.

Browning thought it best to sell.

"Then," said Sedgwick, "there will be no more work for us except to resign as officers of the company, our resignations to take place with the transfer of the property."

"There is yet another matter," said Browning. "How is the division of the proceeds to be made?"

"That all rests with you, Jack," said Sedgwick; "only I think you should pay me back what I advanced to put the property on its feet, and you should keep in mind that this was made a success by our friend Jordan."

"Not to any great extent," said Jordan. "I war merely a hired man working for my board and clothes, and you forget thet because uv it I made a fortune sich ez no gold could buy. Treat me, please, ez tho' I war already wealthy, *exceedingly* wealthy!"

"It is all due to you two," said Jack. "When the old men made good their robbery, I was even. All the rest is yours."

And they wrangled over the matter for a full hour.

Then McGregor spoke. "Let me help you out, my friends. You are offered £1,050,000. It is enough for you all. Divide it into three parts, and settle that way."

Then came another wrangle, but it was settled on that basis, except that each agreed that Captain McGregor should receive fair compensation for bringing Jordan home, and they estimated that to be worth £100,000. That, Jordan insisted should be paid out of his share, and it took an hour to talk him out of it.

Then it required another half hour for the three to bulldoze McGregor into accepting it. The convinc-

ing argument was made by Jordan, who said: " Sup-
posin' you hedn't a-come, whar would I a-bin now?

McGregor went out, and then Browning said:

"I have a little matter to speak of. I sold my
Venezuela mine yesterday for £100,000," and so saying he took a memorandum from his pocket, opened
it, and tossed to Sedgwick and Jordan each a certificate for one-third of the amount, saying: "I feared
the way you were behaving you would spend all
your money, so I went to work to make you a little
stake, as the boys in Nevada say."

Another wrangle then ensued, both Sedgwick and
Jordan declaring that they had had nothing in the
world to do with making the money; but Jack was
obstinate and carried his point.

McGregor returned, and all went to Sedgwick's to
dinner. About the time the coffee was brought, a
messenger rang at the door and left a package for
Mr. Jordan. It was brought in, and then Jordan
said :

" Friends, in Africa I found a prospector ez war
broke. I give him a little outfit ter go down on the
Vaal. He came back after a while and divied with
me, 'nd I want ter divy with yo'."

So saying, he opened the package. Exclamations
of surprise arose on all sides. Before their eyes was
a great heap of diamonds. "I war thinkin'," said
Jordan, "thet inasmuch ez thar war seven uv us, ther
right thing ter do would be ter make seven heaps
of ther stones," and the only change they could
make in his plans was that the division should be

made by one who knew their value. He had secretly had them cut since coming to London. They were really worth £10,000.

Next day the wedding of Jordan and Mrs. Hazleton was celebrated with all the pomp which Grace and Rose could give it. It was followed by a great feast, and numberless rare presents. Jordan never showed off so well. The marriage exalted and transformed him.

After the wedding, Mr. and Mrs. Jordan left for a month's visit to Scotland.

CHAPTER XXXII.

The syndicate that bought the "Wedge of Gold" put some of the stock on the market. A few days later another shipment of bullion was received, another dividend was declared, and the stock advanced to £10 per share. The happy owners gave an entertainment in honor of the mine, and called it "The Wedge of Gold Reception." Sedgwick and Browning with their wives and Captain McGregor attended.

As they returned, the dawn was breaking in the East, and mighty London with its five millions of people began to awaken. There were confused murmurs, which swelled in volume every moment ; these were interspersed with distinct clamors, as one industry after another took up anew its daily work. Then there was the whistle of trains ; the deeper calls and answers of boats on the river ; the louder and louder hum of the awaking millions, until with the coming of the full dawn the roar of the swelling hosts became a full diapason.

"What a monster this great handiwork of man is, Sedgwick," said McGregor ; "I wonder if there is anything else like it in this whole world."

"I guess not," was Sedgwick's reply ; "but, strangely enough, it reminds me of something not at all like it, but which impressed me quite as much as does this. As you say, this is man's handiwork. I saw another dawn once which had little in it save God's handiwork.

"While mining in Virginia City, I determined one summer day to give up work for a week and to make a visit to the high Sierras. One day's ride takes you from the Comstock into the very fastnesses of the mountains. There were five of us in the party. We went to Lake Tahoe, crossed the lake, and kept on to a spring and stream of water beyond, a few miles. We had a camping outfit, and determined to sleep in no house while absent. We spread our beds in a little grassy glen; to the east there was no forest, but on the north and south the trees were immense, and to the west, a mile or two away, the mountains rose abruptly to a height which held the snows in their arms all the summer long.

"The good-night hoot of an owl or some other sound awakened me just as the first streaks of the dawn began to flush the face of the east.

"I sat up, and while my friends were sleeping around me, I watched the transformation scene of that dawn. There were not many birds to awake—our altitude was too high for them—and so the panorama moved on almost in silence. But it was the more impressive because of its stillness. The east grew warmer and warmer, and the solemn night began to spread her black wings, under which she had brooded the world, in preparation for flight. The shadows began to retreat from where they had shrouded the nearest trees. The air grew softer; from it a noiseless breeze just touched the great arms of the pines as though to

waken them and gave to them an almost imperceptible motion.   The stars and planets began to faint in
the heavens.   As the waves of light increased in the east,
the snow on the high mountains to the west took on the
hue of the opal, and when the last shadow fled away
and the sun flashed gloriously above the eastern
horizon, and another day was born, I knew just how
the ancient Fire Worshipers felt when they bowed
their heads in reverence before the splendors of the
rising sun."

It was a good while ago that the events out of
which this story was woven transpired.

Now, at different seasons of the year, these families,
with two gray-haired old ladies and a gray-haired old
man with a sailor's rolling walk, may be seen, sometimes in London, sometimes on a fair estate in Devonshire, sometimes in a stately home in the Miami
Valley, and again down on the Brazos in Texas.

Around and among them are playing broods of
little Jacks, Jims, Toms, Roses, Graces, and Mar-
garets, and older children are away at school.   All
the children call the old ladies " Grandma" and the
gray man with the sailor's walk "Grand-uncle," and all
who see them declare that no other such a happy
company can be found in all the world.

The place on the Brazos is superintended by a
shrewd Irishman, while the village physician, for-
merly a ship surgeon, is named Craig, and his wife's
name is Nora; and the people there say there is not

in all Texas another woman who is more of a lady or has a complexion so clear, a face so fair, or such a wealth of hair, which in color is between flaxen and gold.

www.ingramcontent.com/pod-product-compliance
Lightning Source LLC
Chambersburg PA
CBHW030629030726
47497CB00006B/1700